TO CUT A LONG STORY SHORT

JEFFREY ARCHER is a master storyteller, the author of ten novels which have all been world-wide bestsellers. *Not a Penny More, Not a Penny Less* was his first book, and it achieved instant success. Next came the tense and terrifying thriller *Shall We Tell the President?*, followed by his triumphant bestseller *Kane and Abel*. His first collection of short stories, *A Quiver Full of Arrows*, came next, and then *The Prodigal Daughter*, the superb sequel to *Kane and Abel*. This was followed by *First Among Equals*, considered by the *Scotsman* to be the finest novel about Parliament since Trollope, the thrilling chase story *A Matter of Honour*, his second collection of stories, *A Twist in the Tale*, and the novels *As the Crow Flies* and *Honour Among Thieves*. *Twelve Red Herrings*, his third collection of stories, was followed by the novels *The Fourth Estate* and *The Eleventh Commandment*. A collected edition of his short stories was published in 1997, followed by a new selection, *To Cut a Long Story Short*.

Jeffrey Archer was born in 1940 and educated at Wellington School, Somerset, and Brasenose College, Oxford. He represented Great Britain in the 100 metres in the early sixties, and entered the House of Commons when he won the by-election at Louth in 1969. He wrote his first novel, *Not a Penny More, Not a Penny Less*, in 1974. From September 1985 to October 1986 he was Deputy Chairman of the Conservative Party, and he was created a Life Peer in the Queen's Birthday Honours of 1992. He lives in London and Cambridge with his wife and two sons.

JEFFREY ARCHER

To Cut a
Long Story Short

HarperCollins*Publishers*

HarperCollins*Publishers*
77–85 Fulham Palace Road,
Hammersmith, London w6 8jb

The HarperCollins webside address is:
www.harpercollins.co.uk

This paperback edition 2001
1

First published in Great Britain by
HarperCollins*Publishers* 2000

isbn 978-0-00-784148-6
isbn 978-0-00-784193-6

Set in PostScript Linotype Baskerville by
Rowland Phototypesetting Ltd, Bury St Edmunds, Suffolk

Printed and bound in Great Britain by
Clays Ltd, St Ives plc

To Stephan, Alison and David

CONTENTS

* Based on true incidents

PREFACE

Before you begin this volume of fourteen short stories, as in the past I would like to acknowledge that several of them are based on true incidents. On the contents page you will find these indicated by an asterisk (*).

In my travels around the globe, always searching for some vignette which might have a life of its own, I came across 'Death Speaks', and was so moved by it that I have placed the story at the beginning of the book.

It was originally translated from the Arabic, and despite extensive research, the author remains 'Anon', though the tale appeared in Somerset Maugham's play *Sheppey*, and later as a preface to John O'Hara's *Appointment in Samarra*.

I have rarely come across a better example of the simple art of storytelling. A gift that truly lacks any prejudice, it is bestowed without regard to birth, upbringing or education. You only have to consider the contrasting upbringings of Joseph

Conrad and Walter Scott, of John Buchan and O. Henry, of H.H. Munro and Hans Christian Andersen, to prove my point.

In this, my fourth volume of stories, I have attempted two very short examples of the genre: 'The Letter' and 'Love at First Sight'.

But first, 'Death Speaks':

Death Speaks

There was a merchant in Bagdad who sent his servant to market to buy provisions and in a little while the servant came back, white and trembling, and said, Master, just now when I was in the market-place I was jostled by a woman in the crowd and when I turned I saw it was death that jostled me. She looked at me and made a threatening gesture; now, lend me your horse, and I will ride away from this city and avoid my fate. I will go to Samarra and there death will not find me. The merchant lent him his horse, and the servant mounted it, and he dug his spurs in its flanks and as fast as the horse could gallop he went. Then the merchant went down to the market-place and he saw me standing in the crowd and he came to me and said, Why did you make a threatening gesture to my servant when you saw him this morning? That was not a threatening gesture, I said, it was only a start of

3

surprise. I was astonished to see him in Bagdad, for I had an appointment with him tonight in Samarra.

The Expert Witness

'Damn good drive,' said Toby, as he watched his opponent's ball sail through the air. 'Must be every inch of 230, perhaps even 250 yards,' he added, as he held up his hand to his forehead to shield his eyes from the sun, and continued to watch the ball bouncing down the middle of the fairway.

'Thank you,' said Harry.

'What did you have for breakfast this morning, Harry?' Toby asked when the ball finally came to a halt.

'A row with my wife,' came back his opponent's immediate reply. 'She wanted me to go shopping with her this morning.'

'I'd be tempted to get married if I thought it would improve my golf that much,' said Toby as he addressed his ball. 'Damn,' he added a moment later, as he watched his feeble effort squirt towards the heavy rough no more than a hundred yards from where he stood.

Toby's game did not improve on the back nine, and when they headed for the clubhouse just before lunch, he warned his opponent, 'I shall have to take my revenge in court next week.'

'I do hope not,' said Harry, with a laugh.

'Why's that?' asked Toby as they entered the clubhouse.

'Because I'm appearing as an expert witness on your side,' Harry replied as they sat down for lunch.

'Funny,' Toby said. 'I could have sworn you were against me.'

Sir Toby Gray QC and Professor Harry Bamford were not always on the same side when they met up in court.

'All manner of persons who have anything to do before My Lords the Queen's Justices draw near and give your attendance.' The Leeds Crown Court was now sitting. Mr Justice Fenton presided.

Sir Toby eyed the elderly judge. A decent and fair man, he considered, though his summings-up could be a trifle long-winded. Mr Justice Fenton nodded down from the bench.

Sir Toby rose from his place to open the defence

case. 'May it please Your Lordship, members of the jury, I am aware of the great responsibility that rests on my shoulders. To defend a man charged with murder can never be easy. It is made even more difficult when the victim is his wife, to whom he had been happily married for over twenty years. This the Crown has accepted, indeed formally admitted.

'My task is not made any easier, m'lud,' continued Sir Toby, 'when all the circumstantial evidence, so adroitly presented by my learned friend Mr Rodgers in his opening speech yesterday, would on the face of it make the defendant appear guilty. However,' said Sir Toby, grasping the tapes of his black silk gown and turning to face the jury, 'I intend to call a witness whose reputation is beyond reproach. I am confident that he will leave you, members of the jury, with little choice but to return a verdict of not guilty. I call Professor Harold Bamford.'

A smartly dressed man, wearing a blue double-breasted suit, white shirt and a Yorkshire County Cricket Club tie, entered the courtroom and took his place in the witness box. He was presented with a copy of the New Testament, and read the oath with a confidence that would have left no member of the jury in any doubt that this wasn't his first appearance at a murder trial.

Sir Toby adjusted his gown as he stared across the courtroom at his golfing partner.

'Professor Bamford,' he said, as if he had never set eyes on the man before, 'in order to establish your expertise, it will be necessary to ask you some preliminary questions that may well embarrass you. But it is of overriding importance that I am able to show the jury the relevance of your qualifications as they affect this particular case.'

Harry nodded sternly.

'You were, Professor Bamford, educated at Leeds Grammar School,' said Sir Toby, glancing at the all-Yorkshire jury, 'from where you won an open scholarship to Magdalen College, Oxford, to read Law.'

Harry nodded again, and said, 'That is correct,' as Toby glanced back down at his brief – an unnecessary gesture, as he had often been over this routine with Harry before.

'But you did not take up that offer,' continued Sir Toby, 'preferring to spend your undergraduate days here in Leeds. Is that also correct?'

'Yes,' said Harry. This time the jury nodded along with him. Nothing more loyal or more proud than a Yorkshireman when it comes to things Yorkshire, thought Sir Toby with satisfaction.

'When you graduated from Leeds University, can you confirm for the record that you were awarded a first-class honours degree?'

'I was.'

'And were you then offered a place at Harvard University to study for a masters degree and thereafter for a doctorate?'

Harry bowed slightly and confirmed that he was. He wanted to say, 'Get on with it, Toby,' but he knew his old sparring partner was going to milk the next few moments for all they were worth.

'And for your Ph.D. thesis, did you choose the subject of handguns in relation to murder cases?'

'That is correct, Sir Toby.'

'Is it also true,' continued the distinguished QC, 'that when your thesis was presented to the examining board, it created such interest that it was published by the Harvard University Press, and is now prescribed reading for anyone specialising in forensic science?'

'It's kind of you to say so,' said Harry, giving Toby the cue for his next line.

'But *I* didn't say so,' said Sir Toby, rising to his

full height and staring at the jury. 'Those were the words of none other than Judge Daniel Webster, a member of the Supreme Court of the United States. But allow me to move on. After leaving Harvard and returning to England, would it be accurate to say that Oxford University tried to tempt you once again, by offering you the first Chair of Forensic Science, but that you spurned them a second time, preferring to return to your alma mater, first as a senior lecturer, and later as a professor? Am I right, Professor Bamford?'

'You are, Sir Toby,' said Harry.

'A post you have held for the past eleven years, despite the fact that several universities around the world have made you lucrative offers to leave your beloved Yorkshire and join them?'

At this point Mr Justice Fenton, who had also heard it all before, peered down and said, 'I think I can say, Sir Toby, that you have established the fact that your witness is a pre-eminent expert in his chosen field. I wonder if we could now move on and deal with the case in hand.'

'I am only too happy to do so, m'lud, especially after your generous words. It won't be necessary to heap any more accolades on the good professor's shoulders.' Sir Toby would have loved to have told the judge that he had actually come to the end of his preliminary comments moments before he had been interrupted.

'I will therefore, with your permission, m'lud, move on to the case before us, now that you feel I have established the credentials of this particular witness.' He turned back to face the professor, with whom he exchanged a knowing wink.

'Earlier in the case,' continued Sir Toby, 'my learned friend Mr Rodgers set out in detail the case for the prosecution, leaving no doubt that it rested on a single piece of evidence: namely, the smoking gun that never smoked' – an expression Harry had heard his old friend use many times in the past, and was in no doubt he would use on many more occasions in the future.

'I refer to the gun, covered in the defendant's fingerprints, that was discovered near the body of his unfortunate wife, Mrs Valerie Richards. The prosecution went on to claim that after killing his wife, the defendant panicked and ran out of the house, leaving the firearm in the middle of the room.' Sir Toby swung round to face the jury. 'On this one, flimsy, piece of evidence – and flimsy I shall prove it to be – you, the jury, are being asked to convict a man for murder and place him behind bars for the rest of his life.' He paused to allow the jury to take in the significance of his words.

'So, now I return to you, Professor Bamford, and ask you as a pre-eminent expert in your field – to use m'lud's description of your status – a series of questions.' Harry realised the preamble was finally over, and that he would now be expected to live up to his reputation.

'Let me start by asking you, Professor, is it your experience that after a murderer has shot his victim, he or she is likely to leave the murder weapon at the scene of the crime?'

'No, Sir Toby, it is most unusual,' replied Harry. 'In nine cases out of ten where a handgun is involved, the weapon is never recovered, because the murderer makes sure that he or she disposes of the evidence.'

'Quite so,' said Sir Toby. 'And in the one case out of ten where the gun is recovered, is it common to find fingerprints all over the murder weapon?'

'Almost unknown,' replied Harry. 'Unless the murderer is a complete fool, or is actually caught in the act.'

'The defendant may be many things,' said Sir Toby, 'but he is clearly not a fool. Like you, he was educated at Leeds Grammar School; and he was arrested not at the scene of the crime, but in the home of a friend on the other side of the city.' Sir Toby omitted to add, as prosecuting counsel had pointed out several times in his opening statement, that the defendant was discovered in bed with his mistress, who turned out to be the only alibi he had.

'Now, I'd like to turn to the gun itself, Professor. A Smith and Wesson K4217 B.'

'It was actually a K4127 B,' said Harry, correcting his old friend.

'I bow to your superior knowledge,' said Sir Toby, pleased with the effect his little mistake had made on the jury. 'Now, returning to the handgun. The Home Office laboratory found the murder victim's fingerprints on the weapon?'

'They did, Sir Toby.'

'And, as an expert, does this lead you to form any conclusions?'

'Yes, it does. Mrs Richards's prints were most prominent on the trigger and the butt of the gun, which causes me to believe that she was the last person to handle the weapon. Indeed, the physical evidence suggests that it was she who squeezed the trigger.'

'I see,' said Sir Toby. 'But couldn't the gun have been placed in the hand of Mrs Richards by her murderer, in order to mislead the police?'

'I would be willing to go along with that theory if the police had not also found Mr Richards's prints on the trigger.'

'I'm not sure I fully understand what you're getting at, Professor,' said Sir Toby, fully understanding.

'In almost every case I have been involved in, the first thing a murderer does is to remove his own fingerprints from the murder weapon before he considers placing it in the hand of the victim.'

'I take your point. But correct me if I am wrong,' said Sir Toby. 'The gun was not found in the hand of the victim, but nine feet away from her body, which is where the prosecution claims it was dropped when the defendant fled in panic from his marital home. So, let me ask you, Professor Bamford: if someone committing suicide held a gun to their temple and pulled the trigger, where would you expect the gun to end up?'

'Anywhere between six and ten feet from the body,' Harry replied. 'It's a common mistake – often made in poorly researched films and television programmes – for victims to be shown still

holding onto the gun after they have shot themselves. Whereas what actually happens in the case
of suicide is that the force of the gun's recoil jerks
it from the victim's grip, propelling it several feet
from the body. In thirty years of dealing with sui-
cides involving guns, I have never once known a
weapon to remain in the hand of the victim.'

'So, in your opinion as an expert, Professor, Mrs
Richards's fingerprints and the position of the
weapon would be more consistent with suicide
than with murder.'

'That is correct, Sir Toby.'

'One final question, Professor,' said the defence
QC, tugging his lapels. 'When you have given evidence for the defence in cases such as this in the
past, what percentage of juries have returned a
not guilty verdict?'

'Mathematics was never my strong subject, Sir
Toby, but twenty-one cases out of twenty-four
ended in acquittal.'

Sir Toby turned slowly to face the jury. 'Twenty-
one cases out of twenty-four,' he said, 'ended in
acquittal after you were called as an expert witness.
I think that's around 85 per cent, m'lud. No more
questions.'

Toby caught up with Harry on the courtroom

steps. He slapped his old friend on the back. 'You played another blinder, Harry. I'm not surprised the Crown caved in after you'd given your evidence – I've never seen you in better form. Got to rush, I've a case starting at the Bailey tomorrow, so I'll see you at the first hole, ten o'clock on Saturday. That is, if Valerie will allow it.'

'You'll be seeing me long before then,' murmured the Professor, as Sir Toby jumped into a taxi.

Sir Toby glanced through his notes as he waited for the first witness. The case had begun badly. The prosecution had been able to present a stack of evidence against his client that he was in no position to refute. He wasn't looking forward to the cross-examination of a string of witnesses who would undoubtedly corroborate that evidence.

The judge on this occasion, Mr Justice Fairborough, nodded towards prosecuting counsel. 'Call your first witness, Mr Lennox.'

Mr Desmond Lennox QC rose slowly from his place. 'I am obliged, m'lud. I call Professor Harold Bamford.'

A surprised Sir Toby looked up from his notes

to see his old friend heading confidently towards the witness box. The London jury looked quizzically at the man from Leeds.

Sir Toby had to admit that Mr Lennox established his expert witness's credentials rather well – without once referring to Leeds. Mr Lennox then proceeded to take Harry through a series of questions, which ended up making his client sound like a cross between Jack the Ripper and Dr Crippen.

Mr Lennox finally said, 'No more questions, m'lud,' and sat down with a smug expression on his face.

Mr Justice Fairborough looked down at Sir Toby and asked, 'Do you have any questions for this witness?'

'I most certainly do, m'lud,' said Toby, rising from his place. 'Professor Bamford,' he said, as if it were their first encounter, 'before I come to the case in hand, I think it would be fair to say that my learned friend Mr Lennox made great play of establishing your credentials as an expert witness. You will have to forgive me if I revisit that subject, and clear up one or two small details that puzzled me.'

'Certainly, Sir Toby,' said Harry.

'This first degree you took at . . . er, yes, at Leeds

University. What subject was it that you studied?'

'Geography,' said Harry.

'How interesting. I wouldn't have thought that was an obvious preparation for someone who would go on to become an expert in handguns. However,' he continued, 'allow me to move on to your Ph.D., which was awarded by an American university. Can I ask if that degree is recognised by English universities?'

'No, Sir Toby, but . . .'

'Please confine yourself to answering the questions, Professor Bamford. For example, does Oxford or Cambridge University recognise your Ph.D.?'

'No, Sir Toby.'

'I see. And, as Mr Lennox was at pains to point out, this whole case may well rest on your credentials as an expert witness.'

Mr Justice Fairborough looked down at the defence counsel and frowned. 'It will be up to the jury to make that decision, based on the facts presented to them, Sir Toby.'

'I agree m'lud. I just wished to establish how much credence the members of the jury should place in the opinions of the Crown's expert witness.'

The judge frowned again.

'But if you feel I have made that point, m'lud, I will move on,' said Sir Toby, turning back to face his old friend.

'You told the jury, Professor Bamford – as an expert – that in this particular case the victim couldn't have committed suicide, because the gun was found in his hand.'

'That is correct, Sir Toby. It's a common mistake – often made in poorly researched films and television programmes – for victims to be shown still holding onto the gun after they have shot themselves.'

'Yes, yes, Professor Bamford. We have already been entertained by your great knowledge of television soap operas, when my learned friend was examining you. At least we've found something you're an expert in. But I should like to return to the real world. Can I be clear about one thing, Professor Bamford: you are not suggesting even for a moment, I hope, that your evidence proves that the defendant placed the gun in her husband's hand. If that were so, you wouldn't be an expert, Professor Bamford, but a clairvoyant.'

'I made no such assumption, Sir Toby.'

'I'm grateful to have your support in that. But tell me, Professor Bamford: in your experience, have you ever come across a case in which the murderer placed the gun in the victim's hand, in order to try to suggest that the cause of death was suicide?'

Harry hesitated for a moment.

'Take your time, Professor Bamford. The rest of a woman's life may depend on your reply.'

'I have come across such cases in the past' – he hesitated again – 'on three occasions.'

'On three occasions?' repeated Sir Toby, trying to look surprised, despite the fact that he himself had appeared in all three cases.

'Yes, Sir Toby,' said Harry.

'And, in these three cases, did the jury return a verdict of not guilty?'

'No,' said Harry quietly.

'No?' repeated Sir Toby, facing the jury. 'In how many of the cases did the jury find the defendant not guilty?'

'In two of the cases.'

'And what happened in the third?' asked Sir Toby.

'The man was convicted of murder.'

'And sentenced . . . ?' asked Sir Toby.

'To life imprisonment.'

'I think I'd like to know a little bit more about that case, Professor Bamford.'

'Is this leading anywhere, Sir Toby?' asked Mr Justice Fairborough, staring down at the defence counsel.

'I suspect we are about to find out, m'lud,' said Sir Toby, turning back to the jury, whose eyes were now fixed on the expert witness. 'Professor Bamford, do let the court know the details of that particular case.'

'In that case, the Queen against Reynolds,' said Harry, 'Mr Reynolds served eleven years of his sentence before fresh evidence was produced to show that he couldn't have committed the crime. He was later pardoned.'

'I hope you'll forgive my next question, Professor Bamford, but a woman's reputation, not to mention her freedom, is at stake in this courtroom.' He paused, looked gravely at his old friend and said, 'Did you appear on behalf of the prosecution in that particular case?'

'I did, Sir Toby.'

'As an expert witness for the Crown?'

Harry nodded. 'Yes, Sir Toby.'

'And an innocent man was convicted for a crime

that he did not commit, and ended up serving eleven years in prison?'

Harry nodded again. 'Yes, Sir Toby.'

'No "buts" in that particular case?' asked Sir Toby. He waited for a reply, but Harry didn't speak. He knew he no longer had any credibility as an expert witness in this particular case.

'One final question, Professor Bamford: in the other two cases, to be fair, did the juries' verdicts support your interpretation of the evidence?'

'They did, Sir Toby.'

'You will recall, Professor Bamford, that the Crown made great play of the fact that in the past your evidence has been crucial in cases such as these, in fact – to quote Mr Lennox verbatim – "the decisive factor in proving the Crown's case". However, we now learn that in the three cases in which a gun was found in the victim's hand, you have a 33 per cent failure rate as an expert witness.'

Harry didn't comment, as Sir Toby knew he wouldn't.

'And as a result, an innocent man spent eleven years in jail.' Sir Toby switched his attention to the jury and said quietly, 'Professor Bamford, let us hope that an innocent woman isn't about to spend the rest of her life in jail because of the opinion of an "expert witness" who manages to get it wrong 33 per cent of the time.'

Mr Lennox rose to his feet to protest at the treatment the witness was being made to endure, and Mr Justice Fairborough wagged an admonishing finger. 'That was an improper comment, Sir Toby,' he warned.

But Sir Toby's eyes remained on the jury, who no longer hung on the expert witness's every word, but were now whispering among themselves.

Sir Toby slowly resumed his seat. 'No more questions, m'lud.'

'Damn good shot,' said Toby, as Harry's ball disappeared into the cup on the eighteenth hole. 'Lunch on me again, I fear. You know, I haven't beaten you for weeks, Harry.'

'Oh, I don't know about that, Toby,' said his golfing partner, as they headed back to the clubhouse. 'How would you describe what you did to me in court on Thursday?'

'Yes, I must apologise for that, old chap,' said Toby. 'Nothing personal, as you well know. Mind you, it was damn stupid of Lennox to select you as his expert witness in the first place.'

'I agree,' said Harry. 'I did warn them that no one knew me better than you, but Lennox wasn't interested in what happened on the North-Eastern Circuit.'

'I wouldn't have minded so much,' said Toby, as he took his place for lunch, 'if it hadn't been for the fact . . .'

'Hadn't been for the fact . . . ?' Harry repeated.

'That in both cases, the one in Leeds and the one at the Bailey, any jury should have been able to see that my clients were as guilty as sin.'

The Endgame

Cornelius Barrington hesitated before he made his next move. He continued to study the board with great interest. The game had been going on for over two hours, and Cornelius was confident that he was only seven moves away from checkmate. He suspected that his opponent was also aware of the fact.

Cornelius looked up and smiled across at Frank Vintcent, who was not only his oldest friend but had over the years, as the family solicitor, proved to be his wisest adviser. The two men had many things in common: their age, both over sixty; their background, both middle-class sons of professionals; they had been educated at the same school and at the same university. But there the similarities ended. For Cornelius was by nature an entrepreneur, a risk-taker, who had made his fortune mining in South Africa and Brazil. Frank was a solicitor by profession, cautious, slow to decision, fascinated by detail.

Cornelius and Frank also differed in their physical appearance. Cornelius was tall, heavily built, with a head of silver hair many men half his age would have envied. Frank was slight, of medium stature, and apart from a semicircle of grey tufts, was almost completely bald.

Cornelius had been widowed after four decades of happy married life. Frank was a confirmed bachelor.

Among the things that had kept them close friends was their enduring love of chess. Frank joined Cornelius at The Willows for a game every Thursday evening, and the result usually remained in the balance, often ending in stalemate.

The evening always began with a light supper, but only one glass of wine each would be poured – the two men took their chess seriously – and after the game was over they would return to the drawing room to enjoy a glass of brandy and a cigar; but tonight Cornelius was about to shatter that routine.

'Congratulations,' said Frank, looking up from the board. 'I think you've got me beaten this time. I'm fairly sure there's no escape.' He smiled, placed the red king flat on the board, rose from his place and shook hands with his closest friend.

'Let's go through to the drawing room and have a brandy and a cigar,' suggested Cornelius, as if it were a novel idea.

'Thank you,' said Frank as they left the study and strolled towards the drawing room. As Cornelius passed the portrait of his son Daniel, his heart missed a beat – something that hadn't changed for the past twenty-three years. If his only child had lived, he would never have sold the company.

As they entered the spacious drawing room the two men were greeted by a cheerful fire blazing in the grate, which had been laid by Cornelius's housekeeper Pauline only moments after she had finished clearing up their supper. Pauline also believed in the virtues of routine, but her life too was about to be shattered.

'I should have trapped you several moves earlier,' said Cornelius, 'but I was taken by surprise when you captured my queen's knight. I should have seen that coming,' he added, as he strolled over to the sideboard. Two large cognacs and two Monte Cristo cigars had been laid out on a silver tray. Cornelius picked up the cigar-clipper and passed it across to his friend, then struck a match, leaned over and watched Frank puff away until he was convinced his cigar was alight. He then completed the same routine himself before sinking into his favourite seat by the fire.

Frank raised his glass. 'Well played, Cornelius,' he said, offering a slight bow, although his host would have been the first to acknowledge that over the years his guest was probably just ahead on points.

Cornelius allowed Frank to take a few more puffs before shattering his evening. Why hurry? After all, he had been preparing for this moment for several weeks, and was unwilling to share the secret with his oldest friend until everything was in place.

They both remained silent for some time, relaxed in each other's company. Finally Cornelius placed his brandy on a side table and said, 'Frank, we have been friends for over fifty years. Equally importantly, as my legal adviser you have proved to be a shrewd advocate. In fact, since the untimely death of Millicent there has been no one I rely on more.'

Frank continued to puff away at his cigar without interrupting his friend. From the expression on his face, he was aware that the compliment was nothing more than an opening gambit. He suspected he would have to wait some time before Cornelius revealed his next move.

'When I first set up the company some thirty years ago, it was you who was responsible for executing the original deeds; and I don't believe I've signed a legal document since that day which has not crossed your desk – something that was unquestionably a major factor in my success.'

'It's generous of you to say so,' said Frank, before taking another sip of brandy, 'but the truth is that it was always your originality and enterprise that made it possible for the company to go from strength to strength – gifts that the gods decided not to bestow on me, leaving me with little choice but to be a mere functionary.'

'You have always underestimated your contribution to the company's success, Frank, but I am in no doubt of the role you played over the years.'

'Where is this all leading?' asked Frank with a smile.

'Patience, my friend,' said Cornelius. 'I still have a few moves to make before I reveal the stratagem I have in mind.' He leaned back and took another long puff of his cigar. 'As you know, when I sold the company some four years ago, it had been my intention to slow down for the first time in years.

I had promised to take Millie on an extended holiday to India and the Far East –' he paused '– but that was not to be.'

Frank nodded his head in understanding.

'Her death served to remind me that I am also mortal, and may myself not have much longer to live.'

'No, no, my friend,' protested Frank. 'You still have a good many years to go yet.'

'You may be right,' said Cornelius, 'although funnily enough it was you who made me start to think seriously about the future . . .'

'Me?' said Frank, looking puzzled.

'Yes. Don't you remember some weeks ago, sitting in that chair and advising me that the time had come for me to consider rewriting my will?'

'Yes, I do,' said Frank, 'but that was only because in your present will virtually everything is left to Millie.'

'I'm aware of that,' said Cornelius, 'but it nevertheless served to concentrate the mind. You see, I still rise at six o'clock every morning, but as I no longer have an office to go to, I spend many self-indulgent hours considering how to distribute my wealth now that Millie can no longer be the main beneficiary.'

Cornelius took another long puff of his cigar before continuing. 'For the past month I have been considering those around me – my relatives, friends, acquaintances and employees – and I began to think about the way they have always treated me, which caused me to wonder which of them would show the same amount of devotion, attention and loyalty if I were not worth millions, but was in fact a penniless old man.'

'I have a feeling I'm in check,' said Frank, with a laugh.

'No, no, my dear friend,' said Cornelius. '*You* are absolved from any such doubts. Otherwise I would not be sharing these confidences with you.'

'But are such thoughts not a little unfair on your immediate family, not to mention . . .'

'You may be right, but I don't wish to leave that to chance. I have therefore decided to find out the truth for myself, as I consider mere speculation to be unsatisfactory.' Once again, Cornelius paused to take a puff of his cigar before continuing. 'So indulge me for a moment while I tell you what I have in mind, for I confess that without your cooperation it will be impossible for me to carry out my little subterfuge. But first allow me to refill your glass.' Cornelius rose from his chair, picked up his friend's empty goblet and walked to the sideboard.

'As I was saying,' continued Cornelius, passing the refilled glass back to Frank, 'I have recently been wondering how those around me would behave if I were penniless, and I have come to the conclusion that there is only one way to find out.'

Frank took a long gulp before enquiring, 'What do you have in mind? A fake suicide perhaps?'

'Not quite as dramatic as that,' replied Cornelius. 'But almost, because –' he paused again '– I intend to declare myself bankrupt.' He stared through the haze of smoke, hoping to observe his friend's immediate reaction. But, as so often in the past, the old solicitor remained inscrutable, not least because, although his friend had just made a bold move, he knew the game was far from over.

He pushed a pawn tentatively forward. 'How do you intend to go about that?' he asked.

'Tomorrow morning,' replied Cornelius, 'I want you to write to the five people who have the greatest claim on my estate: my brother Hugh, his wife Elizabeth, their son Timothy, my sister Margaret, and finally my housekeeper Pauline.'

'And what will be the import of this letter?'

asked Frank, trying not to sound too incredulous.

'You will explain to all of them that, due to an unwise investment I made soon after my wife's death, I now find myself in debt. In fact, without their help I may well be facing bankruptcy.'

'But . . .' protested Frank.

Cornelius raised a hand. 'Hear me out,' he pleaded, 'because your role in this real-life game could prove crucial. Once you have convinced them that they can no longer expect anything from me, I intend to put the second phase of my plan into operation, which should prove conclusively whether they really care for me, or simply for the prospect of my wealth.'

'I can't wait to learn what you have in mind,' said Frank.

Cornelius swirled the brandy round in his glass while he collected his thoughts.

'As you are well aware, each of the five people I have named has at some time in the past asked me for a loan. I have never required anything in writing, as I have always considered the repayment of these debts to be a matter of trust. These loans range from £100,000 to my brother Hugh to purchase the lease for his shop – which I understand is doing quite well – to my housekeeper Pauline, who borrowed £500 for a deposit on a second-hand car. Even young Timothy needed £1,000 to pay off his university loan, and as he seems to be progressing well in his chosen profession, it should not be too much to ask him – like all of the others – to repay his debt.'

'And the second test?' enquired Frank.

'Since Millie's death, each of them has performed some little service for me, which they have always insisted they enjoyed carrying out, rather than it being a chore. I'm about to find out if they are willing to do the same for a penniless old man.'

'But how will you know . . .' began Frank.

'I think that will become obvious as the weeks go by. And in any case, there is a third test, which I believe will settle the matter.'

Frank stared across at his friend. 'Is there any point in trying to talk you out of this crazy idea?' he asked.

'No, there is not,' replied Cornelius without hesitation. 'I am resolved in this matter, although I accept that I cannot make the first move, let alone bring it to a conclusion, without your cooperation.'

'If it is truly what you want me to do, Cornelius, then I shall carry out your instructions to the letter, as I have always done in the past. But on this occasion there must be one proviso.'

'And what might that be?' asked Cornelius.

'I shall not charge a fee for this commission, so that I will be able to attest to anyone who should ask that I have not benefited from your shenanigans.'

'But . . .'

'No "buts", old friend. I made a handsome profit from my original shareholding when you sold the company. You must consider this a small attempt to say thank you.'

Cornelius smiled. 'It is I who should be grateful, and indeed I am, as always, conscious of your valued assistance over the years. You are truly a good friend, and I swear I would leave my entire estate to you if you weren't a bachelor, and if I didn't know it wouldn't change your way of life one iota.'

'No, thank you,' said Frank with a chuckle. 'If you did that, I would only have to carry out exactly the same test with a different set of characters.' He paused. 'So, what is your first move?'

Cornelius rose from his chair. 'Tomorrow you will send out five letters informing those concerned that a bankruptcy notice has been served on me, and that I require any outstanding loans to be repaid in full, and as quickly as possible.'

Frank had already begun making notes on a little pad he always carried with him. Twenty minutes later, when he had written down Cornelius's final instruction, he placed the pad back in an inside pocket, drained his glass and stubbed out his cigar.

When Cornelius rose to accompany him to the front door, Frank asked, 'But what is to be the third of your tests, the one you're convinced will prove so conclusive?'

The old solicitor listened carefully as Cornelius outlined an idea of such ingenuity that he departed feeling all the victims would be left with little choice but to reveal their true colours.

The first person to call Cornelius on Saturday morning was his brother Hugh. It must have been only moments after he had opened Frank's letter. Cornelius had the distinct feeling that someone else was listening in on the conversation.

'I've just received a letter from your solicitor,' said Hugh, 'and I simply can't believe it. Please tell me there's been some dreadful mistake.'

'I'm afraid there has been no mistake,'

Cornelius replied. 'I only wish I could tell you otherwise.'

'But how could you, who are normally so shrewd, have allowed such a thing to happen?'

'Put it down to old age,' Cornelius replied. 'A few weeks after Millie died I was talked into investing a large sum of money in a company that specialised in supplying mining equipment to the Russians. All of us have read about the endless supply of oil there, if only one could get at it, so I was confident my investment would show a handsome return. Last Friday I was informed by the company secretary that they had filed a 217 order, as they were no longer solvent.'

'But surely you didn't invest everything you had in the one company?' said Hugh, sounding even more incredulous.

'Not originally, of course,' said Cornelius, 'but I fear I got sucked in whenever they needed a further injection of cash. Towards the end I had to go on investing more, as it seemed to me the only way I would have any chance of getting back my original investment.'

'But doesn't the company have any assets you can lay your hands on? What about all the mining equipment?'

'It's all rusting away somewhere in central Russia, and so far we haven't seen a thimbleful of oil.'

'Why didn't you get out when your losses were still manageable?' asked Hugh.

'Pride, I suppose. Unwilling to admit I'd backed a loser, always believing my money would be safe in the long run.'

'But they must be offering some recompense,' said Hugh desperately.

'Not a penny,' replied Cornelius. 'I can't even afford to fly over and spend a few days in Russia to find out what the true position is.'

'How much time have they given you?'

'A bankruptcy notice has already been served on me, so my very survival depends on how much I can raise in the short term.' Cornelius paused. 'I'm sorry to remind you of this, Hugh, but you will recall that some time ago I loaned you £100,000. So I was rather hoping . . .'

'But you know that every penny of that money has been sunk into the shop, and with High Street sales at an all-time low, I don't think I could lay my hands on more than a few thousand at the moment.'

Cornelius thought he heard someone whispering the words 'And no more' in the background.

'Yes, I can see the predicament you're in,' said Cornelius. 'But anything you can do to help would be appreciated. When you've settled on a sum –' he paused again ' – and naturally you'll have to discuss with Elizabeth just how much you can spare – perhaps you could send a cheque direct to Frank Vintcent's office. He's handling the whole messy business.'

'The lawyers always seem to end up getting their cut, whether you win or lose.'

'To be fair,' said Cornelius, 'Frank has waived his fee on this occasion. And while you're on the phone, Hugh, the people you're sending to refit the kitchen were due to start later this week. It's even more important now that they complete the job as quickly as possible, because I'm putting the house on the market and a new kitchen will help me get a better price. I'm sure you understand.'

'I'll see what I can do to help,' said Hugh, 'but I may have to move that particular team onto another assignment. We've got a bit of a backlog at the moment.'

'Oh? I thought you said money was a little tight right now,' Cornelius said, stifling a chuckle.

'It is,' said Hugh, a little too quickly. 'What I

meant to say was that we're all having to work overtime just to keep our heads above water.'

'I think I understand,' said Cornelius. 'Still, I'm sure you'll do everything you can to help, now you're fully aware of my situation.' He put the phone down and smiled.

The next victim to contact him didn't bother to phone, but arrived at the front door a few minutes later, and wouldn't take her finger off the buzzer until the door had been opened.

'Where's Pauline?' was Margaret's first question when her brother opened the door. Cornelius stared down at his sister, who had put on a little too much make-up that morning.

'I'm afraid she's had to go,' said Cornelius as he bent down to kiss his sister on the cheek. 'The petitioner in bankruptcy takes a rather dim view of people who can't afford to pay their creditors, but still manage to retain a personal entourage. It was considerate of you to pop round so quickly in my hour of need, Margaret, but if you were hoping for a cup of tea, I'm afraid you'll have to make it yourself.'

'I didn't come round for a cup of tea, as I suspect you know only too well, Cornelius. What I want to know is how you managed to fritter away your entire fortune.' Before her brother could deliver some well-rehearsed lines from his script, she added, 'You'll have to sell the house, of course. I've always said that since Millie's death it's far too large for you. You can always take a bachelor flat in the village.'

'Such decisions are no longer in my hands,' said Cornelius, trying to sound helpless.

'What are you talking about?' demanded Margaret, rounding on him.

'Just that the house and its contents have already been seized by the petitioners in bankruptcy. If I'm to avoid going bankrupt, we must hope that the house sells for a far higher price than the estate agents are predicting.'

'Are you telling me there's absolutely nothing left?'

'Less than nothing would be more accurate,' said Cornelius, sighing. 'And once they've evicted me from The Willows, I'll have nowhere to go.' He tried to sound plaintive. 'So I was rather hoping that you would allow me to take up the kind offer you made at Millie's funeral and come and live with you.'

His sister turned away, so that Cornelius was unable to see the expression on her face.

'That wouldn't be convenient at the present time,' she said without explanation. 'And in any case, Hugh and Elizabeth have far more spare rooms in their house than I do.'

'Quite so,' said Cornelius. He coughed. 'And the small loan I advanced you last year, Margaret – I'm sorry to raise the subject, but . . .'

'What little money I have is carefully invested, and my brokers tell me that this is not a time to sell.'

'But the allowance I've provided every month for the past twenty years – surely you have a little salted away?'

'I'm afraid not,' Margaret replied. 'You must understand that being your sister has meant I am expected to maintain a certain standard of living, and now that I can no longer rely on my monthly allowance, I shall have to be even more careful with my meagre income.'

'Of course you will, my dear,' said Cornelius. 'But any little contribution would help, if you felt able . . .'

'I must be off,' said Margaret, looking at her watch. 'You've already made me late for the hair-dresser.'

'Just one more little request before you go, my

dear,' said Cornelius. 'In the past you've always been kind enough to give me a lift into town whenever . . .'

'I've always said, Cornelius, that you should have learned to drive years ago. If you had, you wouldn't expect everyone to be at your beck and call night and day. I'll see what I can do,' she added as he opened the door for her.

'Funny, I don't recall you ever saying that. But then, perhaps my memory is going as well,' he said as he followed his sister out onto the drive. He smiled. 'New car, Margaret?' he enquired innocently.

'Yes,' his sister replied tartly as he opened the door for her. Cornelius thought he detected a slight colouring in her cheeks. He chuckled to himself as she drove off. He was learning more about his family by the minute.

Cornelius strolled back into the house, and returned to his study. He closed the door, picked up the phone on his desk and dialled Frank's office.

'Vintcent, Ellwood and Halfon,' said a prim voice.

'I'd like to speak to Mr Vintcent.'

'Who shall I say is calling?'

'Cornelius Barrington.'

'I'll have to see if he's free, Mr Barrington.'

Very good, thought Cornelius. Frank must have convinced even his receptionist that the rumours were true, because in the past her response had always been, 'I'll put you straight through, sir.'

'Good morning, Cornelius,' said Frank. 'I've just put the phone down on your brother Hugh. That's the second time he's called this morning.'

'What did he want?' asked Cornelius.

'To have the full implications explained to him, and also his immediate obligations.'

'Good,' said Cornelius. 'So can I hope to receive a cheque for £100,000 in the near future?'

'I doubt it,' said Frank. 'From the tone of his voice I don't think that's what he had in mind, but I'll let you know just as soon as I've heard back from him.'

'I shall look forward to that, Frank.'

'I do believe you're enjoying yourself, Cornelius.'

'You bet I am,' he replied. 'I only wish Millie was here to share the fun with me.'

'You know what she would have said, don't you?'

'No, but I have a feeling you're about to tell me.'

'You're a wicked old man.'

'And, as always, she would have been right,' Cornelius confessed with a laugh. 'Goodbye, Frank.' As he replaced the receiver there was a knock at the door.

'Come in,' said Cornelius, puzzled as to who it could possibly be. The door opened and his housekeeper entered, carrying a tray with a cup of tea and a plate of shortbread biscuits. She was, as always, neat and trim, not a hair out of place, and showed no sign of embarrassment. She can't have received Frank's letter yet, was Cornelius's first thought.

'Pauline,' he said as she placed the tray on his desk, 'did you receive a letter from my solicitor this morning?'

'Yes, I did, sir,' Pauline replied, 'and of course I shall sell the car immediately, and repay your £500.' She paused before looking straight at him. 'But I was just wondering, sir . . .'

'Yes, Pauline?'

'Would it be possible for me to work it off in lieu? You see, I need a car to pick up my girls from school.'

For the first time since he had embarked on the enterprise, Cornelius felt guilty. But he knew that if he agreed to Pauline's request, someone would find out, and the whole enterprise would be endangered.

'I'm so sorry, Pauline, but I've been left with no choice.'

'That's exactly what the solicitor explained in his letter,' Pauline said, fiddling with a piece of paper in the pocket of her pinafore. 'Mind you, I never did go much on lawyers.'

This statement made Cornelius feel even more guilty, because he didn't know a more trustworthy person than Frank Vintcent.

'I'd better leave you now, sir, but I'll pop back this evening just to make sure things don't get too untidy. Would it be possible, sir . . . ?'

'Possible . . . ?' said Cornelius.

'Could you give me a reference? I mean, you see, it's not that easy for someone of my age to find a job.'

'I'll give you a reference that would get you a position at Buckingham Palace,' said Cornelius. He immediately sat down at his desk and wrote a glowing homily on the service Pauline Croft had given for over two decades. He read it through, then handed it across to her. 'Thank you, Pauline,' he said, 'for all you have done in the past for Daniel, Millie and, most of all, myself.'

'My pleasure, sir,' said Pauline.

Once she had closed the door behind her, Cornelius could only wonder if water wasn't sometimes thicker than blood.

He sat back down at his desk and began writing some notes to remind him what had taken place that morning. When he had finished he went through to the kitchen to make himself some lunch, and found a salad had been laid out for him.

After lunch, Cornelius took a bus into town – a novel experience. It was some time before he located a bus stop, and then he discovered that the conductor didn't have change for a twenty-pound note. His first call after he had been dropped off in the town centre was to the local estate agent, who didn't seem that surprised to see him. Cornelius was delighted to find how quickly the rumour of his financial demise must be spreading.

'I'll have someone call round to The Willows in the morning, Mr Barrington,' said the young man, rising from behind his desk, 'so we can measure up and take some photographs. May we also have your permission to place a sign in the garden?'

'Please do,' said Cornelius without hesitation,

and barely stopped himself from adding, the bigger the better.

After he'd left the estate agent, Cornelius walked a few yards down the street and called into the local removal firm. He asked another young man if he could make an appointment for them to take away the entire contents of the house.

'Where's it all to go, sir?'

'To Botts' Storeroom in the High Street,' Cornelius informed him.

'That will be no problem, sir,' said the young assistant, picking up a pad from his desk. Once Cornelius had completed the forms in triplicate, the assistant said, 'Sign there, sir,' pointing to the bottom of the form. Then, looking a little nervous, he added, 'We'll need a deposit of £100.'

'Of course,' said Cornelius, taking out his chequebook.

'I'm afraid it will have to be cash, sir,' the young man said in a confidential tone.

Cornelius smiled. No one had refused a cheque from him for over thirty years. 'I'll call back tomorrow,' he said.

On the way back to the bus stop Cornelius stared through the window of his brother's hardware store, and noted that the staff didn't seem all that busy. On arriving back at The Willows, he returned to his study and made some more notes on what had taken place that afternoon.

As he climbed the stairs to go to bed that night, he reflected that it must have been the first afternoon in years that no one had called him to ask how he was. He slept soundly that night.

When Cornelius came downstairs the following morning, he picked up his post from the mat and made his way to the kitchen. Over a bowl of cornflakes he checked through the letters. He had once been told that if it was known you were likely to go bankrupt, a stream of brown envelopes would begin to drop through the letterbox, as shopkeepers and small businessmen tried to get in before anyone else could be declared a preferred creditor.

There were no brown envelopes in the post that morning, because Cornelius had made certain every bill had been covered before he began his journey down this particular road.

Other than circulars and free offers, there was just one white envelope with a London postmark. It turned out to be a handwritten letter from his nephew Timothy, saying how sorry he was to learn of his uncle's problems, and that although he didn't get back to Chudley much nowadays, he would make every effort to travel up to Shropshire at the weekend and call in to see him.

Although the message was brief, Cornelius silently noted that Timothy was the first member of the family to show any sympathy for his predicament.

When he heard the doorbell ring, he placed the letter on the kitchen table and walked out into the hall. He opened the front door to be greeted by Elizabeth, his brother's wife. Her face was white, lined and drained, and Cornelius doubted if she had slept a great deal the previous night.

The moment Elizabeth had stepped into the house she began to pace around from room to room, almost as though she were checking to see that everything was still in place, as if she couldn't accept the words she had read in the solicitor's letter.

Any lingering doubts must have been dispelled when, a few minutes later, the local estate agent appeared on the doorstep, tape measure in hand, with a photographer by his side.

'If Hugh was able to return even part of the hundred thousand I loaned him, that would be most helpful,' Cornelius remarked to his sister-in-law as he followed her through the house.

It was some time before she spoke, despite the fact that she had had all night to consider her response.

'It's not quite that easy,' she eventually replied. 'You see, the loan was made to the company, and the shares are distributed among several people.'

Cornelius knew all three of the several people. 'Then perhaps the time has come for you and Hugh to sell off some of your shares.'

'And allow some stranger to take over the company, after all the work we've put into it over the years? No, we can't afford to let that happen. In any case, Hugh asked Mr Vintcent what the legal position was, and he confirmed that there was no obligation on our part to sell any of our shares.'

'Have you considered that perhaps you have a moral obligation?' asked Cornelius, turning to face his sister-in-law.

'Cornelius,' she said, avoiding his stare, 'it has been your irresponsibility, not ours, that has been the cause of your downfall. Surely you wouldn't expect your brother to sacrifice everything he's worked for over the years, simply to place my family in the same perilous position in which you now find yourself?'

Cornelius realised why Elizabeth hadn't slept the previous night. She was not only acting as spokeswoman for Hugh, but was obviously making the decisions as well. Cornelius had always considered her to be the stronger-willed of the two, and he doubted if he would come face to face with his brother before an agreement had been reached.

'But if there's any other way we might help . . .' Elizabeth added in a more gentle tone, as her hand rested on an ornate gold-leafed table in the drawing room.

'Well, now you mention it,' replied Cornelius, 'I'm putting the house on the market in a couple of weeks' time, and will be looking for . . .'

'That soon?' said Elizabeth. 'And what's going to happen to all the furniture?'

'It will all have to be sold to help cover the debts. But, as I said . . .'

'Hugh has always liked this table.'

'Louis XIV,' said Cornelius casually.

'I wonder what it's worth,' Elizabeth mused, trying to make it sound as if it were of little consequence.

'I have no idea,' said Cornelius. 'If I remember correctly, I paid around £60,000 for it – but that was over ten years ago.'

'And the chess set?' Elizabeth asked, picking up one of the pieces.

'It's a worthless copy,' Cornelius replied. 'You could pick up a set just like it in any Arab bazaar for a couple of hundred pounds.'

'Oh, I always thought...' Elizabeth hesitated before replacing the piece on the wrong square. 'Well, I must be off,' she said, sounding as if her task had been completed. 'We must try not to forget that I still have a business to run.'

Cornelius accompanied her as she began striding back down the long corridor in the direction of the front door. She walked straight by the portrait of her nephew Daniel. In the past she had always stopped to remark on how much she missed him.

'I was wondering...' began Cornelius as they walked out into the hall.

'Yes?' said Elizabeth.

'Well, as I have to be out of here in a couple of weeks, I hoped it might be possible to move in with you. That is, until I find somewhere I can afford.'

'If only you'd asked a week ago,' said Elizabeth, without missing a beat. 'But unfortunately we've just agreed to take in my mother, and the only other room is Timothy's, and he comes home most weekends.'

'Is that so?' said Cornelius.

'And the grandfather clock?' asked Elizabeth, who still appeared to be on a shopping expedition.

'Victorian – I purchased it from the Earl of Bute's estate.'

'No, I meant how much is it worth?'

'Whatever someone is willing to pay for it,' Cornelius replied as they reached the front door.

'Don't forget to let me know, Cornelius, if there's anything I can do to help.'

'How kind of you, Elizabeth,' he said, opening the door to find the estate agent hammering a stake into the ground with a sign on it declaring FOR SALE. Cornelius smiled, because it was the only thing that morning that had stopped Elizabeth in her tracks.

Frank Vintcent arrived on the Thursday evening, carrying a bottle of cognac and two pizzas.

'If I'd realised that losing Pauline was to be part

of the deal, I would never have agreed to go along with your plan in the first place,' Frank said as he nibbled at his microwaved pizza. 'How do you manage without her?'

'Rather badly,' Cornelius admitted, 'although she still drops in for an hour or two every evening. Otherwise this place would look like a pigsty. Come to think of it, how do *you* cope?'

'As a bachelor,' Frank replied, 'you learn the art of survival from an early age. Now, let's stop this small-talk and get on with the game.'

'Which game?' enquired Cornelius with a chuckle.

'Chess,' replied Frank. 'I've had enough of the other game for one week.'

'Then we'd better go through to the library.'

Frank was surprised by Cornelius's opening moves, as he had never known his old friend to be so daring. Neither of them spoke again for over an hour, most of which Frank spent trying to defend his queen.

'This might well be the last game we play with this set,' said Cornelius wistfully.

'No, don't worry yourself about that,' said Frank. 'They always allow you to keep a few personal items.'

'Not when they're worth a quarter of a million pounds,' replied Cornelius.

'I had no idea,' said Frank, looking up.

'Because you're not the sort of man who has ever been interested in worldly goods. It's a sixteenth-century Persian masterpiece, and it's bound to cause considerable interest when it comes under the hammer.'

'But surely you've found out all you need to know by now,' said Frank. 'Why carry on with the exercise when you could lose so much that's dear to you?'

'Because I still have to discover the truth.'

Frank sighed, stared down at the board and moved his queen's knight. 'Checkmate,' he said. 'It serves you right for not concentrating.'

Cornelius spent most of Friday morning in a private meeting with the managing director of Botts and Company, the local fine art and furniture auctioneers.

Mr Botts had already agreed that the sale could take place in a fortnight's time. He had often repeated that he would have preferred a longer period to prepare the catalogue and send out an extensive mailing for such a fine collection, but at least he showed some sympathy for the position Mr Barrington found himself in. Over the years, Lloyd's of London, death duties and impending bankruptcy had proved the auctioneer's best friends.

'We will need to have everything in our store-room as soon as possible,' said Mr Botts, 'so there's enough time to prepare a catalogue, while still allowing the customers to view on three consecutive days before the sale takes place.'

Cornelius nodded his agreement.

The auctioneer also recommended that a full page be taken in the *Chudley Advertiser* the following Wednesday, giving details of what was coming under the hammer, so they could reach those people they failed to contact by post.

Cornelius left Mr Botts a few minutes before midday, and on his way back to the bus stop dropped into the removal company. He handed over £100 in fives and tens, leaving the impression that it had taken him a few days to raise the cash.

While waiting for the bus, he couldn't help noticing how few people bothered to say good morning, or even acknowledge him. Certainly no one crossed the road to pass the time of day.

*　　*　　*

Twenty men in three vans spent the next day loading and unloading as they travelled back and forth between The Willows and the auctioneers' storeroom in the High Street. It was not until the early evening that the last stick of furniture had been removed from the house.

As he walked through the empty rooms, Cornelius was surprised to find himself thinking that, with one or two exceptions, he wasn't going to miss many of his worldly possessions. He retired to the bedroom – the only room in the house that was still furnished – and continued to read the novel Elizabeth had recommended before his downfall.

The following morning he only had one call, from his nephew Timothy, to say he was up for the weekend, and wondered if Uncle Cornelius could find time to see him.

'Time is the one thing I still have plenty of,' replied Cornelius.

'Then why don't I drop round this afternoon?' said Timothy. 'Shall we say four o'clock?'

'I'm sorry I can't offer you a cup of tea,' said Cornelius, 'but I finished the last packet this morning, and as I'm probably leaving the house next week . . .'

'It's not important,' said Timothy, who was unable to mask his distress at finding the house stripped of his uncle's possessions.

'Let's go up to the bedroom. It's the only room that still has any furniture in it – and most of that will be gone by next week.'

'I had no idea they'd taken everything away. Even the picture of Daniel,' Timothy said as he passed an oblong patch of a lighter shade of cream than the rest of the wall.

'And my chess set,' sighed Cornelius. 'But I can't complain. I've had a good life.' He began to climb the stairs to the bedroom.

Cornelius sat in the only chair while Timothy perched on the end of the bed. The old man studied his nephew more closely. He had grown into a fine young man. An open face, with clear brown eyes that served to reveal, to anyone who didn't already know, that he had been adopted. He must have been twenty-seven or twenty-eight – about the same age Daniel would have been if he were still alive. Cornelius had always had a soft spot for his nephew, and had imagined that his affection was reciprocated. He wondered if he was about to be disillusioned once again.

Timothy appeared nervous, shuffling uneasily

from foot to foot as he perched on the end of the bed. 'Uncle Cornelius,' he began, his head slightly bowed, 'as you know, I have received a letter from Mr Vintcent, so I thought I ought to come to see you and explain that I simply don't have £1,000 to my name, and therefore I'm unable to repay my debt at present.'

Cornelius was disappointed. He had hoped that just one of the family . . .

'However,' the young man continued, removing a long, thin envelope from an inside pocket of his jacket, 'on my twenty-first birthday my father presented me with shares of 1 per cent of the company, which I think must be worth at least £1,000, so I wondered if you would consider taking them in exchange for my debt – that is, until I can afford to buy them back.'

Cornelius felt guilty for having doubted his nephew even for a moment. He wanted to apologise, but knew he couldn't if the house of cards was to remain in place for a few more days. He took the widow's mite and thanked Timothy.

'I am aware just how much of a sacrifice this must be for you,' said Cornelius, 'remembering how many times you have told me in the past of your ambition to take over the company when your father eventually retires, and your dreams of expanding into areas he has refused even to contemplate.'

'I don't think he'll ever retire,' said Timothy, with a sigh. 'But I was hoping that after all the experience I've gained working in London he might take me seriously as a candidate for manager when Mr Leonard retires at the end of the year.'

'I fear your chances won't be advanced when he learns that you've handed over 1 per cent of the company to your bankrupt uncle.'

'My problems can hardly be compared with the ones you are facing, Uncle. I'm only sorry I can't hand over the cash right now. Before I leave, is there anything else I can do for you?'

'Yes, there is, Timothy,' said Cornelius, returning to the script. 'Your mother recommended a novel, which I've been enjoying, but my old eyes seem to tire earlier and earlier, and I wondered if you'd be kind enough to read a few pages to me. I've marked the place I've reached.'

'I can remember you reading to me when I was a child,' said Timothy. '*Just William* and *Swallows and Amazons*,' he added as he took the proffered book.

Timothy must have read about twenty pages when he suddenly stopped and looked up.

'There's a bus ticket at page 450. Shall I leave it there, Uncle?'

'Yes, please do,' said Cornelius. 'I put it there to remind me of something.' He paused. 'Forgive me, but I'm feeling a little tired.'

Timothy rose and said, 'I'll come back soon and finish off the last few pages.'

'No need to bother yourself, I'll be able to manage that.'

'Oh, I think I'd better, Uncle, otherwise I'll never find out which one of them becomes Prime Minister.'

The second batch of letters, which Frank Vintcent sent out on the following Friday, caused another flurry of phone calls.

'I'm not sure I fully understand what it means,' said Margaret, in her first communication with her brother since calling round to see him a fortnight before.

'It means exactly what it says, my dear,' said Cornelius calmly. 'All my worldly goods are to come under the hammer, but I am allowing those I consider near and dear to me to select one item that, for sentimental or personal reasons, they would like to see remain in the family. They will then be able to bid for them at the auction next Friday.'

'But we could all be outbid and end up with nothing,' said Margaret.

'No, my dear,' said Cornelius, trying not to sound exasperated. 'The *public* auction will be held in the afternoon. The selected pieces will be auctioned separately in the morning, with only the family and close friends present. The instructions couldn't be clearer.'

'And are we able to see the pieces before the auction takes place?'

'Yes, Margaret,' said her brother, as if addressing a backward child. 'As Mr Vintcent stated clearly in his letter, "Viewing Tuesday, Wednesday, Thursday, 10 a.m. to 4 p.m., before the sale on Friday at eleven o'clock".'

'But we can only select one piece?'

'Yes,' repeated Cornelius, 'that is all the petitioner in bankruptcy would allow. But you'll be pleased to know that the portrait of Daniel, which you have commented on so many times in the past, will be among the lots available for your consideration.'

'Yes, I do like it,' said Margaret. She hesitated for a moment. 'But will the Turner also be up for sale?'

'It certainly will,' said Cornelius. 'I'm being forced to sell everything.'

'Have you any idea what Hugh and Elizabeth are after?'

'No, I haven't, but if you want to find out, why don't you ask them?' he replied mischievously, aware that they scarcely exchanged a word from one year's end to the next.

The second call came only moments after he had put the phone down on his sister.

'At last,' said a peremptory voice, as if it were somehow Cornelius's fault that others might also wish to speak to him.

'Good morning, Elizabeth,' said Cornelius, immediately recognising the voice. 'How nice to hear from you.'

'It's about the letter I received this morning.'

'Yes, I thought it might be,' said Cornelius.

'It's just, well, I wanted to confirm the value of the table – the Louis XIV piece – and, while I'm on the line, the grandfather clock that used to belong to the Earl of Bute.'

'If you go to the auction house, Elizabeth, they

will give you a catalogue, which tells you the high and low estimate for every item in the sale.'

'I see,' said Elizabeth. She remained silent for some time. 'I don't suppose you know if Margaret will be bidding for either of those pieces?'

'I have no idea,' replied Cornelius. 'But it was Margaret who was blocking the line when you were trying to get through, and she asked me a similar question, so I suggest you give her a call.' Another long silence. 'By the way, Elizabeth, you do realise that you can only bid for one item?'

'Yes, it says as much in the letter,' replied his sister-in-law tartly.

'I only ask because I always thought Hugh was interested in the chess set.'

'Oh no, I don't think so,' said Elizabeth. Cornelius wasn't in any doubt who would be doing the bidding on behalf of that family on Friday morning.

'Well, good luck,' said Cornelius. 'And don't forget the 15 per cent commission,' he added as he put the phone down.

Timothy wrote the following day to say he was hoping to attend the auction, as he wanted to pick up a little memento of The Willows and his uncle and aunt.

Pauline, however, told Cornelius as she tidied up the bedroom that she had no intention of going to the auction.

'Why not?' he asked.

'Because I'd be sure to make a fool of myself and bid for something I couldn't afford.'

'Very wise,' said Cornelius. 'I've fallen into that trap once or twice myself. But did you have your eye on anything in particular?'

'Yes, I did, but my savings would never stretch to it.'

'Oh, you can never be sure with auctions,' said Cornelius. 'If no one else joins in the bidding, sometimes you can make a killing.'

'Well, I'll think about it, now I've got a new job.'

'I'm so pleased to hear that,' said Cornelius, who was genuinely disappointed to learn her news.

Neither Cornelius nor Frank was able to concentrate on their weekly chess match that Thursday evening, and after half an hour they abandoned the game and settled on a draw.

'I must confess that I can't wait for things to

return to normal,' said Frank as his host poured him a glass of cooking sherry.

'Oh, I don't know. I find the situation has its compensations.'

'Like what for example?' said Frank, who frowned after his first sip.

'Well, for a start, I'm looking forward to tomorrow's auction.'

'But that could still go badly wrong,' said Frank.

'What can possibly go wrong?' asked Cornelius.

'Well, for a start, have you considered . . . ?' But he didn't bother to complete the sentence, because his friend wasn't listening.

Cornelius was the first to arrive at the auction house the following morning. The room was laid out with 120 chairs in neat rows of twelve, ready for the anticipated packed house that afternoon, but Cornelius thought the real drama would unfold in the morning, when only six people would be in attendance.

The next person to appear, fifteen minutes before the auction was due to begin, was Cornelius's solicitor Frank Vintcent. Observing his client deep in conversation with Mr Botts, who would be conducting the auction, he took a seat towards the back of the room on the right-hand side.

Cornelius's sister Margaret was the next to make an appearance, and she was not as considerate. She charged straight up to Mr Botts and asked in a shrill voice, 'Can I sit anywhere I like?'

'Yes, madam, you most certainly can,' said Mr Botts. Margaret immediately commandeered the centre seat in the front row, directly below the auctioneer's podium.

Cornelius gave his sister a nod before walking down the aisle and taking a chair three rows in front of Frank.

Hugh and Elizabeth were the next to arrive. They stood at the back for some time while they considered the layout of the room. Eventually they strolled up the aisle and occupied two seats in the eighth row, which afforded them a perfect sightline to the podium, while at the same time being able to keep an eye on Margaret. Opening move to Elizabeth, thought Cornelius, who was quietly enjoying himself.

As the hour hand of the clock on the wall behind the auctioneer's rostrum ticked inexorably towards eleven, Cornelius was disappointed that neither Pauline nor Timothy made an appearance.

Just as the auctioneer began to climb the steps

to the podium, the door at the back of the room
eased open and Pauline's head peered round. The
rest of her body remained hidden behind the door
until her eyes settled on Cornelius, who smiled
encouragingly. She stepped inside and closed the
door, but showed no interest in taking a seat,
retreating into a corner instead.

The auctioneer beamed down at the hand-
picked invitees as the clock struck eleven.

'Ladies and gentlemen,' he began, 'I've been in
the business for over thirty years, but this is the
first time I've conducted a private sale, so this is a
most unusual auction even for me. I'd better go
over the ground rules, so that no one can be in
any doubt should a dispute arise later.

'All of you present have some special association,
whether as family or friends, with Mr Cornelius Barrington, whose personal effects are coming under
the hammer. Each of you has been invited to select
one item from the inventory, for which you will be
allowed to bid. Should you be successful you may
not bid for any other lot, but if you fail on the item
of your first choice, you may join in the bidding for
any other lot. I hope that is clear,' he said, as the
door was flung open and Timothy rushed in.

'So sorry,' he said a little breathlessly, 'but my

train was held up.' He quickly took a seat in the back row. Cornelius smiled – every one of his pawns was now in place.

'As there are only five of you eligible to bid,' continued Mr Botts as if there had been no interruption, 'only five items will come under the hammer. But the law states that if anyone has previously left a written bid, that bid must be recognised as part of the auction. I shall make things as easy to follow as possible by saying if I have a bid at the table, from which you should assume it is a bid left at our office by a member of the public. I think it would be only fair to point out,' he added, 'that I have outside bids on four of the five items.

'Having explained the ground rules, I will with your permission begin the auction.' He glanced towards the back of the room at Cornelius, who nodded his assent.

'The first lot I am able to offer is a long-case clock, dated 1892, which was purchased by Mr Barrington from the estate of the late Earl of Bute.

'I shall open the bidding for this lot at £3,000. Do I see £3,500?' Mr Botts asked, raising an eyebrow. Elizabeth looked a little shocked, as three thousand was just below the low estimate and the figure she and Hugh had agreed on that morning.

'Is anyone interested in this lot?' asked Mr Botts, looking directly at Elizabeth, but she remained apparently mesmerised. 'I shall ask once again if anyone wishes to bid £3,500 for this magnificent long-case clock. Fair warning. I see no bids, so I shall have to withdraw this item and place it in the afternoon sale.'

Elizabeth still seemed to be in a state of shock. She immediately turned to her husband and began a whispered conversation with him. Mr Botts looked a little disappointed, but moved quickly on to the second lot.

'The next lot is a charming watercolour of the Thames by William Turner of Oxford. Can I open the bidding at £2,000?'

Margaret waved her catalogue furiously.

'Thank you, madam,' said the auctioneer, beaming down at her. 'I have an outside bid of £3,000. Will anyone offer me £4,000?'

'Yes!' shouted Margaret, as if the room were so crowded that she needed to make herself heard above the din.

'I have a bid of five thousand at the table – will you bid six, madam?' he asked, returning his attention to the lady in the front row.

'I will,' said Margaret equally firmly.

'Are there any other bids?' demanded the auctioneer, glancing around the room – a sure sign that the bids at the table had dried up. 'Then I'm going to let this picture go for £6,000 to the lady in the front row.'

'Seven,' said a voice behind her. Margaret looked round to see that her sister-in-law had joined in the bidding.

'Eight thousand!' shouted Margaret.

'Nine,' said Elizabeth without hesitation.

'Ten thousand!' bellowed Margaret.

Suddenly there was silence. Cornelius glanced across the room to see a smile of satisfaction cross Elizabeth's face, having left her sister-in-law with a bill for £10,000.

Cornelius wanted to burst out laughing. The auction was turning out to be even more entertaining than he could have hoped.

'There being no more bids, this delightful watercolour is sold to Miss Barrington for £10,000,' said Mr Botts as he brought the hammer down with a thump. He smiled down at Margaret, as if she had made a wise investment.

'The next lot,' he continued, 'is a portrait simply entitled *Daniel*, by an unknown artist. It is a well-executed work, and I was hoping to open the bidding at £100. Do I see a bid of one hundred?'

To Cornelius's disappointment, no one in the room seemed to be showing any interest in this lot.

'I am willing to consider a bid of £50 to get things started,' said Mr Botts, 'but I am unable to go any lower. Will anyone bid me £50?'

Cornelius glanced around the room, trying to work out from the expressions on their faces who had selected this item, and why they no longer wished to bid when the price was so reasonable.

'Then I fear I will have to withdraw this lot as well.'

'Does that mean I've got it?' asked a voice from the back. Everyone looked round.

'If you are willing to bid £50, madam,' said Mr Botts, adjusting his spectacles, 'the picture is yours.'

'Yes please,' said Pauline. Mr Botts smiled in her direction as he brought down the hammer. 'Sold to the lady at the back of the room,' he declared, 'for £50.'

'Now I move on to lot number four, a chess set of unknown provenance. What shall I say for this item? Can I start someone off with £100? Thank you, sir.'

Cornelius looked round to see who was bidding. 'I have two hundred at the table. Can I say three hundred?'

Timothy nodded.

'I have a bid at the table of three fifty. Can I say four hundred?'

This time Timothy looked crestfallen, and Cornelius assumed the sum was beyond his limit. 'Then I am going to have to withdraw this piece also and place it in this afternoon's sale.' The auctioneer stared at Timothy, but he didn't even blink. 'The item is withdrawn.'

'And finally I turn to lot number five. A magnificent Louis XIV table, circa 1712, in almost mint condition. Its provenance can be traced back to its original owner, and it has been in the possession of Mr Barrington for the past eleven years. The full details are in your catalogue. I must warn you that there has been a lot of interest in this item, and I shall open the bidding at £50,000.'

Elizabeth immediately raised her catalogue above her head.

'Thank you, madam. I have a bid at the table of sixty thousand. Do I see seventy?' he asked, his eyes fixed on Elizabeth.

Her catalogue shot up again.

'Thank you, madam. I have a bid at the table of eighty thousand. Do I see ninety?' This time Elizabeth seemed to hesitate before raising her catalogue slowly.

'I have a bid at the table of one hundred thousand. Do I see a hundred and ten?'

Everyone in the room was now looking towards Elizabeth, except Hugh, who, head down, was staring at the floor. He obviously wasn't going to have any influence on the bidding. 'If there are no further bids, I shall have to withdraw this lot and place it in the afternoon sale. Fair warning,' declared Mr Botts. As he raised his hammer, Elizabeth's catalogue suddenly shot up.

'One hundred and ten thousand. Thank you, madam. Are there any more bids? Then I shall let this fine piece go for £110,000.' He brought down his hammer and smiled at Elizabeth. 'Congratulations, madam, it is indeed a magnificent example of the period.' She smiled weakly back, a look of uncertainty on her face.

Cornelius turned round and winked at Frank, who remained impassively in his seat. He then rose from his place and made his way to the podium to thank Mr Botts for a job well done. As he turned to leave, he smiled at Margaret and Elizabeth, but neither acknowledged him, as they both seemed to be preoccupied. Hugh, head in hands, continued to stare down at the floor.

As Cornelius walked towards the back of the hall, he could see no sign of Timothy, and assumed that his nephew must have had to return to London. Cornelius was disappointed, as he had hoped the lad might join him for a pub lunch. After such a successful morning he felt a little celebrating was in order.

He had already decided that he wasn't going to attend the afternoon sale, as he had no desire to witness his worldly goods coming under the hammer, even though he wouldn't have room for most of them once he moved into a smaller house. Mr Botts had promised to call him the moment the sale was over and report how much the auction had raised.

Having enjoyed the best meal since Pauline had left him, Cornelius began his journey back from the pub to The Willows. He knew exactly what time the bus would appear to take him home, and arrived at the bus stop with a couple of minutes to spare. He now took it for granted that people would avoid his company.

Cornelius unlocked the front door as the clock

on the nearby church struck three. He was looking forward to the inevitable fall-out when it sank in to Margaret and Elizabeth how much they had really bid. He grinned as he headed towards his study and glanced at his watch, wondering when he might expect a call from Mr Botts. The phone began to ring just as he entered the room. He chuckled to himself. It was too early for Mr Botts, so it had to be Elizabeth or Margaret, who would need to see him urgently. He picked up the phone to hear Frank's voice on the other end of the line.

'Did you remember to withdraw the chess set from the afternoon sale?' Frank asked, without bothering with any formalities.

'What are you talking about?' said Cornelius.

'Your beloved chess set. Have you forgotten that as it failed to sell this morning, it will automatically come up in the afternoon sale? Unless of course you've already given orders to withdraw it, or tipped off Mr Botts about its true value.'

'Oh my God,' said Cornelius. He dropped the phone and ran back out of the door, so he didn't hear Frank say, 'I'm sure a telephone call to Mr Botts's assistant is all that will be needed.'

Cornelius checked his watch as he ran down the path. It was ten past three, so the auction would have only just begun. Running towards the bus stop, he tried to recall what lot number the chess set was. All he could remember was that there were 153 lots in the sale.

Standing at the bus stop, hopping impatiently from foot to foot, he scanned the road in the hope of hailing a passing taxi, when to his relief he saw a bus heading towards him. Although his eyes never left the driver, that didn't make him go any faster.

When it eventually drew up beside him and the doors opened, Cornelius leapt on and took his place on the front seat. He wanted to tell the driver to take him straight to Botts and Co. in the High Street, and to hell with the fare, but he doubted if the other passengers would have fallen in with his plan.

He stared at his watch – 3.17 p.m. – and tried to remember how long it had taken Mr Botts that morning to dispose of each lot. About a minute, a minute and a half perhaps, he concluded. The bus came to a halt at every stop on its short journey into town, and Cornelius spent as much time following the progress of the minute hand on his watch as he did the journey. The driver finally reached the High Street at 3.31 p.m.

Even the door seemed to open slowly. Cornelius leapt out onto the pavement, and despite not having run for years, sprinted for the second time that day. He covered the two hundred yards to the auction house in less than record pace, but still arrived exhausted. He charged into the auction room as Mr Botts declared, 'Lot number 32, a long-case clock originally purchased from the estate of . . .'

Cornelius's eyes swept the room, coming to rest on an auctioneer's clerk who was standing in the corner with her catalogue open, entering the hammer price after each lot had been sold. He walked over to her just as a woman he thought he recognised slipped quickly past him and out of the door.

'Has the chess set come up yet?' asked a still-out-of-breath Cornelius.

'Let me just check, sir,' the clerk replied, flicking back through her catalogue. 'Yes, here it is, lot 27.'

'How much did it fetch?' asked Cornelius.

'£450, sir,' she replied.

Mr Botts called Cornelius later that evening to inform him that the afternoon sale had raised £902,800 – far more than he had estimated.

'Do you by any chance know who bought the chess set?' was Cornelius's only question.

'No,' replied Mr Botts. 'All I can tell you is that it was purchased on behalf of a client. The buyer paid in cash and took the item away.'

As he climbed the stairs to go to bed, Cornelius had to admit that everything had gone to plan except for the disastrous loss of the chess set, for which he realised he had only himself to blame. What made it worse was that he knew Frank would never refer to the incident again.

Cornelius was in the bathroom when the phone rang at 7.30 the following morning. Obviously someone had been lying awake wondering what was the earliest moment they could possibly disturb him.

'Is that you, Cornelius?'

'Yes,' he replied, yawning noisily. 'Who's this?' he added, knowing only too well.

'It's Elizabeth. I'm sorry to call you so early, but I need to see you urgently.'

'Of course, my dear,' Cornelius replied, 'why don't you join me for tea this afternoon?'

'Oh no, it can't wait until then. I have to see you this morning. Could I come round at nine?'

'I'm sorry, Elizabeth, but I already have an appointment at nine.' He paused. 'But I could fit you in at ten for half an hour, then I won't be late for my meeting with Mr Botts at eleven.'

'I could give you a lift into town if that would help,' suggested Elizabeth.

'That's extremely kind of you, my dear,' said Cornelius, 'but I've got used to taking the bus, and in any case I wouldn't want to impose on you. Look forward to seeing you at ten.' He put the phone down.

Cornelius was still in the bath when the phone rang a second time. He wallowed in the warm water until the ringing had ceased. He knew it was Margaret, and he was sure she would call back within minutes.

He hadn't finished drying himself before the phone rang again. He walked slowly to the bed-room, picked up the receiver by his bed and said, 'Good morning Margaret.'

'Good morning, Cornelius,' she said, sounding surprised. Recovering quickly, she added, 'I need to see you urgently.'

'Oh? What's the problem?' asked Cornelius, well aware exactly what the problem was.

'I can't possibly discuss such a delicate matter

over the phone, but I could be with you by ten.'

'I'm afraid I've already agreed to see Elizabeth at ten. It seems that she also has an urgent matter she needs to discuss with me. Why don't you come round at eleven?'

'Perhaps it would be better if I came over immediately,' said Margaret, sounding flustered.

'No, I'm afraid eleven is the earliest I can fit you in, my dear. So it's eleven or afternoon tea. Which would suit you best?'

'Eleven,' said Margaret without hesitation.

'I thought it might,' said Cornelius. 'I'll look forward to seeing you then,' he added before replacing the receiver.

When Cornelius had finished dressing, he went down to the kitchen for breakfast. A bowl of corn-flakes, a copy of the local paper and an unstamped envelope were awaiting him, although there was no sign of Pauline.

He poured himself a cup of tea, tore open the envelope and extracted a cheque made out to him for £500. He sighed. Pauline must have sold her car.

He began to turn the pages of the Saturday supplement, stopping when he reached 'Houses for Sale'. When the phone rang for the third time that morning, he had no idea who it might be.

'Good morning, Mr Barrington,' said a cheerful voice. 'It's Bruce from the estate agents. I thought I'd give you a call to let you know we've had an offer for The Willows that is in excess of the asking price.'

'Well done,' said Cornelius.

'Thank you, sir,' said the agent, with more respect in his voice than Cornelius had heard from anyone for weeks, 'but I think we should hold on for a little longer. I'm confident I can squeeze some more out of them. If I do, my advice would be to accept the offer and ask for a 10 per cent deposit.'

'That sounds like good advice to me,' said Cornelius. 'And once they've signed the contract, I'll need you to find me a new house.'

'What sort of thing are you looking for, Mr Barrington?'

'I want something about half the size of The Willows, with perhaps a couple of acres, and I'd like to remain in the immediate area.'

'That shouldn't be too hard, sir. We have one or two excellent houses on our books at the moment, so I'm sure we'll be able to accommodate you.'

'Thank you,' said Cornelius, delighted to have spoken to someone who had begun the day well.

He was chuckling over an item on the front page of the local paper when the doorbell rang. He checked his watch. It was still a few minutes to ten, so it couldn't be Elizabeth. When he opened the front door he was greeted by a man in a green uniform, holding a clipboard in one hand and a parcel in the other.

'Sign here,' was all the courier said, handing over a biro.

Cornelius scrawled his signature across the bottom of the form. He would have asked who had sent the parcel if he had not been distracted by a car coming up the drive.

'Thank you,' he said. He left the package in the hall and walked down the steps to welcome Elizabeth.

When the car drew up outside the front door, Cornelius was surprised to find Hugh seated in the passenger seat.

'It was kind of you to see us at such short notice,' said Elizabeth, who looked as if she had spent another sleepless night.

'Good morning, Hugh,' said Cornelius, who suspected his brother had been kept awake all night.

'Please come through to the kitchen – I'm afraid it's the only room in the house that's warm.'

As he led them down the long corridor, Elizabeth stopped in front of the portrait of Daniel. 'I'm so glad to see it back in its rightful place,' she said. Hugh nodded his agreement.

Cornelius stared at the portrait, which he hadn't seen since the auction. 'Yes, back in its rightful place,' he said, before taking them through to the kitchen. 'Now, what brings you both to The Willows on a Saturday morning?' he asked as he filled the kettle.

'It's about the Louis XIV table,' said Elizabeth diffidently.

'Yes, I shall miss it,' said Cornelius. 'But it was a fine gesture on your part, Hugh,' he added.

'A fine gesture . . .' repeated Hugh.

'Yes. I assumed it was your way of returning my hundred thousand,' said Cornelius. Turning to Elizabeth, he said, 'How I misjudged you, Elizabeth. I suspect it was your idea all along.'

Elizabeth and Hugh just stared at each other, then both began speaking at once.

'But we didn't . . .' said Hugh.

'We were rather hoping . . .' said Elizabeth. Then they both fell silent.

'Tell him the truth,' said Hugh firmly.

'Oh?' said Cornelius. 'Have I misunderstood what took place at the auction yesterday morning?'

'Yes, I'm afraid you have,' said Elizabeth, any remaining colour draining from her cheeks. 'You see, the truth of the matter is that the whole thing got out of control, and I carried on bidding for longer than I should have done.' She paused. 'I'd never been to an auction before, and when I failed to get the grandfather clock, and then saw Margaret pick up the Turner so cheaply, I'm afraid I made a bit of a fool of myself.'

'Well, you can always put it back up for sale,' said Cornelius with mock sadness. 'It's a fine piece, and sure to retain its value.'

'We've already looked into that,' said Elizabeth. 'But Mr Botts says there won't be another furniture auction for at least three months, and the terms of the sale were clearly printed in the catalogue: settlement within seven days.'

'But I'm sure that if you were to leave the piece with him . . .'

'Yes, he suggested that,' said Hugh. 'But we didn't realise that the auctioneers add 15 per cent to the sale price, so the real bill is for £126,500. And what's worse, if we put it up for sale again they also retain 15 per cent of the price that's bid, so we would end up losing over thirty thousand.'

'Yes, that's the way auctioneers make their money,' said Cornelius with a sigh.

'But we don't have thirty thousand, let alone 126,500,' cried Elizabeth.

Cornelius slowly poured himself another cup of tea, pretending to be deep in thought. 'Umm,' he finally offered. 'What puzzles me is how you think I could help, bearing in mind my current financial predicament.'

'We thought that as the auction had raised nearly a million pounds . . .' began Elizabeth.

'Far higher than was estimated,' chipped in Hugh.

'We hoped you might tell Mr Botts you'd decided to keep the piece; and of course we would confirm that that was acceptable to us.'

'I'm sure you would,' said Cornelius, 'but that still doesn't solve the problem of owing the auctioneer £16,500, and a possible further loss if it fails to reach £110,000 in three months' time.'

Neither Elizabeth nor Hugh spoke.

'Do you have anything you could sell to help raise the money?' Cornelius eventually asked.

'Only our house, and that already has a large mortgage on it,' said Elizabeth.

'But what about your shares in the company? If you sold them, I'm sure they would more than cover the cost.'

'But who would want to buy them,' asked Hugh, 'when we're only just breaking even?'

'I would,' said Cornelius.

Both of them looked surprised. 'And in exchange for your shares,' Cornelius continued, 'I would release you from your debt to me, and also settle any embarrassment with Mr Botts.'

Elizabeth began to protest, but Hugh asked, 'Is there any alternative?'

'Not that I can think of,' said Cornelius.

'Then I don't see that we're left with much choice,' said Hugh, turning to his wife.

'But what about all those years we've put into the company?' wailed Elizabeth.

'The shop hasn't been showing a worthwhile profit for some time, Elizabeth, and you know it. If we don't accept Cornelius's offer, we could be paying off the debt for the rest of our lives.'

Elizabeth remained unusually silent.

'Well, that seems to be settled,' said Cornelius. 'Why don't you just pop round and have a word with my solicitor? He'll see that everything is in order.'

'And will you sort out Mr Botts?' asked Elizabeth.

'The moment you've signed over the shares, I'll deal with the problem of Mr Botts. I'm confident we can have everything settled by the end of the week.'

Hugh bowed his head.

'And I think it might be wise,' continued Cornelius – they both looked up and stared apprehensively at him – 'if Hugh were to remain on the board of the company as Chairman, with the appropriate remuneration.'

'Thank you,' said Hugh, shaking hands with his brother. 'That's generous of you in the circumstances.' As they returned down the corridor Cornelius stared at the portrait of his son once again.

'Have you managed to find somewhere to live?' asked Elizabeth.

'It looks as if that won't be a problem after all, thank you, Elizabeth. I've had an offer for The Willows far in excess of the price I'd anticipated, and what with the windfall from the auction, I'll be able to pay off all my creditors, leaving me with a comfortable sum over.'

'Then why do you need our shares?' asked Elizabeth, swinging back to face him.

'For the same reason you wanted my Louis XIV table, my dear,' said Cornelius as he opened the front door to show them out. 'Goodbye Hugh,' he added as Elizabeth got into the car.

Cornelius would have returned to the house, but he spotted Margaret coming up the drive in her new car, so he stood and waited for her. When she brought the little Audi to a halt, Cornelius opened the car door to allow her to step out.

'Good morning, Margaret,' he said as he accompanied her up the steps and into the house. 'How nice to see you back at The Willows. I can't remember when you were last here.'

'I've made a dreadful mistake,' his sister admitted, long before they had reached the kitchen.

Cornelius refilled the kettle and waited for her to tell him something he already knew.

'I won't beat about the bush, Cornelius. You see, I had no idea there were two Turners.'

'Oh, yes,' said Cornelius matter-of-factly. 'Joseph Mallord William Turner, arguably the finest painter ever to hail from these shores, and William

Turner of Oxford, no relation, and although painting at roughly the same period, certainly not in the same league as the master.'

'But I didn't realise that . . .' Margaret repeated. 'So I ended up paying far too much for the wrong Turner – not helped by my sister-in-law's antics,' she added.

'Yes, I was fascinated to read in the morning paper that you've got yourself into the *Guinness Book of Records* for having paid a record price for the artist.'

'A record I could have done without,' said Margaret. 'I was rather hoping you might feel able to have a word with Mr Botts, and . . .'

'And what . . . ?' asked Cornelius innocently, as he poured his sister a cup of tea.

'Explain to him that it was all a terrible mistake.'

'I'm afraid that won't be possible, my dear. You see, once the hammer has come down, the sale is completed. That's the law of the land.'

'Perhaps you could help me out by paying for the picture,' Margaret suggested. 'After all, the papers are saying you made nearly a million pounds from the auction alone.'

'But I have so many other commitments to consider,' said Cornelius with a sigh. 'Don't forget that once The Willows is sold, I will have to find somewhere else to live.'

'But you could always come and stay with me . . .'

'That's the second such offer I've had this morning,' said Cornelius, 'and as I explained to Elizabeth, after being turned down by both of you earlier, I have had to make alternative arrangements.'

'Then I'm ruined,' said Margaret dramatically, 'because I don't have £10,000, not to mention the 15 per cent. Something else I didn't know about. You see, I'd hoped to make a small profit by putting the painting back up for sale at Christie's.'

The truth at last, thought Cornelius. Or perhaps half the truth.

'Cornelius, you've always been the clever one in the family,' Margaret said, with tears welling up in her eyes. 'Surely you can think of a way out of this dilemma.'

Cornelius paced around the kitchen as if in deep thought, his sister watching his every step. Eventually he came to a halt in front of her. 'I do believe I may have a solution.'

'What is it?' cried Margaret. 'I'll agree to anything.'

'Anything?'

'Anything,' she repeated.

'Good, then I'll tell you what I'll do,' said Cornelius. 'I'll pay for the picture in exchange for your new car.'

Margaret remained speechless for some time. 'But the car cost me £12,000,' she said finally.

'Possibly, but you wouldn't get more than eight thousand for it second-hand.'

'But then how would I get around?'

'Try the bus,' said Cornelius. 'I can recommend it. Once you've mastered the timetable it changes your whole life.' He glanced at his watch. 'In fact, you could start right now; there's one due in about ten minutes.'

'But . . .' said Margaret as Cornelius stretched out his open hand. Then, letting out a long sigh, she opened her handbag and passed the car keys over to her brother.

'Thank you,' said Cornelius. 'Now I mustn't hold you up any longer, or you'll miss the bus, and there won't be another one along for thirty minutes.' He led his sister out of the kitchen and down the corridor. He smiled as he opened the door for her.

'And don't forget to pick up the picture from Mr Botts, my dear,' he said. 'It will look wonderful over the fireplace in your drawing room, and will bring back so many happy memories of our times together.'

Margaret didn't comment as she turned to walk off down the long drive.

Cornelius closed the door and was about to go to his study and call Frank to brief him on what had taken place that morning when he thought he heard a noise coming from the kitchen. He changed direction and headed back down the corridor. He walked into the kitchen, went over to the sink, bent down and kissed Pauline on the cheek.

'Good morning, Pauline,' he said.

'What's that for?' she asked, her hands immersed in soapy water.

'For bringing my son back home.'

'It's only on loan. If you don't behave yourself, it goes straight back to my place.'

Cornelius smiled. 'That reminds me – I'd like to take you up on your original offer.'

'What are you talking about, Mr Barrington?'

'You told me that you'd rather work off the debt than have to sell your car.' He removed her cheque from an inside pocket. 'I know just how many hours you've worked here over the past month,' he said, tearing the cheque in half, 'so let's call it quits.'

'That's very kind of you, Mr Barrington, but I only wish you'd told me that before I sold the car.'

'That's not a problem, Pauline, because I find myself the proud owner of a new car.'

'But how?' asked Pauline as she began to dry her hands.

'It was an unexpected gift from my sister,' Cornelius said, without further explanation.

'But you don't drive, Mr Barrington.'

'I know. So I'll tell you what I'll do,' said Cornelius. 'I'll swap it for the picture of Daniel.'

'But that's not a fair exchange, Mr Barrington. I only paid £50 for the picture, and the car must be worth far more.'

'Then you'll also have to agree to drive me into town from time to time.'

'Does that mean I've got my old job back?'

'Yes – if you're willing to give up your new one.'

'I don't have a new one,' said Pauline with a sigh. 'They found someone a lot younger than me the day before I was due to begin.'

Cornelius threw his arms around her.

'And we'll have less of that for a start, Mr Barrington.'

Cornelius took a pace back. 'Of course you can have your old job back, and with a rise in salary.'

'Whatever you consider is appropriate, Mr Barrington. After all, the labourer is worthy of his hire.'

Cornelius somehow stopped himself from laughing.

'Does this mean all the furniture will be coming back to The Willows?'

'No, Pauline. This house has been far too large for me since Millie's death. I should have realised that some time ago. I'm going to move out and look for something smaller.'

'I could have told you to do that years ago,' Pauline said. She hesitated. 'But will that nice Mr Vintcent still be coming to supper on Thursday evenings?'

'Until one of us dies, that's for sure,' said Cornelius with a chuckle.

'Well, I can't stand around all day chattering, Mr Barrington. After all, a woman's work is never done.'

'Quite so,' said Cornelius, and quickly left the kitchen. He walked back through the hall, picked up the package, and took it through to his study.

He had removed only the outer layer of

wrapping paper when the phone rang. He put the package to one side and picked up the receiver to hear Timothy's voice.

'It was good of you to come to the auction, Timothy. I appreciated that.'

'I'm only sorry that my funds didn't stretch to buying you the chess set, Uncle Cornelius.'

'If only your mother and aunt had shown the same restraint . . .'

'I'm not sure I understand, Uncle.'

'It's not important,' said Cornelius. 'So, what can I do for you, young man?'

'You've obviously forgotten that I said I'd come over and read the rest of that story to you – unless of course you've already finished it.'

'No, I'd quite forgotten about it, what with the drama of the last few days. Why don't you come round tomorrow evening, then we can have supper as well. And before you groan, the good news is that Pauline is back.'

'That's excellent news, Uncle Cornelius. I'll see you around eight tomorrow.'

'I look forward to it,' said Cornelius. He replaced the receiver and returned to the half-opened package. Even before he had removed the final layer of paper, he knew exactly what was inside. His heart began beating faster. He finally raised the lid of the heavy wooden box and stared down at the thirty-two exquisite ivory pieces. There was a note inside: 'A small appreciation for all your kindness over the years. Hugh.'

Then he recalled the face of the woman who had slipped past him at the auction house. Of course, it had been his brother's secretary. The second time he had misjudged someone.

'What an irony,' he said out loud. 'If Hugh had put the set up for sale at Sotheby's, he could have held on to the Louis XIV table and had the same amount left over. Still, as Pauline would have said, it's the thought that counts.'

He was writing a thank-you note to his brother when the phone rang again. It was Frank, reliable as ever, reporting in on his meeting with Hugh.

'Your brother has signed all the necessary documents, and the shares have been transferred as requested.'

'That was quick work,' said Cornelius.

'The moment you gave me instructions last week, I had all the legal papers drawn up. You're still the most impatient client I have. Shall I bring the share certificates round on Thursday evening?'

'No,' said Cornelius. 'I'll drop in this afternoon

and pick them up. That is, assuming Pauline is free to drive me into town.'

'Am I missing something?' asked Frank, sounding a little bewildered.

'Don't worry, Frank. I'll bring you up to date when I see you on Thursday evening.'

Timothy arrived at The Willows a few minutes after eight the following evening. Pauline immediately put him to work peeling potatoes.

'How are your mother and father?' asked Cornelius, probing to discover how much the boy knew.

'They seem fine, thank you Uncle. By the way, my father's offered me the job of shop manager. I begin on the first of next month.'

'Congratulations,' said Cornelius. 'I'm delighted. When did he make the offer?'

'Some time last week,' replied Timothy.

'Which day?'

'Is it important?' asked Timothy.

'I think it might be,' replied Cornelius, without explanation.

The young man remained silent for some time, before he finally said, 'Yes, it was Saturday evening, after I'd seen you.' He paused. 'I'm not sure

Mum's all that happy about it. I meant to write and let you know, but as I was coming back for the auction, I thought I'd tell you in person. But then I didn't get a chance to speak to you.'

'So he offered you the job before the auction took place?'

'Oh yes,' said Timothy. 'Nearly a week before.' Once again, the young man looked quizzically at his uncle, but still no explanation was forthcoming.

Pauline placed a plate of roast beef in front of each of them as Timothy began to reveal his plans for the company's future.

'Mind you, although Dad will remain as Chairman,' he said, 'he's promised not to interfere too much. I was wondering, Uncle Cornelius, now that you own 1 per cent of the company, whether you would be willing to join the board?'

Cornelius looked first surprised, then delighted, then doubtful.

'I could do with your experience,' added Timothy, 'if I'm to go ahead with my expansion plans.'

'I'm not sure your father would consider it a good idea to have me on the board,' said Cornelius, with a wry smile.

'I can't think why not,' said Timothy. 'After all, it was his idea in the first place.'

Cornelius remained silent for some time. He hadn't expected to go on learning more about the players after the game was officially over.

'I think the time has come for us to go upstairs and find out if it's Simon Kerslake or Raymond Gould who becomes Prime Minister,' he eventually said.

Timothy waited until his uncle had poured himself a large brandy and lit a cigar – his first for a month – before he started to read.

He became so engrossed in the story that he didn't look up again until he had turned the last page, where he found an envelope sellotaped to the inside of the book's cover. It was addressed to 'Mr Timothy Barrington'.

'What's this?' he asked.

Cornelius would have told him, but he had fallen asleep.

The doorbell rang at eight, as it did every Thursday evening. When Pauline opened the door, Frank handed her a large bunch of flowers.

'Oh, Mr Barrington will appreciate those,' she said. 'I'll put them in the library.'

'They're not for Mr Barrington,' said Frank, with a wink.

'I'm sure I don't know what's come over you two gentlemen,' Pauline said, scurrying away to the kitchen.

As Frank dug into a second bowl of Irish stew, Cornelius warned him that it could be their last meal together at The Willows.

'Does that mean you've sold the house?' Frank asked, looking up.

'Yes. We exchanged contracts this afternoon, but on the condition that I move out immediately. After such a generous offer, I'm in no position to argue.'

'And how's the search for a new place coming along?'

'I think I've found the ideal house, and once the surveyors have given the all clear, I'll be putting an offer in. I'll need you to push the paperwork through as quickly as possible so that I'm not homeless for too long.'

'I certainly will,' said Frank, 'but in the meantime, you'd better come and camp out with me. I'm all too aware what the alternatives are.'

'The local pub, Elizabeth or Margaret,' said

Cornelius, with a grin. He raised his glass. 'Thank you for the offer. I accept.'

'But there's one condition,' said Frank.

'And what might that be?' asked Cornelius.

'That Pauline comes as part of the package, because I have no intention of spending all my spare time tidying up after you.'

'What do you think about that, Pauline?' asked Cornelius as she began to clear away the plates.

'I'm willing to keep house for both of you gentlemen, but only for one month. Otherwise you'd never move out, Mr Barrington.'

'I'll make sure there are no hold-ups with the legal work, I promise,' said Frank.

Cornelius leant across to him conspiratorially. 'She hates lawyers, you know, but I do think she's got a soft spot for you.'

'That may well be the case, Mr Barrington, but it won't stop me leaving after a month, if you haven't moved into your new house.'

'I think you'd better put down that deposit fairly quickly,' said Frank. 'Good houses come on the market all the time, good housekeepers rarely.'

'Isn't it time you two gentlemen got on with your game?'

'Agreed,' said Cornelius. 'But first, a toast.'

'Who to?' asked Frank.

'Young Timothy,' said Cornelius, raising his glass, 'who will start as Managing Director of Barrington's, Chudley, on the first of the month.'

'To Timothy,' said Frank, raising his glass.

'You know he's asked me to join the board,' said Cornelius.

'You'll enjoy that, and he'll benefit from your experience. But it still doesn't explain why you gave him all your shares in the company, despite him failing to secure the chess set for you.'

'That's precisely why I was willing to let him take control of the company. Timothy, unlike his mother and father, didn't allow his heart to rule his head.'

Frank nodded his approval as Cornelius drained the last drop of wine from the one glass they allowed themselves before a game.

'Now, I feel I ought to warn you,' said Cornelius as he rose from his place, 'that the only reason you have won the last three encounters in a row is simply because I have had other things on my mind. Now that those matters have been resolved, your run of luck is about to come to an end.'

'We shall see,' said Frank, as they marched down the long corridor together. The two men stopped for a moment to admire the portrait of Daniel.

'How did you get that back?' asked Frank.

'I had to strike a mean bargain with Pauline, but we both ended up with what we wanted.'

'But how . . . ?' began Frank.

'It's a long story,' Cornelius replied, 'and I'll tell you the details over a brandy after I've won the game.'

Cornelius opened the library door and allowed his friend to enter ahead of him, so that he could observe his reaction. When the inscrutable lawyer saw the chess set laid out before him, he made no comment, but simply walked across to the far side of the table, took his usual place and said, 'Your move first, if I remember correctly.'

'You're right,' said Cornelius, trying to hide his irritation. He pushed his queen's pawn to Q4.

'Back to an orthodox opening gambit. I see I shall have to concentrate tonight.'

They had been playing for about an hour, no word having passed between them, when Cornelius could bear it no longer. 'Are you not in the least bit curious to discover how I came back into possession of the chess set?' he asked.

'No,' said Frank, his eyes remaining fixed on the board. 'Not in the least bit.'

'But why not, you old dullard?'

'Because I already know,' Frank said as he moved his queen's bishop across the board.

'How can you possibly know?' demanded Cornelius, who responded by moving a knight back to defend his king.

Frank smiled. 'You forget that Hugh is also my client,' he said, moving his king's rook two squares to the right.

Cornelius smiled. 'And to think he need never have sacrificed his shares, if he had only known the true value of the chess set.' He returned his queen to its home square.

'But he did know its true value,' said Frank, as he considered his opponent's last move.

'How could he possibly have found out, when you and I were the only people who knew?'

'Because I told him,' said Frank matter-of-factly.

'But why would you do that?' asked Cornelius, staring across at his oldest friend.

'Because it was the only way I could find out if Hugh and Elizabeth were working together.'

'So why didn't he bid for the set in the morning auction?'

'Precisely because he didn't want Elizabeth to know what he was up to. Once he discovered that

Timothy was also hoping to purchase the set in order to give it back to you, he remained silent.'

'But he could have kept bidding once Timothy had fallen out.'

'No, he couldn't. He had agreed to bid for the Louis XIV table, if you recall, and that was the last item to come under the hammer.'

'But Elizabeth failed to get the long-case clock, so she could have bid for it.'

'Elizabeth is not my client,' said Frank, as he moved his queen across the board. 'So she never discovered the chess set's true value. She believed what you had told her – that at best it was worth a few hundred pounds – which is why Hugh instructed his secretary to bid for the set in the afternoon.'

'Sometimes you can miss the most obvious things, even when they are staring you right in the face,' said Cornelius, pushing his rook five squares forward.

'I concur with that judgement,' said Frank, moving his queen across to take Cornelius's rook. He looked up at his opponent and said, 'I think you'll find that's checkmate.'

The Letter

All the guests were seated around the breakfast table when Muriel Arbuthnot strode into the room, clutching the morning post. She extracted a long white envelope from the pile and handed it over to her oldest chum.

A puzzled look came over Anna Clairmont's face. Who could possibly know that she was spending the weekend with the Arbuthnots? Then she saw the familiar handwriting, and had to smile at his ingenuity. She hoped her husband Robert, who was seated at the far end of the table, hadn't noticed, and was relieved to see that he remained engrossed in his copy of *The Times*.

Anna was trying to wedge her thumb into the corner of the envelope while keeping a wary eye on Robert, when suddenly he glanced across at her and smiled. She returned the smile, dropped the envelope in her lap, picked up her fork and jabbed it into a lukewarm mushroom.

She made no attempt to retrieve the letter until her husband had disappeared back behind his paper. Once he had turned to the business section, she placed the envelope on her right-hand side, picked up the butter knife and slipped it into the thumbed corner. Slowly, she began to slit open the envelope. Having completed the task, she returned the knife to its place by the side of the butter dish.

Before making her next move, she once again glanced across in the direction of her husband, to check that he was still hidden behind his newspaper. He was.

She held down the envelope with her left hand, while carefully extracting the letter with her right. She then placed the envelope in the bag by her side.

She looked down at the familiar Basildon Bond cream notepaper, folded in three. One more casual glance in Robert's direction; as he remained out of sight, she unfolded the two-page letter.

No date, no address, the first page, as always, written on continuation paper.

'*My darling Titania*'. The first night of the *Dream* at Stratford, followed by the first night they had slept together. Two firsts on the same night, he had remarked. *'I am sitting in my bedroom, our bedroom, penning these thoughts only moments after you have left me. This is a third attempt, as I can't find the right words to let you know how I really feel.'*

Anna smiled. For a man who had made his fortune with words, that must have been quite difficult for him to admit.

'Last night you were everything a man could ask from a lover. You were exciting, tender, provocative, teasing, and, for an exquisite moment, a rampant whore.

'It's been over a year since we met at the Selwyns' dinner party in Norfolk, and, as I have often told you, I wanted you to come back home with me that evening. I lay awake all night imagining you lying next to the prune.' Anna glanced across the table to see that Robert had reached the back page of his paper.

'And then there was that chance meeting at Glyndebourne – but it was still to be another eleven days before you were unfaithful for the first time, and then not until the prune was away in Brussels. That night went far too quickly for me.

'I can't imagine what the prune would have made of it, if he had seen you in your maid's outfit. He'd have probably assumed that you always tidied up the drawing room in Lonsdale Avenue in a white see-through blouse, no bra, a skin-tight black leather skirt with a zip up the

front, fishnet stockings and stiletto heels, not forgetting the shocking-pink lipstick.'

Anna looked up again and wondered if she was blushing. If he had really enjoyed himself that much, she would have to go on another shopping trip in Soho as soon as she got back to town. She continued to read the letter.

'My darling, there is no aspect of our lovemaking that I don't relish, but I confess that what turns me on the most is the places you choose when you can only take an hour off work during your lunch break. I can recall every one of them. On the back seat of my Mercedes in that NCP carpark in Mayfair; the service lift in Harrods; the loo at the Caprice. But most exciting of all was that little box in the dress circle at Covent Garden during a performance of Tristan and Isolde. *Once before the first interval and then again during the final act – well, it is a long opera.'*

Anna giggled and quickly placed the letter back into her lap as Robert peered round the side of his newspaper.

'What made you laugh, my dear?' he asked.

'The picture of James Bond landing on the Dome,' she said. Robert looked puzzled. 'On the front of your paper.'

'Ah, yes,' said Robert, glancing at the front page,

but he didn't smile as he returned to the business section.

Anna retrieved the letter.

'What maddens me most about your spending the week-end with Muriel and Reggie Arbuthnot is the thought of you being in the same bed as the prune. I've tried to convince myself that as the Arbuthnots are related to the Royal family, they've probably given you separate bedrooms.'

Anna nodded, wishing she could tell him he had guessed correctly.

'And does he really snore like the QE II *coming into Southampton harbour? I can see him now, sitting on the far side of the breakfast table. Harris tweed jacket, grey trousers, checked shirt, wearing an MCC tie, as thought to be fashionable by* Hare and Hound *circa 1966.'*

This time Anna did burst out laughing, and was only rescued by Reggie Arbuthnot rising from his end of the table to enquire, 'Anyone care to make up a four for tennis? The weather forecast is predicting that the rain will stop long before the morning's out.'

'I'll be happy to join you,' said Anna, secreting the letter back under the table.

'How about you, Robert?' Reggie asked.

Anna watched as her husband folded up *The Times*, placed it on the table in front of him and shook his head.

Oh my God, thought Anna. He *is* wearing a tweed jacket and an MCC tie.

'I'd love to,' said Robert, 'but I'm afraid I have to make several phone calls.'

'On a Saturday morning?' said Muriel, who was standing at the laden sideboard, filling her plate for a second time.

'Afraid so,' replied Robert. 'You see, criminals don't work a five-day, forty-hour week, so they don't expect their lawyers to do so either.' Anna didn't laugh. After all, she had heard him make the same observation every Saturday for the past seven years.

Robert rose from the table, glanced towards his wife and said, 'If you need me, my dear, I'll be in my bedroom.'

Anna nodded and waited for him to leave the room.

She was about to return to her letter when she noticed that Robert had left his glasses on the table. She would take them through to him as soon as she had finished breakfast. She placed the letter on the table in front of her and turned to the second page.

'Let me tell you what I have planned for our anniversary weekend while the prune is away at his conference in Leeds. I've booked us back into the Lygon Arms, so we'll be in the same room in which we spent our first night together. This time I've got tickets for All's Well. But I plan a change of atmosphere once we have returned from Stratford to the privacy of our room in Broadway.

'I want to be tied up to a four-poster bed, with you standing over me in a police sergeant's uniform: truncheon, whistle, handcuffs, wearing a tight black outfit with silver buttons down the front, which you will undo slowly to reveal a black bra. And, my darling, you're not to release me until I have made you scream at the top of your voice, the way you did in that underground carpark in Mayfair.

'Until then,

'Your loving Oberon.'

Anna raised her head and smiled, wondering where she could get her hands on a police sergeant's uniform. She was about to turn back to the front page and read the letter again when she noticed the P.S.

'P.S. I wonder what the prune is up to right now.'

Anna looked up to see that Robert's glasses were no longer on the table.

'What scoundrel could write such an outrageous

letter to a married woman?' demanded Robert as he adjusted his glasses.

Anna turned, horrified to see her husband standing behind her and staring down at the letter, beads of sweat appearing on his forehead.

'Don't ask me,' said Anna coolly, as Muriel appeared by her side, tennis racket in hand. Anna folded her letter, passed it over to her oldest friend, winked and said, 'Fascinating, my dear, but for your sake I do hope Reggie never finds out.'

Crime Pays

Kenny Merchant – that wasn't his real name, but then, little was real about Kenny – had selected Harrods on a quiet Monday morning as the venue for the first part of the operation.

Kenny was dressed in a pinstriped suit, white shirt and Guards tie. Few of the shop's customers would have realised it was a Guards tie, but he was confident that the assistant he had selected to serve him would recognise the crimson and dark-blue stripes immediately.

The door was held open for him by a commissionaire who had served in the Coldstream Guards, and who on spotting the tie immediately saluted him. The same commissionaire had not saluted him on any of his several visits during the previous week, but to be fair, Kenny had been dressed then in a shiny, well-worn suit, open-necked shirt and dark glasses. But last week had only been for reconnaissance; today he planned to be arrested.

Although Harrods has over a hundred thousand customers a week, the quietest period is always between ten and eleven on a Monday morning. Kenny knew every detail about the great store, in the way a football fan knows all the statistics of his favourite team.

He knew where all the CCTV cameras were placed, and could recognise any of the security guards at thirty paces. He even knew the name of the assistant who would be serving him that morning, although Mr Parker had no idea that he had been selected as a tiny cog in Kenny's well-oiled machine.

When Kenny appeared at the jewellery department that morning, Mr Parker was briefing a young assistant on the changes he required to the shelf display.

'Good morning, sir,' he said, turning to face his first customer of the day. 'How can I help you?'

'I was looking for a pair of cufflinks,' Kenny said, in the clipped tones he hoped made him sound like a Guards officer.

'Yes, of course sir,' said Mr Parker.

It amused Kenny to see the deferential treatment he received as a result of the Guards tie, which he had been able to purchase in the men's department the previous day for an outlay of £23.

'Any particular style?' asked the sales assistant.

'I'd prefer silver.'

'Of course, sir,' said Mr Parker, who proceeded to place on the counter several boxes of silver cufflinks.

Kenny already knew the pair he wanted, as he had picked them out the previous Saturday afternoon. 'What about those?' he asked, pointing to the top shelf. As the sales assistant turned away, Kenny checked the TV surveillance camera and took a pace to his right, to be sure that they could see him more clearly. While Mr Parker reached up to remove the cufflinks, Kenny slid the chosen pair off the counter and slipped them into his jacket pocket before the assistant turned back round.

Out of the corner of his eye, Kenny saw a security guard moving swiftly towards him, while at the same time speaking into his walkie-talkie.

'Excuse me, sir,' said the guard, touching his elbow. 'I wonder if you would be kind enough to accompany me.'

'What's this all about?' demanded Kenny, trying to sound annoyed, as a second security guard appeared on his other side.

'Perhaps it might be wise if you were to accompany us, so that we can discuss the matter privately,' suggested the second guard, holding onto his arm a little more firmly.

'I've never been so insulted in my life,' said Kenny, now speaking at the top of his voice. He took the cufflinks out of his pocket, replaced them on the counter and added, 'I had every intention of paying for them.'

The guard picked up the box. To his surprise the irate customer then accompanied him to the interview room without uttering another word.

On entering the little green-walled room, Kenny was asked to take a seat on the far side of a desk. One guard returned to his duties on the ground floor while the other remained by the door. Kenny knew that on an average day, forty-two people were arrested for shoplifting at Harrods, and over 90 per cent of them were prosecuted.

A few moments later, the door opened and a tall, thin man with a weary look on his face entered the room. He took a seat on the other side of the desk and glanced across at Kenny before pulling open a drawer and removing a green form.

'Name?' he said.

'Kenny Merchant,' Kenny replied without hesitation.

'Address?'

'42 St Luke's Road, Putney.'

'Occupation?'

'Unemployed.'

Kenny spent several more minutes accurately answering the tall man's enquiries. When the inquisitor reached his final question, he spent a moment studying the silver cufflinks before filling in the bottom line. Value: £90. Kenny knew all too well the significance of that particular sum.

The form was then swivelled round for Kenny to sign, which to the inquisitor's surprise he did with a flourish.

The guard then accompanied Kenny to an adjoining room, where he was kept waiting for almost an hour. The guard was surprised that Kenny didn't ask what would happen next. All the others did. But then, Kenny knew exactly what was going to happen next, despite the fact that he had never been charged with shoplifting before.

About an hour later the police arrived and he was driven, along with five others, to Horseferry Road Magistrates' Court. There followed another long wait before he came up in front of the magistrate. The charge was read out to him and he pleaded guilty. As the value of the cufflinks was under £100, Kenny knew he would receive a fine rather than a custodial sentence, and he waited patiently for the magistrate to ask the same question he had when Kenny had sat at the back of the court and listened to several cases the previous week.

'Is there anything else you would like me to take into consideration before I pass sentence?'

'Yes, sir,' said Kenny. 'I stole a watch from Selfridges last week. It's been on my conscience ever since, and I would like to return it.' He beamed up at the magistrate.

The magistrate nodded and, looking down at the defendant's address on the form in front of him, ordered that a constable should accompany Mr Merchant to his home and retrieve the stolen merchandise. For a moment the magistrate almost looked as if he was going to praise the convicted criminal for his act of good citizenship, but like Mr Parker, the guard and the inquisitor, he didn't realise he was simply another cog in a bigger wheel.

Kenny was driven to his home in Putney by a young constable, who told him that he'd only been on the job for a few weeks. Then you're in for a bit of a shock, thought Kenny as he unlocked the front door of his home and invited the officer in.

'Oh my God,' said the young man the moment he stepped into the sitting room. He turned, ran back out of the flat and immediately called his station sergeant on the car radio. Within minutes, two patrol cars were parked outside Kenny's home in St Luke's Road. Chief Inspector Travis marched through the open door to find Kenny sitting in the hall, holding up the stolen watch.

'To hell with the watch,' said the Chief Inspector. 'What about this lot?' he said, his arms sweeping around the sitting room.

'It's all mine,' said Kenny. 'The only thing I admit to stealing, and am now returning, is one watch. Timex Masterpiece, value £44, taken from Selfridges.'

'What's your game, laddie?' asked Travis.

'I have no idea what you mean,' said Kenny innocently.

'You know exactly what I mean,' said the Chief Inspector. 'This place is full of expensive jewellery, paintings, *objets d'art* and antique furniture' – around £300,000-worth, Kenny would have liked to have told him – 'and I don't believe any of it belongs to you.'

'Then you'll have to prove it, Chief Inspector, because should you fail to do so, the law assumes that it belongs to me. And that being the case, I will be able to dispose of it as I wish.' The Chief Inspector frowned, informed Kenny of his rights and arrested him for theft.

When Kenny next appeared in court, it was at the Old Bailey, in front of a judge. Kenny was dressed appropriately for the occasion in a pin-striped suit, white shirt and Guards tie. He stood in the dock charged with the theft of goods to the value of £24,000.

The police had made a complete inventory of everything they found in the flat, and spent the next six months trying to trace the owners of the treasure trove. But despite advertising in all the recognised journals, and even showing the stolen goods extensively on television's *Crimewatch*, as well as putting them on display for the public to view, over 80 per cent of the items remained unclaimed.

Chief Inspector Travis tried to bargain with Kenny, saying he would recommend a lenient sentence if he would cooperate and reveal who the property belonged to.

'It all belongs to me,' repeated Kenny.

'If that's going to be your game, don't expect any help from us,' said the Chief Inspector.

Kenny hadn't expected any help from Travis in the first place. It had never been part of his original plan.

Kenny had always believed that if you penny-pinch when it comes to selecting a lawyer, you could well end up paying dearly for it. So when he stood in the dock he was represented by a leading firm of solicitors and a silky barrister called Arden Duveen, QC, who wanted £10,000 on his brief.

Kenny pleaded guilty to the indictment, aware that when the police gave evidence they would be unable to mention any of the goods that had remained unclaimed, and which the law therefore assumed belonged to him. In fact, the police had already reluctantly returned the property that they were unable to prove had been stolen, and Kenny had quickly passed it on to a dealer for a third of its value, compared with the tenth he had been offered by a fence six months before.

Mr Duveen, QC, defending, pointed out to the judge that not only was it his client's first offence, but that he had invited the police to accompany him to his home, well aware that they would discover the stolen goods and that he would be arrested. Could there be better proof of a repentant and remorseful man, he asked.

Mr Duveen went on to point out to the court that Mr Merchant had served nine years in the armed services, and had been honourably discharged following active service in the Gulf, but that since leaving the army he seemed unable to settle down to civilian life. Mr Duveen did not claim this as an excuse for his client's behaviour, but he wished the court to know that Mr Merchant had vowed never to commit such a crime again, and therefore pleaded with the judge to impose a lenient sentence.

Kenny stood in the dock, his head bowed.

The judge lectured him for some time on how evil his crime had been, but added that he had taken into consideration all the mitigating circumstances surrounding this case, and had settled on a prison sentence of two years.

Kenny thanked him, and assured him that he would not be bothering him again. He knew that the next crime he had planned could not end up with a prison sentence.

Chief Inspector Travis watched as Kenny was

taken down, then, turning to the prosecuting counsel, asked, 'How much do you imagine that bloody man has made by keeping to the letter of the law?'

'About a hundred thousand would be my bet,' replied the Crown's silk.

'More than I'd be able to put by in a lifetime,' the Chief Inspector commented, before uttering a string of words that no one present felt able to repeat to their wives over dinner that evening.

Prosecuting counsel was not far out. Kenny had deposited a cheque at the Hongkong and Shanghai Bank earlier that week for £86,000.

What the Chief Inspector couldn't know was that Kenny had completed only half of his plan, and that now the seed money was in place, he was ready to prepare for an early retirement. Before he was taken away to prison, he made one further request of his solicitor.

While Kenny was holed up in Ford Open Prison he used his time well. He spent every spare moment going over various Acts of Parliament that were currently being debated in the House of Commons. He quickly dismissed several Green Papers, White Papers and Bills on health, education and the social services, before he came across the Data Protection Bill, each clause of which he set about studying as assiduously as any Member of the House of Commons at the report stage of the Bill. He followed each new amendment that was placed before the House, and each new clause as it was passed. Once the Act had become law in 1992, he sought a further interview with his solicitor.

The solicitor listened carefully to Kenny's questions and, finding himself out of his depth, admitted he would have to seek counsel's opinion. 'I will get in touch with Mr Duveen immediately,' he said.

While Kenny waited for his QC's judgement, he asked to be supplied with copies of every business magazine published in the United Kingdom.

The solicitor tried not to look puzzled by this request, as he had done when he had been asked to supply every Act of Parliament currently being debated in the House of Commons. During the next few weeks, bundles and bundles of magazines arrived at the prison, and Kenny spent all his spare time cutting out any advertisements that appeared in three magazines or more.

A year to the day after Kenny had been

sentenced, he was released on parole following his exemplary behaviour. When he walked out of Ford Open Prison, having served only half his term, the one thing he took with him was a large brown envelope containing three thousand advertisements and the written opinion of leading counsel on clause 9, paragraph 6, subsection (a) of the Data Protection Act 1992.

A week later, Kenny took a flight to Hong Kong.

The Hong Kong police reported back to Chief Inspector Travis that Mr Merchant had booked into a small hotel, and spent his days visiting local printers, seeking quotes for the publication of a magazine entitled *Business Enterprise UK*, and the retail price of headed notepaper and envelopes. The magazine, they quickly discovered, would contain a few articles on finance and shares, but the bulk of its pages would be taken up with small advertisements.

The Hong Kong police confessed themselves puzzled when they discovered how many copies of the magazine Kenny had ordered to be printed.

'How many?' asked Chief Inspector Travis.

'Ninety-nine.'

'Ninety-nine? There has to be a reason,' was Travis's immediate response.

He was even more puzzled when he discovered that there was already a magazine called *Business Enterprise*, and that it published 10,000 copies a month.

The Hong Kong police later reported that Kenny had ordered 2,500 sheets of headed paper, and 2,500 brown envelopes.

'So what's he up to?' demanded Travis.

No one in Hong Kong or London could come up with a convincing suggestion.

Three weeks later, the Hong Kong police reported that Mr Merchant had been seen at a local post office, despatching 2,400 letters to addresses all over the United Kingdom.

The following week, Kenny flew back to Heathrow.

Although Travis kept Kenny under surveillance, the young constable was unable to report anything untoward, other than that the local postman had told him Mr Merchant was receiving around twenty-five letters a day, and that like clockwork he would drop into Lloyd's Bank in the King's Road around noon and deposit several cheques for amounts ranging from two hundred to two thousand pounds. The constable didn't report that Kenny gave him a wave every morning just before entering the bank.

After six months the letters slowed to a trickle, and Kenny's visits to the bank almost came to a halt.

The only new piece of information the Constable was able to pass on to Chief Inspector Travis was that Mr Merchant had moved from his small flat in St Luke's Road, Putney, to an imposing four-storey mansion in Chester Square, SW1.

Just as Travis turned his attention to more pressing cases, Kenny flew off to Hong Kong again. 'Almost a year to the day,' was the Chief Inspector's only comment.

The Hong Kong police reported back to the Chief Inspector that Kenny was following roughly the same routine as he had the previous year, the only difference being that this time he had booked himself into a suite at the Mandarin. He had selected the same printer, who confirmed that his client had made another order for *Business Enterprise UK*. The second issue had some new articles, but would contain only 1,971 advertisements.

'How many copies is he having published this time?' asked the Chief Inspector.

'The same as before,' came back the reply. 'Ninety-nine. But he's only ordered two thousand sheets of headed paper and two thousand envelopes.'

'What is he up to?' repeated the Chief Inspector. He received no reply.

Once the magazine had rolled off the presses, Kenny returned to the post office and sent out 1,971 letters, before taking a flight back to London, care of British Airways, first class.

Travis knew Kenny must be breaking the law somehow, but he had neither the staff nor the resources to follow it up. And Kenny might have continued to milk this particular cow indefinitely had a complaint from a leading company on the stock exchange not landed on the Chief Inspector's desk.

A Mr Cox, the company's financial director, reported that he had received an invoice for £500 for an advertisement his firm had never placed.

The Chief Inspector visited Mr Cox in his City office. After a long discussion, Cox agreed to assist the police by pressing charges.

The Crown took the best part of six months to prepare its case before sending it to the CPS for consideration. They took almost as long before deciding to prosecute, but once they had, the Chief Inspector drove straight to Chester Square and personally arrested Kenny on a charge of fraud.

Mr Duveen appeared in court the following morning, insisting that his client was a model citizen. The judge granted Kenny bail, but demanded that he lodge his passport with the court.

'That's fine by me,' Kenny told his solicitor. 'I won't be needing it for a couple of months.'

The trial opened at the Old Bailey six weeks later, and once again Kenny was represented by Mr Duveen. While Kenny stood to attention in the dock, the clerk of the court read out seven charges of fraud. On each charge he pleaded not guilty. Prosecuting counsel made his opening statement, but the jury, as in so many financial trials, didn't look as if they were following his detailed submissions.

Kenny accepted that twelve good men and women true would decide whether they believed him or Mr Cox, as there wasn't much hope that they would understand the niceties of the 1992 Data Protection Act.

When Mr Cox read out the oath on the third day, Kenny felt he was the sort of man you could trust with your last penny. In fact, he thought he might even invest a few thousand in his company.

Mr Matthew Jarvis, QC, counsel for the Crown, took Mr Cox through a series of gentle questions designed to show him to be a man of such probity that he felt it was nothing less than his public duty to ensure that the evil fraud perpetrated by the defendant was stamped out once and for all.

Mr Duveen rose to cross-examine him.

'Let me begin, Mr Cox, by asking you if you ever saw the advertisement in question.'

Mr Cox stared down at him in righteous indignation.

'Yes, of course I did,' he replied.

'Was it of a quality that in normal circumstances would have been acceptable to your company?'

'Yes, but . . .'

'No "buts", Mr Cox. It either was, or it was not, of a quality acceptable to your company.'

'It was,' replied Mr Cox, through pursed lips.

'Did your company end up paying for the advertisement?'

'Certainly not,' said Mr Cox. 'A member of my staff queried the invoice, and immediately brought it to my attention.'

'How commendable,' said Duveen. 'And did that same member of staff spot the wording concerning payment of the invoice?'

'No, it was I who spotted that,' said Mr Cox, looking towards the jury with a smile of satisfaction.

'Most impressive, Mr Cox. And can you still recall the exact wording on the invoice?'

'Yes, I think so,' said Mr Cox. He hesitated, but only for a moment. ' "If you are dissatisfied with the product, there is no obligation to pay this invoice." '

' "No obligation to pay this invoice," ' repeated Duveen.

'Yes,' Mr Cox replied. 'That's what it stated.'

'So you didn't pay the bill?'

'No, I did not.'

'Allow me to sum up your position, Mr Cox. You received a free advertisement in my client's magazine, of a quality that would have been acceptable to your company had it been in any other periodical. Is that correct?'

'Yes, but . . .' began Mr Cox.

'No more questions, m'lud.'

Duveen had avoided mentioning those clients who *had* paid for their advertisements, as none of them was willing to appear in court for fear of the adverse publicity that would follow. Kenny felt his QC had destroyed the prosecution's star witness, but Duveen warned him that Jarvis would try to do the same to him the moment he stepped into the witness box.

The judge suggested a break for lunch. Kenny didn't eat – he just perused the Data Protection Act once again.

When the court resumed after lunch, Mr Duveen informed the judge that he would be calling only the defendant.

Kenny entered the witness box dressed in a dark-blue suit, white shirt and Guards tie.

Mr Duveen spent some considerable time allowing Kenny to take him through his army career and the service he had given to his country in the Gulf, without touching on the service he had more recently given at Her Majesty's pleasure. He then proceeded to guide Kenny through the evidence in brief. By the time Duveen had resumed his place, the jury were in no doubt that they were dealing with a businessman of unimpeachable rectitude.

Mr Matthew Jarvis QC rose slowly from his place, and made great play of rearranging his papers before asking his first question.

'Mr Merchant, allow me to begin by asking you about the periodical in question, *Business Enterprise UK*. Why did you select that particular name for your magazine?'

'It represents everything I believe in.'

'Yes, I'm sure it does, Mr Merchant, but isn't the truth that you were trying to mislead potential advertisers into confusing your publication with *Business Enterprise*, a magazine of many years' standing and an impeccable reputation. Isn't that what you were really up to?'

'No more than *Woman* does with *Woman's Own*, or *House and Garden* with *Homes and Gardens*,' Kenny retorted.

'But all the magazines you have just mentioned sell many thousands of copies. How many copies of *Business Enterprise UK* did you publish?'

'Ninety-nine,' replied Kenny.

'Only ninety-nine? Then it was hardly likely to top the bestsellers' list, was it? Please enlighten the court as to why you settled on that particular figure.'

'Because it is fewer than a hundred, and the

Data Protection Act 1992 defines a publication as consisting of at least one hundred copies. Clause 2, subsection 11.'

'That may well be the case, Mr Merchant, which is all the more reason,' suggested Mr Jarvis, 'that to expect clients to pay £500 for an unsolicited advertisement in your magazine was outrageous.'

'Outrageous, perhaps, but not a crime,' said Kenny, with a disarming smile.

'Allow me to move on, Mr Merchant. Perhaps you could explain to the court on what you based your decision, when it came to charging each company.'

'I found out how much their accounts departments were authorised to spend without having to refer to higher authority.'

'And what deception did you perpetrate to discover that piece of information?'

'I called the accounts department and asked to speak to the billing clerk.'

A ripple of laughter ran through the courtroom. The judge cleared his throat theatrically and demanded the court come to order.

'And on that alone you based your decision on how much to charge?'

'Not entirely. You see, I did have a rate card.

Prices varied between £2,000 for a full-colour page and £200 for a quarter-page, black and white. I think you'll find we're fairly competitive – if anything, slightly below the national average.'

'Certainly you were below the national average for the number of copies produced,' snapped Mr Jarvis.

'I've known worse.'

'Perhaps you can give the court an example,' said Mr Jarvis, confident that he had trapped the defendant.

'The Conservative Party.'

'I'm not following you, Mr Merchant.'

'They hold a dinner once a year at Grosvenor House. They sell around five hundred programmes and charge £5,000 for a full-page advertisement in colour.'

'But at least they allow potential advertisers every opportunity to refuse to pay such a rate.'

'So do I,' retorted Kenny.

'So, you do not accept that it is against the law to send invoices to companies who were never shown the product in the first place?'

'That may well be the law in the United Kingdom,' said Kenny, 'even in Europe. But it does not apply if the magazine is produced in Hong Kong, a British colony, and the invoices are despatched from that country.'

Mr Jarvis began sifting through his papers.

'I think you'll find it's amendment 9, clause 4, as amended in the Lords at report stage,' said Kenny.

'But that is not what their Lordships intended when they drafted that particular amendment,' said Jarvis, moments after he had located the relevant clause.

'I am not a mind-reader, Mr Jarvis,' said Kenny, 'so I cannot be sure what their Lordships intended. I am only interested in keeping to the letter of the law.'

'But you broke the law by receiving money in England and not declaring it to the Inland Revenue.'

'That is not the case, Mr Jarvis. *Business Enterprise UK* is a subsidiary of the main company, which is registered in Hong Kong. In the case of a British colony, the Act allows subsidiaries to receive the income in the country of distribution.'

'But you made no attempt to distribute the magazine, Mr Merchant.'

'A copy of *Business Enterprise UK* was placed in the British Library and several other leading institutions, as stipulated in clause 19 of the Act.'

'That may be true, but there is no escaping the fact, Mr Merchant, that you were demanding money under false pretences.'

'Not if you state clearly on the invoice that if the client is dissatisfied with the product, they are not required to make any payment.'

'But the wording on the invoice is so small that you would need a magnifying glass to see it.'

'Consult the Act, Mr Jarvis, as I did. I could not find anything to indicate what size the lettering should be.'

'And the colour?'

'The colour?' asked Kenny, feigning surprise.

'Yes, Mr Merchant, the colour. Your invoices were printed on dark-grey paper, while the lettering was light grey.'

'Those are the company colours, Mr Jarvis, as anyone would know who had looked at the cover of the magazine. And there is nothing in the Act to suggest what colour should be used when sending out invoices.'

'Ah,' said prosecuting counsel, 'but there is a clause in the Act stating in unambiguous terms that the wording should be placed in a prominent position. Clause 3, paragraph 14.'

'That is correct, Mr Jarvis.'

'And do you feel that the back of the paper could be described as a prominent position?'

'I certainly do,' said Kenny. 'After all, there wasn't anything else on the back of the page. I do also try to keep to the spirit of the law.'

'Then so will I,' snapped Jarvis. 'Because once a company has paid for an advertisement in *Business Enterprise UK*, is it not also correct that that company must be supplied with a copy of the magazine?'

'Only if requested – clause 42, paragraph 9.'

'And how many companies requested a copy of *Business Enterprise UK*?'

'Last year it was 107. This year it dropped to ninety-one.'

'And did they all receive copies?'

'No. Unfortunately, in some cases they didn't last year, but this year I was able to fulfil every order.'

'So you broke the law on that occasion?'

'Yes, but only because I was unable to print a hundred copies of the magazine, as I explained earlier.'

Mr Jarvis paused to allow the judge to complete a note. 'I think you'll find it's clause 84, paragraph 6, m'lud.'

The judge nodded.

'Finally, Mr Merchant, let me turn to something you lamentably failed to tell your defence counsel when he was questioning you.'

Kenny gripped the side of the witness box.

'Last year you sent out 2,400 invoices. How many companies sent back payments?'

'Around 45 per cent.'

'How many, Mr Merchant?'

'1,130,' admitted Kenny.

'And this year, you sent out only 1,900 invoices. May I ask why five hundred companies were reprieved?'

'I decided not to invoice those firms that had declared poor annual results and had failed to offer their shareholders a dividend.'

'Most commendable, I'm sure. But how many still paid the full amount?'

'1,090,' said Kenny.

Mr Jarvis stared at the jury for some time before asking, 'And how much profit did you make during your first year?'

The courtroom was as silent as it had been at any point during the eight-day trial as Kenny considered his reply. '£1,412,000,' he eventually replied.

'And this year?' asked Mr Jarvis quietly.

'It fell a little, which I blame on the recession.'

'How much?' demanded Mr Jarvis.

'A little over £1,200,000.'

'No more questions, m'lud.'

Both leading counsels made robust final statements, but Kenny sensed that the jury would wait to hear the judge's summing-up on the following day before they came to their verdict.

Mr Justice Thornton took a considerable time to sum the case up. He pointed out to the jury that it was his responsibility to explain to them the law as it applied in this particular case.

'And we are certainly dealing with a man who has studied the letter of the law. And that is his privilege, because it is parliamentarians who make the law, and it is not for the courts to try and work out what was in their minds at the time.

'To that end I must tell you that Mr Merchant is charged on seven counts, and on six of them I must advise you to return a verdict of "not guilty", because I direct you that Mr Merchant has not broken the law.

'On the seventh charge – that of failing to supply copies of his magazine, *Business Enterprise UK*, to those customers who had paid for an advertisement and then requested a copy – he admitted that, in a few cases, he failed so to do. Members of the jury, you may feel that he certainly broke the law on that occasion, even though he rectified the position a year later – and then I suspect only because the number of requests had fallen below one hundred copies. Members of the jury will possibly recall that particular clause of the Data Protection Act, and its significance.' Twelve blank expressions didn't suggest that they had much idea what he was talking about.

The judge ended with the words, 'I hope you will not take your final decision lightly, as there are several parties beyond this courtroom who will be awaiting your verdict.'

The defendant had to agree with that sentiment as he watched the jury file out of the courtroom, accompanied by the ushers. He was taken back down to his cell, where he declined lunch, and spent over an hour lying on a bunk before he was asked to return to the dock and learn his fate.

Once Kenny had climbed the stairs and was back in the dock, he only had to wait a few minutes before the jury filed back into their places.

The judge took his seat, looked down towards the clerk of the court and nodded. The clerk then turned his attention to the foreman of the jury and read out each of the seven charges.

On the first six counts of fraud and deception, the foreman followed the instructions of the judge and delivered verdicts of 'not guilty'.

The clerk then read out the seventh charge: failure to supply a copy of the magazine to those companies who, having paid for an advertisement in the said magazine and requested a copy of the said magazine, failed to receive one. 'How do you find the defendant on this charge – guilty or not guilty?' asked the clerk.

'Guilty,' said the foreman, and resumed his seat.

The judge turned his attention to Kenny, who was standing to attention in the dock.

'Like you, Mr Merchant,' he began, 'I have spent a considerable time studying the Data Protection Act 1992, and in particular the penalties for failing to adhere to clause 84, paragraph 1. I have decided that I am left with no choice but to inflict on you the maximum penalty the law allows in this particular case.' He stared down at Kenny, looking as if he was about to pronounce the death sentence.

'You will be fined £1,000.'

Mr Duveen did not rise to seek leave for appeal

or time to pay, because it was exactly the verdict Kenny had predicted before the trial opened. He had made only one error during the past two years, and he was happy to pay for it. Kenny left the dock, wrote out a cheque for the amount demanded and passed it across to the clerk of the court.

Having thanked his legal team, he checked his watch and quickly left the courtroom. The Chief Inspector was waiting for him in the corridor.

'So that should finally put paid to your little business enterprise,' said Travis, running along-side him.

'I can't imagine why,' said Kenny, as he con-tinued jogging down the corridor.

'Because Parliament will now have to change the law,' said the Chief Inspector, 'and this time it will undoubtedly tie up all your little loop-holes.'

'Not in the near future would be my bet, Chief Inspector,' Kenny said as he left the building and began jogging down the courtroom steps. 'As Parliament is about to rise for the summer recess, I can't see them finding time for new amendments to the Data Protection Act much before February or March of next year.'

'But if you try to repeat the exercise, I'll arrest

you the moment you get off the plane,' Travis said as Kenny came to a halt on the pavement.

'I don't think so, Chief Inspector.'

'Why not?'

'I can't imagine the CPS will be willing to go through another expensive trial, if all they're likely to end up with is a fine of £1,000. Think about it, Chief Inspector.'

'Well, I'll get you the following year,' said Travis.

'I doubt it. You see, by then Hong Kong will no longer be a Crown Colony, and I will have moved on,' said Kenny as he climbed into a taxi.

'Moved on?' said the Chief Inspector, looking puzzled.

Kenny pulled the taxi window down, smiled at Travis and said, 'If you've nothing better to do with your time, Chief Inspector, I recommend that you study the new Financial Provisions Act. You wouldn't believe how many loopholes there are in it. Goodbye, Chief Inspector.'

'Where to, guv?' asked the taxi driver.

'Heathrow. But could we stop at Harrods on the way? There's a pair of cufflinks I want to pick up.'

Chalk and Cheese

'Such a talented child,' said Robin's mother, as she poured her sister another cup of tea. 'The headmaster said on speech day that the school hadn't produced a finer artist in living memory.'

'You must be so proud of him,' said Miriam, before sipping her tea.

'Yes, I confess I am,' admitted Mrs Summers, almost purring. 'Of course, although everyone knew he would win the Founder's Prize, even his art master was surprised when he was offered a place at the Slade before he had sat his entrance exam. It's only sad that his father didn't live long enough to enjoy his triumph.'

'And how's John getting on?' enquired Miriam, as she selected a jam tart.

Mrs Summers sighed as she considered her older son. 'John will finish his Business Management course at Manchester some time in the summer, but he doesn't seem able to make up his mind what he wants to do.' She paused as she dropped another lump of sugar in her tea. 'Heaven knows what will become of him. He talks about going into business.'

'He always worked so hard at school,' said Miriam.

'Yes, but he never quite managed to come top of anything, and he certainly didn't leave with any prizes. Did I tell you that Robin has been offered the chance of a one-man show in October? It's only a local gallery, of course, but as he pointed out, every artist has to start somewhere.'

John Summers travelled back to Peterborough to attend his brother's first one-man show. His mother would never have forgiven him had he failed to put in an appearance. He had just learned the result of his Business Management examinations. He had been awarded a 2.1 degree, which wasn't bad considering he had been Vice President of the student union, with a President who had rarely made an appearance once he'd been elected. He wouldn't tell Mother about his degree, as it was Robin's special day.

After years of being told by his mother what a brilliant artist his brother was, John had come to assume it would not be long before the rest of the world acknowledged the fact. He often reflected about how different the two of them were; but then, did people know how many brothers Picasso had? No doubt one of them went into business.

It took John some time to find the little back street where the gallery was located, but when he did he was pleased to discover it packed with friends and wellwishers. Robin was standing next to his mother, who was suggesting the words 'magnificent', 'outstanding', 'truly talented' and even 'genius' to a reporter from the *Peterborough Echo*.

'Oh, look, John has arrived,' she said, leaving her little coterie for a moment to acknowledge her other son.

John kissed her on the cheek and said, 'Robin couldn't have a better send-off to his career.'

'Yes, I'm bound to agree with you,' his mother concurred. 'And I'm sure it won't be long before you can bask in his glory. You'll be able to tell everyone that you're Robin Summers's elder brother.'

Mrs Summers left John to have another photograph taken with Robin, which gave him the opportunity to stroll around the room and study his brother's canvases. They consisted mainly of the portfolio he had put together during his last year at school. John, who readily confessed his ignorance when it came to art, felt it must be his own inadequacy that caused him not to appreciate his brother's obvious talent, and he felt guilty that they weren't the kind of pictures he would want to see hanging in his home. He stopped in front of a portrait of his mother, which had a red dot next to it to indicate that it had been sold. He smiled, confident that he knew who had bought it.

'Don't you think it captures the very essence of her soul?' said a voice from behind him.

'It certainly does,' said John, as he swung round to face his brother. 'Well done. I'm proud of you.'

'One of the things I most admire about you,' said Robin, 'is that you have never envied my talent.'

'Certainly not,' said John. 'I delight in it.'

'Then let's hope that some of my success rubs off on you, in whatever profession you should decide to follow.'

'Let's hope so,' said John, not sure what else he could say.

Robin leaned forward and lowered his voice. 'I

don't suppose you could lend me a pound? I'll pay it back, of course.'

'Of course.'

John smiled – at least some things never changed. It had begun years earlier, with sixpence in the playground, and had ended up with a ten-shilling note on Speech Day. Now he needed a pound. Of only one thing could John be certain: Robin would never return a penny. Not that John begrudged his younger brother the money. After all, it wouldn't be long before their roles would surely be reversed. John removed his wallet, which contained two pound-notes and his train ticket back to Manchester. He extracted one of the notes and handed it over to Robin.

John was going to ask him a question about another picture – an oil called *Barabbas in Hell* – but his brother had already turned on his heel and rejoined his mother and the adoring entourage.

When John left Manchester University he was immediately offered a job as a trainee with Reynolds and Company, by which time Robin had taken up residence in Chelsea. He had moved into a set of rooms which his mother described to Miriam as small, but certainly in the most fashionable part of town. She didn't add that he was having to share them with five other students.

'And John?' enquired Miriam.

'He's joined a company in Birmingham that makes wheels; or at least I think that's what they do,' she said.

John settled into digs on the outskirts of Solihull, in a very unfashionable part of town. They were conveniently situated, close to a factory that expected him to clock in by eight o'clock from Monday to Saturday while he was still a trainee.

John didn't bore his mother with the details of what Reynolds and Company did, as manufacturing wheels for the nearby Longbridge car plant didn't have quite the same cachet as being an *avant garde* artist residing in bohemian Chelsea.

Although John saw little of his brother during Robin's days at the Slade, he always travelled down to London to view the end-of-term shows.

In their freshman year, students were invited to exhibit two of their works, and John admitted – only to himself – that when it came to his brother's efforts, he didn't care for either of them. But then, he accepted that he had no real knowledge of art. When the critics seemed to agree with John's judgement, their mother explained it away as

Robin being ahead of his time, and assured him that it wouldn't be long before the rest of the world came to the same conclusion. She also pointed out that both pictures had been sold on the opening day, and suggested that they had been snapped up by a well-known collector who knew a rising talent when he saw one.

John didn't get the chance to engage in a long conversation with his brother, as he seemed pre-occupied with his own set, but he did return to Birmingham that night with £2 less in his wallet than he'd arrived with.

At the end of his second year, Robin showed two new pictures at the end-of-term show – *Knife and Fork in Space* and *Death Pangs*. John stood a few paces away from the canvases, relieved to find from the expressions on the faces of those who stopped to study his brother's work that they were left equally puzzled, not least by the sight of two red dots that had been there since the opening day.

He found his mother seated in a corner of the room, explaining to Miriam why Robin hadn't won the second-year prize. Although her enthusiasm for Robin's work had not dimmed, John felt she looked frailer than when he had last seen her.

'How are you getting on, John?' asked Miriam

when she looked up to see her nephew standing there.

'I've been made a trainee manager, Aunt Miriam,' he replied, as Robin came across to join them.

'Why don't you join us for dinner?' suggested Robin. 'It will give you a chance to meet some of my friends.' John was touched by the invitation, until the bill for all seven of them was placed in front of him.

'It won't be long before I can afford to take you to the Ritz,' Robin declared after a sixth bottle of wine had been consumed.

Sitting in a third-class compartment on the journey back to Birmingham New Street, John was thankful that he had purchased a return ticket, because after he had loaned his brother £5 his wallet was empty.

John didn't return to London again until Robin's graduation. His mother had written insisting that he attend, as all the prizewinners would be announced, and she had heard a rumour that Robin would be among them.

When John arrived at the exhibition it was already in full swing. He walked slowly round the hall, stopping to admire some of the canvases. He spent a considerable time studying Robin's latest efforts. There was no plaque to suggest that he had won any of the star prizes – in fact he wasn't even 'specially commended'. But, perhaps more importantly, on this occasion there were no red dots. It served to remind John that his mother's monthly allowance was no longer keeping up with inflation.

'The judges have their favourites,' his mother explained, as she sat alone in a corner looking even frailer than she had when he last saw her. John nodded, feeling that this was not the time to let her know that the company had given him another promotion.

'Turner never won any prizes when he was a student,' was his mother's only other comment on the subject.

'So what does Robin plan to do next?' asked John.

'He's moving into a studio flat in Pimlico, so he can remain with his set – most essential when you're still making your name.' John didn't need to ask who would be paying the rent while Robin was 'still making his name'.

When Robin invited John to join them for dinner, he made some excuse about having to get back to Birmingham. The hangers-on looked disappointed, until John extracted a £10 note from his wallet.

Once Robin had left college, the two brothers rarely met.

It was some five years later, when John had been invited to address a CBI conference in London on the problems facing the car industry, that he decided to make a surprise visit to his brother and invite him out to dinner.

When the conference closed, John took a taxi over to Pimlico, suddenly feeling uneasy about the fact that he had not warned Robin he might drop by.

As he climbed the stairs to the top floor, he began to feel even more apprehensive. He pressed the bell, and when the door was eventually opened it was a few moments before he realised that the man standing in front of him was his brother. He could not believe the transformation after only five years.

Robin's hair had turned grey. There were bags under his eyes, his skin was puffy and blotched, and he must have put on at least three stone.

'John,' he said. 'What a surprise. I had no idea you were in town. Do come in.'

What hit John as he entered the flat was the smell. At first he wondered if it could be paint, but as he looked around he noticed that the half-finished canvases were outnumbered by the empty wine bottles.

'Are you preparing for an exhibition?' asked John as he stared down at one of the unfinished works.

'No, nothing like that at the moment,' said Robin. 'Lots of interest, of course, but nothing definite. You know what London dealers are like.'

'To be honest, I don't,' said John.

'Well, you have to be either fashionable or news-worthy before they'll consider offering you wall space. Did you know that Van Gogh never sold a picture in his lifetime?'

Over dinner in a nearby restaurant John learned a little more about the vagaries of the art world, and what some of the critics thought of Robin's work. He was pleased to discover that his brother had not lost any of his self-confidence, or his belief that it was only a matter of time before he would be recognised.

Robin's monologue continued throughout the entire meal, and it wasn't until they were back at his flat that John had a chance to mention that he had fallen in love with a girl named Susan, and was about to get married. Robin certainly hadn't enquired about his progress at Reynolds and Co., where he was now the deputy managing director.

Before John left for the station, he settled Robin's bills for several unpaid meals and also slipped his brother a cheque for £100, which neither of them bothered to suggest was a loan. Robin's parting words as John stepped into the taxi were, 'I've just submitted two paintings for the Summer Exhibition at the Royal Academy, which I'm confident will be accepted by the hanging committee, in which case you must come up for the opening day.'

At Euston, John popped into Menzies to buy an evening paper, and noticed on the top of the remainders pile a book entitled *An Introduction to the World of Art from Fra Angelico to Picasso*. As the train pulled out of the station he opened the first page, and by the time he had reached Caravaggio it was pulling into New Street, Birmingham.

He heard a tap at the window and saw Susan smiling up at him.

'That must have been some book,' she said, as they walked down the platform arm in arm.

'It certainly was. I only hope I can get my hands on Volume II.'

The two brothers were brought together twice during the following year. The first was a sad occasion, when they attended their mother's funeral. After the service was over, they returned to Miriam's home for tea, where Robin informed his brother that the Academy had accepted both his entries for the Summer Exhibition.

Three months later John travelled to London to attend the opening day. By the time he entered the hallowed portals of the Royal Academy for the first time, he had read a dozen art books, ranging from the early Renaissance to Pop. He had visited every gallery in Birmingham, and couldn't wait to explore the galleries in the back streets of Mayfair.

As he strolled around the spacious rooms of the Academy, John decided the time had come for him to invest in his first picture. Listen to the experts, but in the end trust your eye, Godfrey Barker had written in the *Telegraph*. His eye told him Bernard Dunstan, while the experts were suggesting William Russell Flint. The eyes won, because Dunstan cost £75, while the cheapest Russell Flint was £600.

John strode from room to room searching for the two oils by his brother, but without the aid of the Academy's little blue book he would never have found them. They had been hung in the middle gallery in the top row, nearly touching the ceiling. He noticed that neither of them had been sold.

After he had been round the exhibition twice and settled on the Dunstan, he went over to the sales counter and wrote out a deposit for the purchases he wanted. He checked his watch: it was a few minutes before twelve, the hour at which he had agreed to meet his brother.

Robin kept him waiting for forty minutes, and then, without the suggestion of an apology, guided him around the exhibition for a third time. He dismissed both Dunstan and Russell Flint as society painters, without giving a hint of who he did consider talented.

Robin couldn't hide his disappointment when they came across his pictures in the middle gallery. 'What chance do I have of selling either of them while they're hidden up there?' he said in disgust. John tried to look sympathetic.

Over a late lunch, John took Robin through the implications of their mother's will, as the family solicitors had failed to elicit any response to their several letters addressed to Mr Robin Summers.

'On principle, I never open anything in a brown envelope,' explained Robin.

Well, at least that couldn't be the reason Robin had failed to turn up to his wedding, John thought. Once again, he returned to the details of his mother's will.

'The bequests are fairly straightforward,' he said. 'She's left everything to you, with the exception of one picture.'

'Which one?' Robin immediately asked.

'The one you did of her when you were still at school.'

'It's one of the best things I've ever done,' said Robin. 'It must be worth at least £50, and I've always assumed that she would leave it to me.'

John wrote out a cheque for the sum of £50. When he returned to Birmingham that night, he didn't let Susan know how much he had paid for the two pictures. He placed the Dunstan of *Venice* in the drawing room above the fireplace, and the one of his mother in his study.

When their first child was born, John suggested that Robin might be one of the godparents.

'Why?' asked Susan. 'He didn't even bother to come to our wedding.'

John could not disagree with his wife's reasoning, and although Robin was invited to the christening he neither responded nor turned up, despite the invitation being sent in a white envelope.

It must have been about two years later that John received an invitation from the Crewe Gallery in Cork Street to Robin's long-awaited one-man show. It actually turned out to be a two-man show, and John certainly would have snapped up one of the works by the other artist, if he hadn't felt it would offend his brother.

He did in fact settle on an oil he wanted, made a note of its number, and the following morning asked his secretary to call the gallery and reserve it in her name.

'I'm afraid the Peter Blake you were after was sold on the opening night,' she informed him.

He frowned. 'Could you ask them how many of Robin Summers's pictures have sold?'

The secretary repeated the question, and cupping her hand over the mouthpiece, told him, 'Two.'

John frowned for a second time.

The following week, John had to return to London to represent his company at the Motor Show at Earls Court. He decided to drop into the Crewe Gallery to see how his brother was selling. No change. Only two red dots on the wall, while Peter Blake was almost sold out.

John left the gallery disappointed on two counts, and headed back towards Piccadilly. He almost walked straight past her, but as soon as he noticed the delicate colour of her cheeks and her graceful figure it was love at first sight. He stood staring at her, afraid she might turn out to be too expensive.

He stepped into the gallery to take a closer look. She was tiny, delicate and exquisite.

'How much?' he asked softly, staring at the woman seated behind the glass table.

'The Vuillard?' she enquired.

John nodded.

'£1,200.'

As if in a daydream, he removed his chequebook and wrote out a sum that he knew would empty his account.

The Vuillard was placed opposite the Dunstan, and thus began a love affair with several painted ladies from all over the world, although John never admitted to his wife how much these framed mistresses were costing him.

Despite the occasional picture to be found hanging in obscure corners of the Summer Exhibition, Robin didn't have another one-man show for several years. When it comes to artists whose canvases remain unsold, dealers are unsympathetic to the suggestion that they could represent a sound investment because they might be recognised after they are dead – mainly because by that time the gallery owners will also be dead.

When the invitation for Robin's next one-man show finally appeared, John knew he had little choice but to attend the opening.

John had recently been involved in a management buy-out of Reynolds and Company. With car sales increasing every year during the seventies, so did the necessity to put wheels on them, which allowed him to indulge in his new hobby as an amateur art collector. He had recently added Bonnard, Dufy, Camoin and Luce to his collection, still listening to the advice of experts, but in the end trusting his eye.

John stepped out of the train at Euston and gave the cabby at the front of the queue the address he needed to be dropped at. The cabby scratched his head for a moment before setting off in the direction of the East End.

When John stepped into the gallery, Robin rushed across to greet him with the words, 'And here is someone who has never doubted my true worth.' John smiled at his brother, who offered him a glass of white wine.

John glanced around the little gallery, to observe knots of people who seemed more interested in gulping down mediocre wine than in taking any interest in mediocre pictures. When would his brother learn that the last thing you need at an opening are other unknown artists accompanied by their hangers-on?

Robin took him by the arm and guided him from group to group, introducing him to people who couldn't have afforded to buy one of the frames, let alone one of the canvases.

The longer the evening dragged on, the more sorry John began to feel for his brother, and on this occasion he happily fell into the dinner trap. He ended up entertaining twelve of Robin's companions, including the owner of the gallery, who John feared wouldn't be getting much more out of the evening than a three-course meal.

'Oh, no,' he tried to assure John. 'We've already sold a couple of pictures, and a lot of people have shown interest. The truth is that the critics have never fully understood Robin's work, as I'm sure no one is more aware than you.'

John looked on sadly as his brother's friends added such comments as 'never been properly recognised', 'unappreciated talent', and 'should have been elected to the RA years ago'. At this suggestion Robin rose unsteadily to his feet and declared, 'Never! I shall be like Henry Moore and David Hockney. When the invitation comes, I shall turn them down.' More cheering, followed by even more drinking of John's wine.

When the clock chimed eleven, John made some excuse about an early-morning meeting. He offered his apologies, settled the bill and left for the Savoy. In the back seat of the taxi, he finally accepted something he had long suspected: his brother simply didn't have any talent.

It was to be some years before John heard from Robin again. It seemed that there were no London galleries who were willing to display his work, so he felt it was nothing less than his duty to leave for the South of France and join up with a group of friends who were equally talented and equally misunderstood.

'It will give me a new lease of life,' he explained in a rare letter to his brother, 'a chance to fulfil my true potential, which has been held up for far too long by the pygmies of the London art establishment. And I wondered if you could possibly . . .'

John transferred £5,000 to an account in Vence, to allow Robin to disappear to warmer climes.

The takeover bid for Reynolds and Co. came out of the blue, although John had always accepted that they were an obvious target for any Japanese car company trying to gain a foothold in Europe. But even he was surprised when their biggest rivals in Germany put in a counter-bid.

He watched as the value of his shares climbed each day, and not until Honda finally outbid Mercedes did he accept that he would have to make a decision. He opted to cash in his shares and leave the company. He told Susan that he wanted to take a trip around the world, visiting only those cities that boasted great art galleries. First stop the Louvre, followed by the Prado, then the Uffizi, the Hermitage in St Petersburg, and finally on to New

York, leaving the Japanese to put wheels on cars.

John wasn't surprised to receive a letter from Robin with a French postmark, congratulating him on his good fortune and wishing him every success in his retirement, while pointing out that he himself had been left with no choice but to battle on until the critics finally came to their senses.

John transferred another £10,000 to the account in Vence.

John had his first heart attack in New York while admiring a Bellini at the Frick.

He told Susan that night as she sat by his bedside that he was thankful they had already visited the Metropolitan and the Whitney.

The second heart attack came soon after they had arrived back in Warwickshire. Susan felt obliged to write to Robin in the South of France and warn him that the doctors' prognosis was not encouraging.

Robin didn't reply. His brother died three weeks later.

The funeral was well attended by John's friends and colleagues, but few of them recognised the heavily built man who demanded to be seated in the front row. Susan and the children knew exactly why he had turned up, and it wasn't to pay his respects.

'He promised I would be taken care of in his will,' Robin told the grieving widow only moments after they had left the graveside. He later sought out the two boys in order to deliver the same message, though he had had little contact with them during the past thirty years. 'You see,' he explained, 'your dad was one of the few people who understood my true worth.'

Over tea back at the house, while others consoled the widow, Robin strolled from room to room, studying the pictures his brother had collected over the years. 'A shrewd investment,' he assured the local vicar, 'even if they do lack originality or passion.' The vicar nodded politely.

When Robin was introduced to the family solicitor, he immediately asked, 'When are you expecting to announce the details of the will?'

'I have not yet discussed with Mrs Summers the arrangements for when the will should be read. However, I anticipate it being towards the end of next week.'

Robin booked himself into the local pub, and rang the solicitor's office every morning until he confirmed that he would be divulging the contents of the will at three o'clock on the following Thursday.

Robin appeared at the solicitor's offices a few minutes before three that afternoon, the first time he had been early for an appointment in years. Susan arrived shortly afterwards, accompanied by the boys, and they took their seats on the other side of the room without acknowledging him.

Although the bulk of John Summers's estate had been left to his wife and the two boys, he had made a special bequest to his brother Robin.

'During my lifetime I was fortunate enough to put together a collection of paintings, some of which are now of considerable value. At the last count, there were eighty-one in all. My wife Susan may select twenty of her choice, my two boys Nick and Chris may then also select twenty each, while my younger brother Robin is to be given the remaining twenty-one, which should allow him to live in a style worthy of his talent.'

Robin beamed with satisfaction. His brother had gone to his deathbed never doubting his true worth.

When the solicitor had completed the reading of the will, Susan rose from her place and walked across the room to speak to Robin.

'We will choose the pictures we wish to keep in the family, and having done so, I will have the remaining twenty-one sent over to you at the Bell and Duck.'

She turned and left before Robin had a chance to reply. Silly woman, he thought. So unlike his brother – she wouldn't recognise real talent if it were standing in front of her.

Over dinner at the Bell and Duck that evening, Robin began to make plans as to how he would spend his new-found wealth. By the time he had consumed the hostelry's finest bottle of claret, he had made the decision that he would limit himself to placing one picture with Sotheby's and one with Christie's every six months, which would allow him to live in a style worthy of his talent, to quote his brother's exact words.

He retired to bed around eleven, and fell asleep thinking about Bonnard, Vuillard, Dufy, Camoin and Luce, and what twenty-one such masterpieces might be worth.

He was still sound asleep at ten o'clock the following morning, when there was a knock on the door.

'Who is it?' he mumbled irritably from under the blanket.

'George, the hall porter, sir. There's a van out-side. The driver says he can't release the goods until you've signed for them.'

'Don't let him go!' shouted Robin. He leapt out of bed for the first time in years, threw on his old shirt, trousers and shoes, and bolted down the stairs and out into the courtyard.

A man in blue overalls, clipboard in hand, was leaning against a large van.

Robin marched towards him. 'Are you the gentleman who's expecting a delivery of twenty-one paintings?' the van driver asked.

'That's me,' said Robin. 'Where do I sign?'

'Right there,' said the van driver, placing his thumb below the word 'Signature'.

Robin scribbled his name quickly across the form and then followed the driver to the back of the van. He unlocked the doors and pulled them open.

Robin was speechless.

He stared at a portrait of his mother, that was stacked on top of twenty other pictures by Robin Summers, painted *circa* 1951 to 1999.

A Change of Heart

There is a man from Cape Town who travels to the black township of Crossroads every day. He spends the morning teaching English at one of the local schools, the afternoon coaching rugby or cricket according to the season, and his evenings roaming the streets trying to convince the young that they shouldn't form gangs or commit crimes, and that they should have nothing to do with drugs. He is known as the Crossroads Convert.

No one is born with prejudice in their hearts, although some people are introduced to it at an early age. This was certainly true of Stoffel van den Berg. Stoffel was born in Cape Town, and never once in his life travelled abroad. His ancestors had emigrated from Holland in the eighteenth century, and Stoffel grew up accustomed to having black servants who were there to carry out his slightest whim.

If the boys – none of the servants appeared to be graced with a name, whatever their age – didn't obey Stoffel's orders, they were soundly beaten or simply not fed. If they carried out a job well, they weren't thanked, and were certainly never praised. Why bother to thank someone who has only been put on earth to serve you?

When Stoffel attended his first primary school in the Cape this unthinking prejudice was simply reinforced, with classrooms full of white children being taught only by white teachers. The few blacks he ever came across at school were cleaning lavatories that they would never be allowed to use themselves.

During his school days Stoffel proved to be above average in the classroom, excelling in maths, but in a class of his own on the playing field.

By the time Stoffel was in his final year of school, this six-foot-two-inch, fair-haired Boer was playing fly half for the 1st XV in the winter and opening the batting for the 1st XI during the summer. There was already talk of him playing either rugby or cricket for the Springboks even before he had applied for a place at any university. Several college scouts visited the school in his final year to offer him scholarships, and on the advice of his headmaster, supported by his father, he settled on Stellenbosch.

Stoffel's unerring progress continued from the moment he arrived on the campus. In his freshman year he was selected to open the batting for the university eleven when one of the regular openers was injured. He didn't miss a match for the rest of the season. Two years later, he captained an undefeated varsity side, and went on to score a century for Western Province against Natal.

On leaving university, Stoffel was recruited by Barclays Bank to join their public relations department, although it was made clear to him at the interview that his first priority was to ensure that Barclays won the Inter-Bank Cricket Cup.

He had been with the bank for only a few weeks when the Springbok selectors wrote to inform him that he was being considered for the South African cricket squad which was preparing for the forthcoming tour by England. The bank was delighted, and told him he could take as much time off as he needed to prepare for the national side. He dreamed of scoring a century at Newlands, and perhaps one day even at Lord's.

He followed with interest the Ashes series that was taking place in England. He had only read about players like Underwood and Snow, but their reputations did not worry him. Stoffel intended to despatch their bowling to every boundary in the country.

The South African papers were also following the Ashes series with keen interest, because they wanted to keep their readers informed of the strengths and weaknesses of the opposition their team would be facing in a few weeks' time. Then, overnight, these stories were transferred from the back pages to the front, when England selected an all-rounder who played for Worcester called Basil D'Oliveira. Mr D'Oliveira, as the press called him, made the front pages because he was what the South Africans classified as 'Cape Coloured'. Because he had not been allowed to play first-class cricket in his native South Africa, he had emigrated to England.

The press in both countries began to speculate on the South African government's attitude should D'Oliveira be selected by the MCC as a member of the touring side to visit South Africa.

'If the English were stupid enough to select him,' Stoffel told his friends at the bank, 'the tour would have to be cancelled.' After all, he couldn't be expected to play against a coloured man.

The South Africans' best hope was that Mr D'Oliveira would fail in the final Test at The Oval, and would not be considered for the coming tour, and thus the problem would simply go away.

D'Oliveira duly obliged in the first innings, scoring only eleven runs and taking no Australian wickets. But in the second innings he played a major role in winning the match and squaring the series, scoring a chanceless 158. Even so, he was controversially left out of the touring team for South Africa. But when another player pulled out because of injury, he was selected as his replacement.

The South African government immediately made their position clear: only white players would be welcome in their land. Robust diplomatic exchanges took place over the following weeks, but as the MCC refused to remove D'Oliveira from the party the tour had to be cancelled. It was not until after Nelson Mandela became President in 1994 that an official English team once again set foot in South Africa.

Stoffel was shattered by the decision, and although he played regularly for Western Province and ensured that Barclays retained the Inter-Bank Cup, he doubted if he would ever be awarded a Test cap.

But, despite his disappointment, Stoffel remained in no doubt that the government had made the right decision. After all, why should the English imagine they could dictate who should visit South Africa?

It was while he was playing against Transvaal that he met Inga. Not only was she the most beautiful creature he had ever set eyes on, but she also fully agreed with his sound views on the superiority of the white race. They were married a year later.

When sanctions began to be imposed on South Africa by country after country, Stoffel continued to back the government, proclaiming that the decadent Western politicians had all become liberal weaklings. Why didn't they come to South Africa and see the country for themselves, he would demand of anyone who visited the Cape. That way they would soon discover that he didn't beat his servants, and that the blacks received a fair wage, as recommended by the government. What more could they hope for? In fact, he could never understand why the government didn't hang Mandela and his terrorist cronies for treason.

Piet and Marike nodded their agreement whenever their father expressed these views. He explained to them over breakfast again and again that you couldn't treat people who had recently fallen out of trees as equals. After all, it wasn't how God had planned things.

When Stoffel stopped playing cricket in his late thirties, he took over as head of the bank's public relations department, and was invited to join the board. The family moved into a large house a few miles down the Cape, overlooking the Atlantic.

While the rest of the world continued to enforce sanctions, Stoffel only became more convinced that South Africa was the one place on earth that had got things right. He regularly expressed these views, both in public and in private.

'You should stand for Parliament,' a friend told him. 'The country needs men who believe in the South African way of life, and aren't willing to give in to a bunch of ignorant foreigners, most of whom have never even visited the country.'

To begin with, Stoffel didn't take such suggestions seriously. But then the National Party's Chairman flew to Cape Town especially to see him.

'The Political Committee were hoping you would allow your name to go forward as a prospective candidate at the next general election,' he told Stoffel.

Stoffel promised he would consider the idea, but explained that he would need to speak to his wife and fellow board members at the bank before he could come to a decision. To his surprise, they all encouraged him to take up the offer. 'After all, you are a national figure, universally popular, and no one can be in any doubt about your attitude to apartheid.' A week later, Stoffel phoned the National Party Chairman to say that he would be honoured to stand as a candidate.

When he was selected to fight the safe seat of Noordhoek, he ended his speech to the adoption committee with the words, 'I'll go to my grave knowing apartheid must be right, for blacks as well as for whites.' He received a standing ovation.

That all changed on 18 August 1989.

Stoffel left the bank a few minutes early that evening, because he was due to address a meeting at his local town hall. The election was now only weeks away, and the opinion polls were indicating that he was certain to become the Member for the Noordhoek constituency.

As he stepped out of the lift he bumped into Martinus de Jong, the bank's General Manager.

'Another half-day, Stoffel?' he asked with a grin.

'Hardly. I'm off to address a meeting in the constituency, Martinus.'

'Quite right, old fellow,' de Jong replied. 'And don't leave them in any doubt that no one can afford to waste their vote this time – that is, if they don't want this country to end up being run by the blacks. By the way,' he added, 'we don't need assisted places for blacks at universities either. If we allow a bunch of students in England to dictate the bank's policy, we'll end up with some black wanting my job.'

'Yes, I read the memo from London. They're acting like a herd of ostriches. Must dash, Martinus, or I'll be late for my meeting.'

'Yes, sorry to have held you up, old fellow.'

Stoffel checked his watch and ran down the ramp to the carpark. When he joined the traffic in Rhodes Street, it quickly became clear that he had not managed to avoid the bumper-to-bumper exodus of people heading out of town for the weekend.

Once he had passed the city limits, he moved quickly into top gear. It was only fifteen miles to Noordhoek, although the terrain was steep and the road winding. But as Stoffel knew every inch of the journey, he was usually parked outside his front door in under half an hour.

He glanced at the clock on the dashboard. With luck, he would still be home with enough time to shower and change before he had to head off for the meeting.

As he swung south onto the road which would take him up into the hills, Stoffel pressed his foot down hard on the accelerator, nipping in and out to overtake slow-moving lorries and cars that weren't as familiar with the road as he was. He scowled as he shot past a black driver who was struggling up the hill in a clapped-out old van that shouldn't have been allowed on the road.

Stoffel accelerated round the next bend to see a lorry ahead of him. He knew there was a long, straight section of road before he would encounter another bend, so he had easily enough time to overtake. He put his foot down and pulled out to overtake, surprised to discover how fast the lorry was travelling.

When he was about a hundred yards from the next bend, a car appeared around the corner. Stoffel had to make an instant decision. Should he slam his foot on the brake, or on the accelerator? He pressed his foot hard down until the accelerator was touching the floor, assuming the other fellow would surely brake. He eased ahead of the lorry, and the moment he had overtaken it, he swung in as quickly as he could, but still he couldn't avoid clipping the mudguard of the oncoming car. For an instant he saw the terrified eyes of the other driver, who had slammed on his brakes, but the steep gradient didn't help him. Stoffel's car rammed into the safety barrier before bouncing back onto the other side of the road, eventually coming to a halt in a clump of trees.

That was the last thing he remembered, before he regained consciousness five weeks later.

Stoffel looked up to find Inga standing at his bedside. When she saw his eyes open, she grasped his hand and then rushed out of the room to call for a doctor.

The next time he woke they were both standing by his bedside, but it was another week before the surgeon was able to tell him what had happened following the crash.

Stoffel listened in horrified silence when he learned that the other driver had died of head injuries soon after arriving at the hospital.

'You're lucky to be alive,' was all Inga said.

'You certainly are,' said the surgeon, 'because only moments after the other driver died, your heart also stopped beating. It was just your luck that a suitable donor was in the next operating theatre.'

'Not the driver of the other car?' said Stoffel.

The surgeon nodded.

'But . . . wasn't he black?' asked Stoffel in disbelief.

'Yes, he was,' confirmed the surgeon. 'And it may come as a surprise to you, Mr van den Berg, that your body doesn't realise that. Just be thankful that his wife agreed to the transplant. If I recall her words' – he paused – 'she said, "I can't see the point in both of them dying." Thanks to her, we were able to save your life, Mr van den Berg.' He hesitated and pursed his lips, then said quietly, 'But I'm sorry to have to tell you that your other internal injuries were so severe that despite the success of the heart transplant, the prognosis is not at all good.'

Stoffel didn't speak for some time, but eventually asked, 'How long do I have?'

'Three, possibly four years,' replied the surgeon. 'But only if you take it easy.'

Stoffel fell into a deep sleep.

It was another six weeks before Stoffel left the hospital, and even then Inga insisted on a long period of convalescence. Several friends came to visit him at home, including Martinus de Jong, who assured him that his job at the bank would be waiting for him just as soon as he had fully recovered.

'I shall not be returning to the bank,' Stoffel said quietly. 'You will be receiving my resignation in the next few days.'

'But why?' asked de Jong. 'I can assure you . . .'

Stoffel waved his hand. 'It's kind of you, Martinus, but I have other plans.'

The moment the doctor said Stoffel could leave the house, he asked Inga to drive him to Crossroads, so he could visit the widow of the man he had killed.

The tall, fair-haired white couple walked among the shacks of Crossroads, watched by sullen, resigned eyes. When they reached the little hovel where they had been told the driver's wife lived, they stopped.

Stoffel would have knocked on the door if there

had been one. He peered through the gap and into the darkness to see a young woman with a baby in her arms, cowering in the far corner.

'My name is Stoffel van den Berg,' he told her. 'I have come to say how sorry I am to have been the cause of your husband's death.'

'Thank you, master,' she replied. 'No need to visit me.'

As there wasn't anything to sit on, Stoffel lowered himself to the ground and crossed his legs.

'I also wanted to thank you for giving me the chance to live.'

'Thank you, master.'

'Is there anything I can do for you?' He paused. 'Perhaps you and your child would like to come and live with us?'

'No, thank you, master.'

'Is there nothing I can do?' asked Stoffel helplessly.

'Nothing, thank you, master.'

Stoffel rose from his place, aware that his presence seemed to disturb her. He and Inga walked back through the township in silence, and did not speak again until they had reached their car.

'I've been so blind,' he said as Inga drove him home.

'Not just you,' his wife admitted, tears welling up in her eyes. 'But what can we do about it?'

'I know what I must do.'

Inga listened as her husband described how he intended to spend the rest of his life.

The next morning Stoffel called in at the bank, and with the help of Martinus de Jong worked out how much he could afford to spend over the next three years.

'Have you told Inga that you want to cash in your life insurance?'

'It was her idea,' said Stoffel.

'How do you intend to spend the money?'

'I'll start by buying some second-hand books, old rugby balls and cricket bats.'

'We could help by doubling the amount you have to spend,' suggested the General Manager.

'How?' asked Stoffel.

'By using the surplus we have in the sports fund.'

'But that's restricted to whites.'

'And you're white,' said the General Manager.

Martinus was silent for some time before he added, 'Don't imagine that you're the only person whose eyes have been opened by this tragedy. And you are far better placed to . . .' he hesitated.

'To . . . ?' repeated Stoffel.

'Make others, more prejudiced than yourself, aware of their past mistakes.'

That afternoon Stoffel returned to Crossroads. He walked around the township for several hours before he settled on a piece of land surrounded by tin shacks and tents.

Although it wasn't flat, or the perfect shape or size, he began to pace out a pitch, while hundreds of young children stood staring at him.

The following day some of those children helped him paint the touchlines and put out the corner flags.

For four years, one month and eleven days, Stoffel van den Berg travelled to Crossroads every morning, where he would teach English to the children in what passed for a school.

In the afternoons, he taught the same children the skills of rugby or cricket, according to the season. In the evenings, he would roam the streets trying to persuade teenagers that they shouldn't form gangs, commit crime or have anything to do with drugs.

Stoffel van den Berg died on 24 March 1994, only days before Nelson Mandela was elected as

President. Like Basil D'Oliveira, he had played a small part in defeating apartheid.

The funeral of the Crossroads Convert was attended by over two thousand mourners who had travelled from all over the country to pay their respects.

The journalists were unable to agree whether there had been more blacks or more whites in the congregation.

Too Many Coincidences

Whenever Ruth looked back on the past three years – and she often did – she came to the conclusion that Max must have planned everything right down to the last detail – yes, even before they'd met.

They first bumped into each other by accident – or that's what Ruth assumed at the time – and to be fair to Max it wasn't the two of them, but their boats, that had bumped into each other.

Sea Urchin was easing its way into the adjoining mooring in the half-light of the evening when the two bows touched. Both skippers quickly checked to see if there had been any damage to their boat, but as both had large inflatable buoys slung over their sides, neither had come to any harm. The owner of *The Scottish Belle* gave a mock salute and disappeared below deck.

Max poured himself a gin and tonic, picked up a paperback that he had meant to finish the previous summer, and settled down in the bow. He began to thumb through the pages, trying to recall the exact place he had reached, when the skipper of *The Scottish Belle* reappeared on the deck.

The older man gave the same mock salute, so Max lowered his book and said, 'Good evening. Sorry about the bump.'

'No harm done,' the skipper replied, raising his glass of whisky.

Max rose from his place and, walking across to the side of the boat, thrust out a hand and said, 'My name's Max Bennett.'

'Angus Henderson,' the older man replied, with a slight Edinburgh burr.

'You live in these parts, Angus?' asked Max casually.

'No,' replied Angus. 'My wife and I live on Jersey, but our twin boys are at school here on the south coast, so we sail across at the end of every term and take them back for their holidays. And you? Do you live in Brighton?'

'No, London, but I come down whenever I can find the time to do a spot of sailing, which I fear isn't often enough – as you've already discovered,' he added with a chuckle, as a woman appeared from below the deck of *The Scottish Belle*.

Angus turned and smiled. 'Ruth, this is Max Bennett. We literally bumped into each other.'

Max smiled across at a woman who could have passed as Henderson's daughter, as she was at least twenty years younger than her husband. Although not beautiful, she was striking, and from her trim, athletic build she looked as if she might work out every day. She gave Max a shy smile.

'Why don't you join us for a drink?' suggested Angus.

'Thank you,' said Max, and clambered across onto the larger boat. He leaned forward and shook Ruth's hand. 'How nice to meet you, Mrs Henderson.'

'Ruth, please. Do you live in Brighton?' she asked.

'No,' said Max. 'I was just telling your husband that I only come down for the odd weekend to do a little sailing. And what do you do on Jersey?' he asked, turning his attention back to Angus. 'You certainly weren't born there.'

'No, we moved there from Edinburgh after I retired seven years ago. I used to manage a small broking business. All I do nowadays is keep an eye on one or two of my family properties to make sure they're showing a worthwhile return, sail a little and play the occasional round of golf. And you?' he enquired.

'Not unlike you, but with a difference.'

'Oh? What's that?' asked Ruth.

'I also look after property, but it belongs to other people. I'm a junior partner with a West End estate agent.'

'How are property prices in London at the moment?' asked Angus after another gulp of whisky.

'It's been a bad couple of years for most agents – no one wants to sell, and only foreigners can afford to buy. And anybody whose lease comes up for renewal demands that their rent should be lowered, while others are simply defaulting.'

Angus laughed. 'Perhaps you should move to Jersey. At least that way you would avoid . . .'

'We ought to think about getting changed, if we're not going to be late for the boys' concert,' interrupted Ruth.

Henderson checked his watch. 'Sorry, Max,' he said. 'Nice to talk to you, but Ruth's right. Perhaps we'll bump into each other again.'

'Let's hope so,' replied Max. He smiled, placed his glass on a nearby table and clambered back onto his own boat as the Hendersons disappeared below deck.

Once again, Max picked up his much-thumbed novel, and although he finally found the right place, he discovered he couldn't concentrate on the words. Thirty minutes later the Hendersons reappeared, suitably dressed for a concert. Max gave them a casual wave as they stepped onto the quay and into a waiting taxi.

When Ruth appeared on the deck the following morning, clutching a cup of tea, she was disappointed to find that *Sea Urchin* was no longer moored next to them. She was about to disappear back below deck when she thought she recognised a familiar boat entering the harbour.

She didn't move as she watched the sail become larger and larger, hoping that Max would moor in the same spot as he had the previous evening. He waved when he saw her standing on the deck. She pretended not to notice.

Once he'd fixed the moorings, he called across, 'So, where's Angus?'

'Gone to pick up the boys and take them off to a rugby match. I'm not expecting him back until this evening,' she added unnecessarily.

Max tied a bowline to the jetty, looked up and said, 'Then why don't you join me for lunch, Ruth? I know a little Italian restaurant that the tourists haven't come across yet.'

Ruth pretended to be considering his offer, and eventually said, 'Yes, why not?'

'Shall we meet up in half an hour?' Max suggested.

'Suits me,' replied Ruth.

Ruth's half-hour turned out to be nearer fifty minutes, so Max returned to his paperback, but once again made little progress.

When Ruth did eventually reappear, she had changed into a black leather mini-skirt, a white blouse and black stockings, and had put on a little too much make-up, even for Brighton.

Max looked down at her legs. Not bad for thirty-eight, he thought, even if the skirt was a little too tight and certainly too short.

'You look great,' he said, trying to sound convincing. 'Shall we go?'

Ruth joined him on the quay, and they strolled towards the town, chatting inconsequentially until he turned down a side street, coming to a halt in front of a restaurant called Venitici. When he opened the door to let her in, Ruth couldn't hide her disappointment at discovering how crowded the room was. 'We'll never get a table,' she said.

'Oh, I wouldn't be so sure of that,' said Max, as the maître d' headed towards them.

'Your usual table, Mr Bennett?'

'Thank you, Valerio,' he said, as they were guided to a quiet table in the corner of the room.

Once they were seated, Max asked, 'What would you like to drink, Ruth? A glass of champagne?'

'That would be nice,' she said, as if it were an everyday experience for her. In fact she rarely had a glass of champagne before lunch, as it would never have crossed Angus's mind to indulge in such extravagance, except perhaps on her birthday.

Max opened the menu. 'The food here is always excellent, especially the gnocchi, which Valerio's wife makes. Simply melts in your mouth.'

'Sounds great,' said Ruth, not bothering to open her menu.

'And a mixed salad on the side, perhaps?'

'Couldn't be better.'

Max closed his menu and looked across the table. 'The boys can't be yours,' he said. 'Not if they're at boarding school.'

'Why not?' asked Ruth coyly.

'Why . . . because of Angus's age. I suppose I just

assumed they must be his by a previous marriage.'

'No,' said Ruth, laughing. 'Angus didn't marry until he was in his forties, and I was very flattered when he asked me to be his wife.'

Max made no comment.

'And you?' asked Ruth, as a waiter offered her a choice of four different types of bread.

'Been married four times,' Max said.

Ruth looked shocked, until he burst out laughing.

'In truth, never,' he said quietly. 'I suppose I just haven't bumped into the right girl.'

'But you're still young enough to have any woman you like,' said Ruth.

'I'm older than you,' said Max gallantly.

'It's different for a man,' said Ruth wistfully.

The maître d' reappeared by their side, a little pad in his hand.

'Two gnocchi and a bottle of your Barolo,' said Max, handing back the menu. 'And a side salad large enough for both of us: asparagus, avocado, lettuce heart – you know what I like.'

'Of course, Mr Bennett,' replied Valerio.

Max turned his attention back to his guest. 'Doesn't someone of your age find Jersey a little dull?' he asked as he leaned across the table and pushed back a strand of blonde hair that had fallen across her forehead.

Ruth smiled shyly. 'It has its advantages,' she replied a little unconvincingly.

'Like what?' pressed Max.

'Tax at 20 per cent.'

'That sounds like a good reason for Angus being on Jersey – but not you. In any case, I'd still rather be in England and pay 40 per cent.'

'Now that he's retired and living on a fixed income, it suits us. If we'd stayed in Edinburgh, we couldn't have maintained the same standard of living.'

'So, Brighton's as good as it gets,' said Max, with a grin.

The maître d' reappeared carrying two plates of gnocchi, which he placed in front of them, while another waiter deposited a large side salad in the centre of the table.

'I'm not complaining,' said Ruth, as she sipped her champagne. 'Angus has always been very considerate. I want for nothing.'

'Nothing?' Max repeated, as a hand disappeared under the table and rested on her knee.

Ruth knew that she should have removed it immediately, but she didn't.

When Max eventually took his hand away and began to concentrate on the gnocchi, Ruth tried to act as if nothing had happened.

'Anything worth seeing in the West End?' she asked casually. 'I'm told *An Inspector Calls* is good.'

'It certainly is,' replied Max. 'I went to the opening night.'

'Oh, when was that?' asked Ruth innocently.

'About five years ago,' Max replied.

Ruth laughed. 'So, now that you know just how out of date I am, you can tell me what I should be seeing.'

'There's a new Tom Stoppard opening next month.' He paused. 'If you were able to escape for a couple of days, we could go and see it together.'

'It's not that easy, Max. Angus expects me to stay with him on Jersey. We don't come to the mainland all that often.'

Max stared down at her empty plate. 'It looks as if the gnocchi lived up to my claims.'

Ruth nodded her agreement.

'You should try the *crême brulée*, also made by the patron's wife.'

'Certainly not. This trip already means I'm going to be out of the gym for at least three days, so I'll settle for a coffee,' said Ruth, as another glass of champagne was placed by her side. She frowned.

'Just pretend it's your birthday,' Max said, as the hand disappeared back under the table – this time resting a few inches higher up her thigh.

Looking back, that was the moment when she should have got up and walked out.

'So, how long have you been an estate agent?' she asked instead, still trying to pretend nothing was happening.

'Since I left school. I started at the bottom of the firm, making the tea, and last year I became a partner.'

'Congratulations. Where is your office?'

'Right in the centre of Mayfair. Why don't you drop in some time? Perhaps when you're next in London.'

'I don't get to London all that often,' Ruth said.

When Max spotted a waiter heading towards their table, he removed the hand from her leg. Once the waiter had placed two cappuccinos in front of them, Max smiled up at him and said, 'And perhaps I could have the bill.'

'Are you in a hurry?' Ruth asked.

'Yes,' he replied. 'I've just remembered that I have a bottle of vintage brandy hidden away on board *Sea Urchin*, and this might be the ideal occasion to open it.' He leaned across the table and took her hand. 'You know, I've been saving this particular bottle for something or someone special.'

'I don't think that would be wise.'

'Do you always do everything that is wise?' asked Max, not letting go of her hand.

'It's just that I really ought to be getting back to *The Scottish Belle.*'

'So you can hang around for three hours, waiting for Angus to return?'

'No. It's just that . . .'

'You're afraid I might try to seduce you.'

'Is that what you had in mind?' asked Ruth, releasing his hand.

'Yes, but not before we sample the brandy,' said Max, as he was passed the bill. He flicked over the little white slip, pulled out his wallet and placed four £10 notes on the silver tray.

Angus had once told her that anyone who pays cash in a restaurant either doesn't need a credit card or earns too little to qualify for one.

Max rose from his place, thanked the head waiter a little too ostentatiously, and slipped him a £5 note when the door was held open for them. They didn't speak as they crossed the road on the way back to the quay. Ruth thought she saw someone jumping off *Sea Urchin*, but when she looked again there was no one in sight. When they reached the boat, Ruth had planned to say goodbye, but she found herself following Max on board and down to the cabin below.

'I hadn't expected it to be so small,' she said, when she reached the bottom step. She turned a complete circle and ended up in Max's arms. She gently pushed him away.

'It's ideal for a bachelor,' was his only comment, as he poured two large brandies. He passed over one of the goblets to Ruth, placing his other arm around her waist. He pulled her gently towards him, allowing their bodies to touch. He leaned forward and kissed her on the lips, before releasing her to take a sip of brandy.

He watched as she raised the glass to her lips, and then once again took her in his arms. This time when they kissed, their lips parted, and she made little effort to stop him undoing the top button of her blouse.

Every time she tried to resist he would break off, waiting for her to take another sip before returning to his task. It took several more sips before he managed to remove the white blouse and locate the zip on the tight-fitting mini-skirt, but by then she was no longer even pretending to try to stop him.

'You're only the second man I've ever made love to,' she said quietly as she lay on the floor afterwards.

'You were a virgin when you met Angus?' said Max in disbelief.

'He wouldn't have married me if I hadn't been,' she replied quite simply.

'And there's been no one else during the past twenty years?' he said as he poured himself another brandy.

'No,' she replied, 'although I have a feeling that Gerald Prescott, the boys' housemaster at their old prep school, fancies me. But he's never got beyond a peck on the cheek, and staring at me with forlorn eyes.'

'But do you fancy him?'

'Yes, I do actually. He's rather nice,' Ruth admitted for the first time in her life. 'But he's not the sort of man who would make the first move.'

'More fool him,' said Max, taking her into his arms again.

Ruth glanced at her watch. 'Oh my God, is that

really the time? Angus could be back at any moment.'

'Don't panic, my darling,' said Max. 'We still have enough time for another brandy, and perhaps even another orgasm – whichever you fancy most.'

'Both, but I don't want to risk him finding us together.'

'Then we'll have to save it for another time,' said Max, putting the cork firmly back in the bottle.

'Or for the next girl,' said Ruth, as she began pulling her tights on.

Max picked up a biro from the side table and wrote on the label of the bottle, 'To be drunk only when I'm with Ruth'.

'Will I see you again?' she asked.

'That will be up to you, my darling,' replied Max, before kissing her again. When he released her, she turned and climbed up the steps and onto the deck, quickly disappearing out of sight.

Once she was back on *The Scottish Belle*, she tried to erase the memory of the last two hours, but when Angus reappeared later that evening with the boys, she realised that forgetting Max wasn't going to be quite that easy.

When she emerged on the deck the following

morning, *Sea Urchin* was nowhere to be seen.

'Were you looking for anything in particular?' Angus asked when he joined her.

She turned and smiled at him. 'No. It's just that I can't wait to get back to Jersey,' she replied.

It must have been about a month later that she picked up the phone and found Max on the other end of the line. She felt the same breathless feeling she had experienced the first time they had made love.

'I'm coming over to Jersey tomorrow, to look at a piece of property for a client. Any chance of seeing you?'

'Why don't you join us for dinner?' Ruth heard herself saying.

'Why don't you join me at my hotel?' he replied. 'And don't let's bother with dinner.'

'No, I think it might be wiser if you came over for dinner. On Jersey, even the letterboxes chatter.'

'If that's the only way I'm going to be able to see you, then I'll settle for dinner.'

'Eight o'clock?'

'Eight o'clock will be just fine,' he said, and put the phone down.

When Ruth heard the phone click she realised

that she hadn't given him their address, and she couldn't phone him back, because she didn't know his number.

When she warned Angus that they would have a guest for dinner the next night, he seemed pleased. 'Couldn't be better timing,' he said. 'There's something I need Max to advise me on.'

Ruth spent the following morning shopping in St Helier, selecting only the finest cuts of meat, the freshest vegetables, and a bottle of claret that she knew Angus would have considered highly extravagant.

She spent the afternoon in the kitchen, explaining to the cook exactly how she wanted the meal prepared, and even longer that evening in the bedroom, choosing and then rejecting what she might wear that night. She was still naked when the doorbell rang a few minutes after eight.

Ruth opened the bedroom door and listened from the top of the stairs as her husband welcomed Max. How old Angus sounded, she thought, as she listened to the two men chatting. She still hadn't discovered what he wanted to speak to Max about, as she didn't wish to appear too interested.

She returned to the bedroom and settled on a dress that a friend had once described as seductive.

'Then it will be wasted on this island,' she remembered replying.

The two men rose from their places when Ruth walked into the drawing room, and Max stepped forward and kissed her on both cheeks in the same way Gerald Prescott always did.

'I've been telling Max about our cottage in the Ardennes,' said Angus, even before they had sat down again, 'and our plans to sell it, now that the twins will be going away to university.'

How typical of Angus, thought Ruth. Get the business out of the way before you even offer your guest a drink. She went over to the sideboard and poured Max a gin and tonic without thinking what she was doing.

'I've asked Max if he would be kind enough to visit the cottage, value it, and advise when would be the best time to put it on the market.'

'That sounds sensible enough,' said Ruth. She avoided looking directly at Max, for fear that Angus might realise how she felt about their guest.

'I could travel on to France tomorrow,' said Max, 'if you'd like me to. I've nothing else planned for the weekend,' he added. 'I could report back to you on Monday.'

'That sounds good to me,' Angus responded.

He paused and sipped the malt whisky his wife had handed him. 'I was thinking, my dear, it might expedite matters if you went along as well.'

'No, I'm sure Max can handle . . .'

'Oh no,' said Angus. 'It was he who suggested the idea. After all, you could show him round the place, and he wouldn't have to keep calling back if he had any queries.'

'Well, I'm rather busy at the moment, what with . . .'

'The bridge society, the health club and . . . No, I think they'll all somehow manage to survive without you for a few days,' said Angus with a smile.

Ruth hated being made to sound so provincial in front of Max. 'All right,' she said. 'If you think it will help, I'll accompany Max to the Ardennes.' This time she did look up at him.

The Chinese would have been impressed by the inscrutability of Max's expression.

The trip to the Ardennes took them three days and, more memorably, three nights. By the time they returned to Jersey, Ruth just hoped it wasn't too obvious that they were lovers.

After Max had presented Angus with a detailed report and valuation, the old man accepted his advice that the property should be placed on the market a few weeks before the beginning of the summer season. The two men shook hands on the deal, and Max said he would be in touch the moment anyone showed some interest.

Ruth drove him to the airport, and her final words before he disappeared through Customs were, 'Could you make it a little less than a month before I hear from you again?'

Max rang the following day to inform Angus that he had placed the property in the hands of two reputable agencies in Paris whom his company had dealt with for many years. 'Before you ask,' he added, 'I'm splitting my fee, so there will be no extra charge.'

'A man after my own heart,' said Angus. He put the phone down before Ruth had a chance to have a word with Max.

Over the next few days, Ruth always picked up the phone before Angus could get to it, but Max didn't call again that week. When he eventually phoned on the following Monday, Angus was sitting in the same room.

'I can't wait to tear your clothes off again, my darling,' were Max's opening words.

She replied, 'I'm pleased to hear that, Max, but

I'll pass you straight over to Angus, so you can tell him the news.' As she handed the phone across to her husband, she only hoped that Max did have some news to pass on.

'So, what's this news you've got for me?' asked Angus.

'We've had an offer of 900,000 francs for the property,' said Max, 'which is almost £100,000. But I'm not going to settle yet, as two other parties have also asked to view it. The French agents are recommending that we accept anything over a million francs.'

'If that's also your advice, I'm happy to go along with it,' said Angus. 'And if you close the deal, Max, I'll fly over and sign the contract. I've been promising Ruth a trip to London for some time.'

'Good. It would be nice to see you both again,' said Max, before ringing off.

He phoned again at the end of the week, and although Ruth managed a whole sentence before Angus appeared at her side, she didn't have time to respond to his sentiments.

'£107,600?' said Angus. 'That's far better than I'd expected. Well done, Max. Why don't you draw up the contracts, and the moment you've got the deposit in the bank, I'll fly over.' Angus put the phone down and, turning to Ruth, said, 'Well, it looks as if it might not be too long before we make that promised trip to London.'

After checking into a small hotel in Marble Arch, Ruth and Angus joined Max at a restaurant in South Audley Street that Angus had never heard of. And when he saw the prices on the menu, he knew he wouldn't have selected it if he had. But the staff were very attentive, and seemed to know Max well.

Ruth found the dinner frustrating, because all Angus wanted to talk about was the deal, and once Max had satisfied him on that front, he went on to discuss his other properties in Scotland.

'They seem to be showing a poor return on capital investment,' Angus said. 'Perhaps you could check them out, and advise me on what I should do?'

'I'd be delighted,' said Max, as Ruth looked up from her *foie gras* and stared at her husband. 'Are you feeling all right, my dear?' she asked. 'You've turned quite white.'

'I've got a pain down my right side,' complained Angus. 'It's been a long day, and I'm not used to these swanky restaurants. I'm sure it's nothing a good night's sleep won't sort out.'

'That may be the case, but I still think we should go straight back to the hotel,' Ruth said, sounding concerned.

'Yes, I agree with Ruth,' chipped in Max. 'I'll settle the bill and ask the doorman to find us a taxi.'

Angus rose unsteadily to his feet and walked slowly across the restaurant, leaning heavily on Ruth's arm. When Max joined them in the street a few moments later, Ruth and the doorman were helping Angus into a taxi.

'Good night, Angus,' said Max. 'I hope you're feeling better in the morning. Don't hesitate to call me if I can be of any assistance.' He smiled and closed the taxi door.

By the time Ruth had managed to get her husband into bed, he didn't look any better. Although she knew he wouldn't approve of the extra expense, she called for the hotel doctor.

The doctor arrived within the hour, and after a full examination he surprised Ruth by asking for the details of what Angus had eaten for dinner. She tried to recollect the courses he had chosen, but all she could remember was that he had fallen in with Max's suggestions. The doctor advised that Mr Henderson should be visited by a specialist first thing in the morning.

'Poppycock,' said Angus weakly. 'There's nothing wrong with me that our local GP won't sort out just as soon as we're back on Jersey. We'll get the first flight home.'

Ruth agreed with the doctor, but knew there was no point in arguing with her husband. When he eventually fell asleep, she went downstairs to phone Max and warn him that they would be returning to Jersey in the morning. He sounded concerned, and repeated his offer to do anything he could to help.

When they boarded the aircraft the following morning and the chief steward saw the state Angus was in, it took all Ruth's powers of persuasion to convince him to allow her husband to remain on the flight. 'I must get him back to his own doctor as quickly as possible,' she pleaded. The steward reluctantly acquiesced.

Ruth had already phoned ahead to arrange for a car to meet them – something else Angus would not have approved of. But by the time the plane landed, Angus was no longer in any state to offer an opinion.

As soon as Ruth had got him back to the house and into his own bed, she immediately called their GP. Dr Sinclair carried out the same examination as the London doctor had put him through, and he too asked what Angus had eaten the night before. He came to the same conclusion: Angus must see a specialist immediately.

An ambulance came to pick him up later that afternoon and take him to the Cottage Hospital. When the specialist had completed his examination, he asked Ruth to join him in his room. 'I'm afraid the news is not good, Mrs Henderson,' he told her. 'Your husband has suffered a heart attack, possibly aggravated by a long day and something he ate that didn't agree with him. In the circumstances, I think it might be wise to bring the children back from school.'

Ruth returned home later that night, not knowing who she could turn to. The phone rang, and when she picked it up she recognised the voice immediately.

'Max,' she blurted out, 'I'm so glad you called. The specialist says Angus hasn't long to live, and that I ought to bring the boys back home.' She paused. 'I don't think I'm up to telling them what's happened. You see, they adore their father.'

'Leave it to me,' said Max quietly. 'I'll ring the headmaster, go down and pick them up tomorrow morning, and fly over to Jersey with them.'

'That's so kind of you, Max.'

'It's the least I could do in the circumstances,' said Max. 'Now try and get some rest. You sound exhausted. I'll call back as soon as I know which flight we're on.'

Ruth returned to the hospital and spent most of the night sitting by her husband's bedside. The only other visitor, who Angus insisted on seeing, was the family solicitor. Ruth arranged for Mr Craddock to come the following morning, while she was at the airport picking up Max and the twins.

Max strode out of the customs hall, the two boys walking on either side of him. Ruth was relieved to find that they were far calmer than she was. Max drove the three of them to the hospital. She was disappointed that Max planned to return to England on the afternoon flight, but as he explained, he felt this was a time for her to be with her family.

Angus died peacefully in the St Helier Cottage Hospital the following Friday. Ruth and the twins were at his bedside.

Max flew over for the funeral, and the next day accompanied the twins back to school. When Ruth waved them goodbye she wondered if she would ever hear from Max again.

He phoned the next morning to ask how she was.

'Lonely, and feeling a little guilty that I miss you more than I should.' She paused. 'When are you next planning to come to Jersey?'

'Not for some time. Try not to forget that it was you who warned me that even the letterboxes chatter on Jersey.'

'But what shall I do? The boys are away at school, and you're stuck in London.'

'Why don't you join me in town? It will be a lot easier to lose ourselves over here, and frankly no one will recognise you in London.'

'Perhaps you're right. Let me think about it, and then I'll call you.'

Ruth flew into Heathrow a week later, and Max was at the airport to greet her. She was touched by how thoughtful and gentle he was, never once complaining about her long silences, or the fact that she didn't want to make love.

When he drove her back to the airport on Monday morning, she clung on to him.

'You know,' she said, 'I didn't even get to see your flat or your office.'

'I think it was sensible that you booked into a hotel this time. You can always see my office next time you come over.'

She smiled for the first time since the funeral. When they parted at the airport, he took her in his arms and said, 'I know it's early days, my darling, but I want you to know how much I love you and hope that at some time in the future you might feel me worthy of taking Angus's place.'

She returned to St Helier that evening continually repeating his words, as if they were the lyrics of a song she could not get out of her mind.

It must have been about a week later that she received a phone call from Mr Craddock, the family solicitor, who suggested that she drop into his office and discuss the implications of her late husband's will. She made an appointment to see him the following morning.

Ruth had assumed that as she and Angus had always led a comfortable life, her standard of living would continue much as before. After all, Angus was not the sort of man who would leave his affairs unresolved. She recalled how insistent he had been that Mr Craddock should visit him at the hospital.

Ruth had never shown any interest in Angus's

business affairs. Although he was always careful with his money, if she had ever wanted something, he had never refused her. In any case, Max had just deposited a cheque for over £100,000 in Angus's account, so she set off for the solicitor's office the following morning confident that her late husband would have left quite enough for her to live on.

She arrived a few minutes early. Despite this, the receptionist accompanied her straight through to the senior partner's room. When she walked in, she found three men seated around the board-room table. They immediately rose from their places, and Mr Craddock introduced them as part-ners of the firm. Ruth assumed they must have come to pay their respects, but they resumed their seats and continued to study the thick files placed in front of them. For the first time, Ruth became anxious. Surely Angus's estate was in order?

The senior partner took his seat at the top of the table, untied a bundle of documents and extracted a thick parchment, then looked up at his late client's wife.

'Firstly, may I express on behalf of the firm the sadness we all felt when we learned of Mr Hender-son's death,' he began.

'Thank you,' said Ruth, bowing her head.

'We asked you to come here this morning so that we could advise you of the details of your late husband's will. Afterwards, we shall be happy to answer any questions you might have.'

Ruth went cold, and began trembling. Why hadn't Angus warned her that there were likely to be problems?

The solicitor read through the preamble, finally coming to the bequests.

'I leave all my worldly goods to my wife Ruth, with the exception of the following bequests:

'a) £200 each to both of my sons Nicholas and Ben, which I would like them to spend on something in my memory.

'b) £500 to the Scottish Royal Academy, to be used for the purchase of a picture of their choice, which must be by a Scottish artist.

'c) £1,000 to George Watson College, my old school, and a further £2,000 to Edinburgh University.'

The solicitor continued with a list of smaller bequests, ending with a gift of £100 to the Cottage Hospital which had taken such good care of Angus during the last few days of his life.

The senior partner looked up at Ruth and asked, 'Do you have any questions, Mrs Henderson, which we might advise you on? Or will you be happy for us to administer your affairs in the same way as we did your late husband's?'

'To be honest, Mr Craddock, Angus never discussed his affairs with me, so I'm not sure what all this means. As long as there's enough for the boys and myself to go on living in the way we did when he was alive, I'm happy for you to continue to administer our affairs.'

The partner seated on Mr Craddock's right said, 'I had the privilege of advising Mr Henderson since he first arrived on the island some seven years ago, Mrs Henderson, and would be happy to answer any questions you may have.'

'That's extremely kind of you,' said Ruth, 'but I have no idea what questions to ask, other than perhaps to know roughly how much my husband was worth.'

'That is not quite so easy to answer,' Mr Craddock said, 'because he left so little in cash. However, it has been my responsibility to calculate a figure for probate,' he added, opening one of the files in front of him. 'My initial judgement, which is perhaps on the conservative side, would suggest a sum of somewhere between eighteen and twenty million.'

'Francs?' said Ruth in a whisper.

'No, pounds, madam,' said Mr Craddock matter-of-factly.

After some considerable thought, Ruth decided that she would not let anyone know of her good fortune, including the children. When she flew into London the following weekend, she told Max that Angus's solicitors had briefed her on the contents of Angus's will and the value of his estate.

'Any surprises?' Max asked.

'No, not really. He left the boys a couple of hundred pounds each, and with the £100,000 you managed to raise on the sale of our house in the Ardennes, there should be just about enough to keep the wolves from the door, as long as I'm not too extravagant. So I fear you'll have to go on working if you still want me to be your wife.'

'Even more. I would have hated the idea of living off Angus's money. In fact, I've got some good news for you. The firm has asked me to look into the possibility of opening a branch in St Helier early in the new year. I've told them that I'll only consider the offer on one condition.'

'And what's that?' asked Ruth.

'That one of the locals agrees to be my wife.'

Ruth took him in her arms, never more confident that she had found the right man to spend the rest of her life with.

Max and Ruth were married at the Chelsea register office three months later, with only the twins as witnesses, and even they had been reluctant to attend. 'He'll never take the place of our father,' Ben had told his mother with considerable feeling. Nicholas had nodded his agreement.

'Don't worry,' said Max, as they drove to the airport. 'Only time will sort out that problem.'

As they flew out of Heathrow to begin their honeymoon, Ruth mentioned that she had been a little disappointed that none of Max's friends had attended the ceremony.

'We don't need to attract unpleasant comments so soon after Angus's death,' he told her. 'It might be wise to let a little time go by before I launch you on London society.' He smiled and took her hand. Ruth accepted his assurance, and put aside any anxieties she might have had.

The plane touched down at Venice airport three hours later, and they were whisked away on a motorboat to a hotel overlooking St Mark's Square. Everything seemed so well organised, and

Ruth was surprised at how willing her new husband was to spend hours in the fashion shops helping her select numerous outfits. He even chose a dress for her that she considered far too expensive. For a whole week of lazing about on gondolas, he never once left her side for a moment.

On the Friday, Max hired a car and drove his bride south to Florence, where they strolled back and forth over the bridges together, visiting the Uffizi, the Pitti Palace and the Accademia. In the evenings they ate too much pasta and joined in the dancing in the market square, often returning to their hotel just as the sun was rising. They reluctantly flew on to Rome for the third week, where the hotel bedroom, the Coliseum, the opera house and the Vatican occupied most of their spare moments. The three weeks passed so quickly that Ruth couldn't recall the individual days.

She wrote to the boys every evening before going to bed, describing what a wonderful holiday she was having, always emphasising how kind Max was. She so much wanted them to accept him, but feared that might take more than time.

When she and Max returned to St Helier, he continued to be considerate and attentive. The only disappointment for Ruth was that he didn't have much success in finding premises for the new branch of his company. He would disappear at around ten every morning, but seemed to spend more time at the golf club than he did in town. 'Networking,' he would explain, 'because that's what will matter once the branch is open.'

'When do you think that will be?' Ruth asked.

'Not too much longer now,' he assured her. 'You have to remember that the most important thing in my business is to open in the right location. It's much better to wait for a prime site than to settle for second best.'

But as the weeks passed, Ruth became anxious that Max didn't seem to be getting any nearer to finding that prime site. Whenever she raised the subject he accused her of nagging, which meant that she didn't feel able to bring it up again for at least another month.

When they had been married for six months, she suggested that they might take a weekend off and visit London. 'It would give me a chance to meet some of your friends and catch up with the theatre, and you could report back to your company.'

Each time, Max found some new excuse for not falling in with her plans. But he did agree that they should return to Venice to celebrate their first wedding anniversary.

Ruth hoped the two-week break would revive the memories of their previous visit, and might even inspire Max, when he returned to Jersey, to finally settle on some premises. As it was, the anniversary couldn't have been in greater contrast to the honeymoon they had shared the year before.

It was raining as the plane touched down at Venice airport, and they stood shivering in a long queue as they waited for a taxi. When they arrived at the hotel, Ruth discovered that Max thought she had organised the booking. He lost his temper with the innocent manager, and stormed out of the building. After they had trudged around in the rain with their luggage for over an hour, they ended up in a backstreet hotel that could only supply a small room with single beds, above the bar.

Over drinks that evening, Max confessed that he had left his credit cards in Jersey, so he hoped Ruth wouldn't mind covering the bills until they got home. She seemed to have been covering most of the bills lately anyway, but decided now was not the time to raise the subject.

In Florence, Ruth hesitantly mentioned over breakfast that she hoped he would have more luck in finding premises for his company once they returned to Jersey, and enquired innocently if the firm was becoming at all anxious about his lack of progress.

Max immediately flew into a rage and walked out of the breakfast room, telling her to stop nagging him all the time. She didn't see him for the rest of the day.

In Rome it continued to rain, and Max didn't help matters by regularly going off without warning, sometimes arriving back at the hotel long after she had gone to bed.

Ruth was relieved when the plane took off for Jersey. Once they were back in St Helier she made every effort not to nag, and to try to be supportive and understanding about Max's lack of progress. But however hard she tried, her efforts were met either with long sullen silences or bouts of temper.

As the months passed, they seemed to grow further and further apart, and Ruth no longer bothered to ask how the search for premises was going. She had long ago assumed that the whole idea had been abandoned, and could only wonder if Max had ever been given such an assignment in the first place.

It was over breakfast one morning that Max suddenly announced that the firm had decided against opening a branch in St Helier, and had written to tell him that if he wanted to remain as a partner, he would have to return to London and resume his old position.

'And if you refuse?' asked Ruth. 'Is there an alternative?'

'They've made it all too clear that they would expect me to hand in my resignation.'

'I'd be quite happy to move to London,' Ruth suggested, hoping that might solve their problems.

'No, I don't think that would help,' said Max, who had obviously already decided what the solution was. 'I think it would be better if I spent the week in London, and then flew back to be with you at weekends.'

Ruth did not think that was a good idea, but she knew that any protest would be pointless.

Max flew to London the following day.

Ruth couldn't remember the last time they had made love, and when Max didn't return to Jersey for their second wedding anniversary she accepted an invitation to join Gerald Prescott for dinner.

The twins' old housemaster was, as always, kind and considerate, and when they were alone he did no more than kiss Ruth on the cheek. She decided to tell him about the problems she was having with Max, and he listened attentively, occasionally nodding his understanding. As Ruth looked across the table at her old friend, she felt the sad first thoughts of divorce. She dismissed them quickly from her mind.

When Max returned home the following weekend, Ruth decided to make a special effort. She spent the morning shopping in the market, selecting fresh ingredients for his favourite dish, coq au vin, and picking out a vintage claret to complement it. She wore the dress he had chosen for her in Venice, and drove to the airport to meet him off the plane. He didn't arrive on his usual flight, but strolled through the barrier two hours later, explaining that he had been held up at Heathrow. He didn't apologise for the hours she had spent pacing around the airport lounge, and when they eventually arrived back home and sat down for dinner, he made no comment on the meal, the wine or her dress.

When Ruth had finished clearing away after dinner, she hurried up to the bedroom to find he was pretending to be fast asleep.

Max spent most of Saturday at the golf club, and on Sunday he took the afternoon flight back to London. His last words before departing for the airport were that he couldn't be sure when he would be returning.

Second thoughts of divorce.

As the weeks passed, with only the occasional phone call from London and the odd snatched weekend together, Ruth started seeing more and more of Gerald. Although he never attempted to do anything more than kiss her on the cheek at the beginning and end of their clandestine meetings, and certainly never placed a hand on her thigh, it was she who finally decided 'the time had come' to seduce him.

'Will you marry me?' she asked, as she watched him getting dressed at six the next morning.

'But you're already married,' Gerald gently reminded her.

'You know perfectly well that it's a sham, and has been for months. I was swept off my feet by Max's charm, and behaved like a schoolgirl.

Heaven knows I'd read enough novels about marrying on the rebound.'

'I'd marry you tomorrow, old girl, given half the chance,' Gerald said, smiling. 'You know I've adored you from the first day we met.'

'Although you're not down on one knee, Gerald, I shall consider that an acceptance,' said Ruth, laughing. She paused and looked at her lover, standing in the half-light. 'When I next see Max I'll ask him for a divorce,' she added quietly.

Gerald took off his clothes and climbed back into bed.

It was to be another month before Max returned to the island, and although he took the late flight, Ruth was waiting for him when he walked in the front door. When he leaned down to kiss her on the cheek, she turned away.

'I want a divorce,' she said matter-of-factly.

Max followed her into the drawing room without saying a word. He slumped down into a chair and remained silent for some time. Ruth sat patiently waiting for his response.

'Is there another man?' he eventually asked.

'Yes,' she replied.

'Do I know him?'

'Yes.'

'Gerald?' he asked, looking up at her.

'Yes.'

Once again Max fell into a morose silence.

'I'll be only too happy to make it easy for you,' said Ruth. 'You can sue me for divorce on the grounds of my adultery with Gerald, and I won't put up a fight.'

She was surprised by Max's response. 'I'd like a little time to think about it,' he said. 'Perhaps it would be sensible for us not to do anything until the boys come home at Christmas.'

Ruth reluctantly agreed, but was puzzled, because she couldn't remember when he had last mentioned the boys in her presence.

Max spent the night in the spare room, and flew back to London the following morning, accompanied by two packed suitcases.

He didn't return to Jersey for several weeks, during which time Ruth and Gerald began to plan their future together.

When the twins returned from university for the Christmas holidays, they sounded neither surprised nor disappointed that their mother would be getting a divorce.

Max made no attempt to join the family for the festive season, but flew over to Jersey the day after the boys had returned to university. He took a taxi straight to the house, but stayed for only an hour.

'I am willing to agree to a divorce,' he told Ruth, 'and I intend to start proceedings just as soon as I return to London.'

Ruth simply nodded her agreement.

'If you want things to go through quickly and smoothly, I suggest you appoint a London solicitor. That way I won't have to keep flying back and forth to Jersey, which will only hold things up.'

Ruth put up no objection to the idea, as she had reached the stage where she didn't want to place any obstacles in Max's way.

A few days after Max had returned to the mainland, Ruth was served with divorce papers from a London law firm she had never heard of. She instructed Angus's old solicitors in Chancery Lane to handle the proceedings, explaining over the phone to a junior partner that she wanted to get it over with as quickly as possible.

'Are you hoping for a maintenance settlement of any kind?' the solicitor asked.

'No,' said Ruth, trying not to laugh. 'I don't

want anything other than for the whole matter to be settled quickly, on the grounds of my adultery.'

'If those are your instructions, madam, I'll draw up the necessary papers and have them ready for you to sign within the next few days.'

When the decree nisi was served, Gerald suggested they celebrate by taking a holiday. Ruth agreed to the idea, just as long as they didn't have to go anywhere near Italy.

'Let's sail around the Greek islands,' said Gerald. 'That way there will be less chance of bumping into any of my pupils, not to mention their parents.' They flew to Athens the next day.

When they sailed into the harbour at Skyros, Ruth said, 'I'd never thought I would spend my third wedding anniversary with another man.'

Gerald took her in his arms. 'Try to forget Max,' he said. 'He's history.'

'Well, nearly,' Ruth said. 'I was rather hoping that the divorce would have been absolute before we left Jersey.'

'Have you any idea what's caused the hold-up?' Gerald asked.

'Heaven knows,' Ruth replied, 'but whatever it is, Max will have his reasons.' She paused. 'You know, I never did get to see his office in Mayfair, or meet any of his colleagues or friends. It's almost as if it was all a figment of my imagination.'

'Or his,' said Gerald, putting an arm around her waist. 'But don't let's waste any more time talking about Max. Let's think about Greeks, and bacchanalian orgies.'

'Is that what you teach those innocent little children in their formative years?'

'No, it's what they teach me,' Gerald replied.

For the next three weeks the two of them sailed around the Greek islands, eating too much moussaka, drinking too much wine, and hoping that too much sex would keep their weight down. By the end of their holiday Gerald was a little too red, and Ruth was dreading being reintroduced to her bathroom scales. The holiday could not have been more fun; not only because Gerald was such a good sailor, but because, as Ruth discovered, even during a storm he could make her laugh.

Once they were back on Jersey, Gerald drove Ruth to the house. When she opened the front door she was greeted by a pile of letters. She sighed. They could all wait until tomorrow, she decided.

Ruth spent a restless night tossing and turning. After snatching a few hours' sleep, she decided that she might as well get up and make herself a cup of tea. She began to thumb through the post, only stopping when she came to a long buff envelope marked 'Urgent' and bearing a London postmark.

She tore it open and extracted a document that brought a smile to her face: 'A decree absolute has been granted between the aforesaid parties: Max Donald Bennett and Ruth Ethel Bennett.'

'That settles that once and for all,' she said out loud, and immediately phoned Gerald to tell him the good news.

'Disappointing,' he said.

'Disappointing?' she repeated.

'Yes, my darling. You have no idea how much my street cred has risen since the boys at school discovered I've been on holiday with a married woman.'

Ruth laughed. 'Behave yourself, Gerald, and try to get used to the idea of being a respectable married man.'

'Can't wait,' he said. 'But must dash. It's one thing to be living in sin; it's quite another to be late for morning prayers.'

Ruth went up to the bathroom and stood gingerly on the scales. She groaned when she saw where the little indicator finally stopped. She decided she would have to spend at least an hour in the gym that morning. The phone rang just as she was stepping into the bath. She got back out and grabbed a towel, thinking it must be Gerald again.

'Good morning, Mrs Bennett,' said a rather formal voice. How she hated even the sound of that name.

'Good morning,' she replied.

'It's Mr Craddock, madam. I've been trying to get in touch with you for the past three weeks.'

'Oh, I'm so sorry,' said Ruth, 'but I only returned from a holiday in Greece last night.'

'Yes, I see. Well, perhaps we could meet as soon as it's convenient?' he said, showing no interest in her holiday.

'Yes, of course, Mr Craddock. I could pop into your office around twelve, if that would suit you.'

'Any time you decide will suit us, Mrs Bennett,' said the formal voice.

Ruth worked hard in the gym that morning, determined to lose the surplus pounds she had put on in Greece – respectable married woman or not, she still wanted to be slim. By the time she'd come off the running machine, the gym clock was chiming twelve. Despite hurrying through to the locker room and showering and changing as quickly as possible, she was still thirty-five minutes late for Mr Craddock.

Once again the receptionist ushered her through to the senior partner's office, without her having to see the inside of a waiting room. As she entered, she found Mr Craddock pacing around the room.

'I'm sorry to have kept you,' she said, feeling a little guilty, as two of the partners rose from their places at the boardroom table.

This time Mr Craddock did not suggest a cup of tea, but simply ushered her into a chair at the other end of the table. Once she was seated, he resumed his place, glanced down at a pile of papers lying in front of him and extracted a single sheet.

'Mrs Bennett, we have received a summons from your husband's solicitors demanding a full settlement following your divorce.'

'But we never discussed a settlement at any time,' said Ruth in disbelief. 'It was never part of the deal.'

'That may well be the case,' said the senior partner, looking down at the papers. 'But unfortunately, you agreed to the divorce being granted

on the grounds of your adultery with a Mr Gerald'
– he checked the name – 'Prescott, at a time when
your husband was working in London.'

'That's true, but we only agreed to that in order
to speed matters up. You see, we both wanted the
divorce to go through as quickly as possible.'

'I'm sure that was the case, Mrs Bennett.'

She would always hate that name.

'However, by agreeing to Mr Bennett's terms,
he became the innocent party in this action.'

'But that is no longer relevant,' said Ruth,
'because this morning I received confirmation
from my London solicitors that I have been
granted a decree absolute.'

The partner seated on Mr Craddock's right
turned and looked directly at her.

'May I be permitted to ask if it was at Mr Bennett's suggestion that you instructed a solicitor
from the mainland to handle your divorce proceedings?'

Ah, so that's what's behind all this, thought
Ruth. They're just annoyed that I didn't consult
them. 'Yes,' she replied firmly. 'It was simply a
matter of convenience, as Max was living in
London at the time, and didn't want to have to
keep flying back and forth to the island.'

'It certainly turned out to be most convenient for Mr Bennett,' said the senior partner. 'Did your husband ever discuss a financial settlement with you?'

'Never,' said Ruth even more firmly. 'He had no idea what I was worth.'

'I have a feeling,' continued the partner seated on Mr Craddock's left, 'that Mr Bennett knew only too well how much you were worth.'

'But that's not possible,' insisted Ruth. 'You see, I never once discussed my finances with him.'

'Nevertheless, he has presented a claim against you, and seems to have made a remarkably accurate assessment of the value of your late husband's estate.'

'Then you must refuse to pay a penny, because it was never part of our agreement.'

'I accept that what you are telling us is correct, Mrs Bennett. But I fear that as you were the guilty party, we have no defence to offer.'

'How can that be possible?' demanded Ruth.

'The law of divorce on Jersey is unequivocal on the subject,' said Mr Craddock. 'As we would have been happy to advise you, had you consulted us.'

'What law?' asked Ruth, ignoring the barbed comment.

'Under the law of Jersey, once it has been accepted that one of the parties is innocent in divorce proceedings, that person – whatever their sex – is automatically entitled to one third of the other's estate.'

Ruth began trembling. 'Are there no exceptions?' she asked quietly.

'Yes,' replied Mr Craddock.

Ruth looked up hopefully.

'If you have been married for less than three years, the law does not apply. You were, however, Mrs Bennett, married for three years and eight days.' He paused, readjusted his spectacles and added, 'I have a feeling that Mr Bennett was not only aware of exactly how much you were worth, but also knew the laws of divorce as they apply on Jersey.'

Three months later, after both sides of solicitors had agreed on the value of Ruth Ethel Bennett's estate, Max Donald Bennett received a cheque for £6,270,000 in full and final settlement.

Whenever Ruth looked back on the past three years – and she often did – she came to the conclusion that Max must have planned everything right down to the last detail. Yes, even before they had bumped into each other.

Love at First Sight

Andrew was running late, and would have grabbed a taxi if it hadn't been the rush hour. He entered the crowded Metro and dodged in and out of the hordes of commuters as they headed down the escalator on their way home.

Andrew wasn't on his way home. After only four stops he would re-emerge from the bowels of the earth to keep an appointment with Ely Bloom, the Chief Executive of Chase Manhattan in Paris. Although Andrew had never met Bloom, like all his colleagues at the bank, he was well aware of his reputation. He didn't 'take a meeting' with anyone unless there was a good reason.

Andrew had spent the forty-eight hours since Bloom's secretary had called to make the appointment trying to work out what that good reason could possibly be. A simple switch from Crédit Suisse to Chase seemed the obvious answer – but it was unlikely to be that simple if Bloom was involved. Was he about to make Andrew an offer he couldn't refuse? Would he expect him to return to New York after he had spent less than two years in Paris? So many questions floated through his mind. He knew he should stop speculating, as they would all be answered at six o'clock. He would have run down the escalator, but it was too crowded.

Andrew knew he had a few chips stacked on his side of the table – he had headed up the foreign exchange desk at Crédit Suisse for almost two years, and it was common knowledge that he was outperforming all of his rivals. The French bankers had simply shrugged their shoulders when they were told of Andrew's success, while his American rivals just tried to persuade him to leave his present position and join them. Whatever Bloom might offer him, Andrew was confident Crédit Suisse would match it. Whenever he had received other approaches during the past twelve months he had dismissed them with the same polite, boyish grin – but he knew that this time would be different. Bloom wasn't a man who could be bought off with a polite, boyish grin.

Andrew didn't want to move banks, as he was well satisfied with the package Crédit Suisse had given him – and at his age, what young man wouldn't enjoy working in Paris? However, it was that time of the year when annual bonuses were being considered, so he was happy to be seen 'taking a meeting' with Ely Bloom in the American Bar at the Georges V. It would be only a matter of hours before someone reported the sighting to his superiors.

When Andrew stepped onto the platform of the Metro, it was so crowded that he wondered if he would be able to get on the first train that pulled into the station. He checked his watch: 5.37. He should still be well in time for the meeting, but as he had no intention of being late for Mr Bloom, he began to slip through any tiny opening or gap that appeared until he found himself at the front of the mêlée, well placed to climb on board the next train. Even if he didn't reach an agreement with Mr Bloom, the man was going to be an important figure in the banking world for years to come, so there was no point in turning up late and making a bad impression.

Andrew waited impatiently for the next train to emerge from the tunnel. He stared across the track at the opposite platform, and tried to concentrate on what questions Bloom might ask.

What is your present salary?

Can you break your contract?

Are you on a bonus scheme?

Are you willing to return to New York?

The southbound platform was just as crowded as the one he was standing on, and Andrew's concentration was broken when his eyes settled on a young woman who was glancing at her watch. Perhaps she also had an appointment she couldn't afford to be late for.

When she raised her head, he immediately forgot Ely Bloom. He just stared into those deep brown eyes. She remained unaware of her admirer. She must have been about five foot eight, with the most perfect oval face, olive skin that would never require make-up, and a mop of curly black hair that no hairdresser could possibly have permed. I'm on the wrong side of the track, he told himself, and it's too late to do anything about it.

She wore a beige-coloured raincoat, the tied belt leaving no question as to how slim and graceful her figure was, and her legs – or as much as he could see of them – completed a perfect package. Better than any Mr Bloom could offer.

She checked her watch again and then looked

up, suddenly aware that he was staring at her.

He smiled. She blushed and lowered her head just as two trains glided into the station from opposite ends of the platform. Everyone standing behind Andrew pushed forward to claim a place on the waiting train.

When it pulled out of the station, Andrew was the only person left on the platform. He stared across at the train on the other side, and watched it slowly accelerate out of the station. When it had disappeared into the tunnel, Andrew smiled again. Only one person remained on the opposite platform, and this time she returned his smile.

You may ask how I know this story to be true. The answer is simple. I was told it at Andrew and Claire's tenth wedding anniversary earlier this year.

Both Sides Against the Middle

'There's one problem I haven't touched on,' said Billy Gibson. 'But first, let me refill your glass.'

For the past hour the two men had sat quietly in the corner of the King William Arms discussing the problems of running a police station on the border of Northern Ireland and Eire. Billy Gibson was retiring after thirty years in the force, the past six of them as Chief of Police. His successor, Jim Hogan, had been brought in from Belfast, and the talk was that if he made a good fist of it, his next stop would be as Chief Constable.

Billy took a long draught, and settled back before he began his story.

'No one can be quite sure of the truth about the house that straddles the border, but, as with all good Irish stories, there are always several half-truths circulating at any one time. I need to tell you a little of the house's history before I come to the problem I'm having with its present owners.

To do that I must mention, if only in passing, one Patrick O'Dowd, who worked in the planning department of Belfast City Council.'

'A nest of vipers at the best of times,' chipped in the new Chief.

'And those were not the best of times,' said the retiring Chief, before taking another sip of Guinness. His thirst quenched, he continued his story.

'No one has ever understood why O'Dowd granted planning permission for a house to be built on the border in the first place. It was not until it had been completed that someone in the rates department in Dublin got hold of an Ordnance Survey map, and pointed out to the authorities in Belfast that the border ran right through the middle of the sitting room. Old lags in the village say the local builder misread the plans, but others assure me that he knew exactly what he was doing.

'At the time, no one cared too much, because the man the house was built for – Bertie O'Flynn, a widower – was a godfearing man who attended Mass at St Mary's in the South, and sipped his Guinness at the Volunteer in the North. I think it's also worth mentioning,' said the Chief, 'that Bertie had no politics.

'Dublin and Belfast managed to reach a rare compromise, and agreed that as the house's front door was in the North, Bertie should pay his taxes to the Crown, but as his kitchen and half-acre of garden were in the South, he should pay his rates to the local council on the other side of the border. For years this agreement caused no difficulties, until dear old Bertie departed this life and left the house to his son, Eamonn. To cut a long story short, Eamonn was, is, and always will be a bad lot.

'The boy had been sent to school in the North, although he attended church in the South, and he showed little interest in either. In fact, by the age of eleven, the only thing he didn't know about smuggling was how to spell it. By the time he turned thirteen, he was buying cartons of cigarettes in the North, and trading them for crates of Guinness in the South. At the age of fifteen, he was earning more money than his headmaster, and when he left school he was already running a flourishing business, importing spirits and wine from the South while exporting cannabis and condoms from the North.

'Whenever his probation officer knocked on the front door in the North, he retreated to his kitchen in the South. If the local Garda was seen walking up the garden path, Eamonn disappeared into the dining room, and stayed there until they got bored and drove away. Bertie, who always ended up having to answer the door, got heartily sick of it, which I suspect in the end was the reason he gave up the ghost.

'Now, when I took up my appointment as Chief of Police six years ago, I decided to make it my personal ambition to put Eamonn O'Flynn behind bars. But what with the problems I've had to handle on the border and normal policing duties, the truth is I never got round to it. I'd even started to turn a blind eye, until O'Flynn met Maggie Crann, a well-known prostitute from the South, who was looking to expand her trade in the North. A house with four upstairs bedrooms, two on either side of the border, seemed to be the answer to her prayers – even if from time to time one of her half-naked customers had to be moved from one side of the house to the other rather quickly, to avoid being arrested.

'When the Troubles escalated, my opposite number south of the border and I agreed to treat the house as a "no go" area – that was, until Eamonn opened a casino in the South in a new conservatory which was never to grow a flower –

planning permission agreed by Dublin – with the cashier's office situated in a newly constructed garage that could take a fleet of buses, but has not yet housed a vehicle of any description – planning permission agreed by Belfast.'

'Why didn't you oppose planning permission?' asked Hogan.

'We did, but it quickly became clear that Maggie had customers in both departments.' Billy sighed. 'But the final blow came when the farmland surrounding the house came up for sale. No one else got a look-in, and O'Flynn ended up with sixty-five acres, in which he could post lookouts. That gives him more than enough time to move any incriminating evidence from one side of the house to the other, long before we can reach the front door.'

The glasses were empty. 'My round,' said the younger man. He went up to the bar and ordered two more pints.

When he returned, he asked his next question even before he had placed the glasses on the table.

'Why haven't you applied for a search warrant? With the number of laws he must be breaking, surely you could have closed the place down years ago?'

'Agreed,' said the Chief, 'but whenever I apply for a warrant, he's the first person to hear about it. By the time we arrive, all we find is a happily married couple living alone in a peaceful farmhouse.'

'But what about your opposite number in the South? It must be in his interests to work with you and . . .'

'You'd think so, wouldn't you? But there have been five of them in the past seven years, and what with not wishing to harm their promotion prospects, their desire for an easy life, or straightforward bribery, not one of them has been willing to cooperate. The current Garda Chief is only months away from retirement, and won't do anything that might harm his pension. No,' continued Billy, 'whichever way you look at it, I've failed. And I can tell you, unlike my opposite number, if I could sort out Eamonn O'Flynn once and for all, I would even be willing to forgo my pension.'

'Well, you still have another six weeks, and after all you've told me, I'd be relieved if O'Flynn was off the patch before I took over. So let's see if I can come up with a solution that will solve both our problems.'

'I'd agree to anything, short of murdering the

man – and don't think that hasn't crossed my mind.'

Jim Hogan laughed, looked at his watch and said, 'I must be getting back to Belfast.'

The old Chief nodded, downed his last drop of Guinness and accompanied his colleague to the carpark at the back of the pub. Hogan didn't speak again until he was seated behind the wheel of his car. He turned on the engine and wound the window down.

'Are you going to have a farewell party?'

'Yes,' said the Chief. 'On the Saturday before I retire. Why do you ask?'

'Because I always think a farewell party is an occasion to let bygones be bygones,' said Jim, without explanation.

The Chief looked puzzled as Jim drove out of the carpark, turned right, and headed north towards Belfast.

Eamonn O'Flynn was somewhat surprised to receive the invitation, as he hadn't expected to feature on the Chief of Police's guest list.

Maggie studied the embossed card inviting them to Chief Gibson's farewell party at the Queen's Arms in Ballyroney.

'Are you going to accept?' she asked

'Why would I want to do that,' responded Eamonn, 'when the bastard has spent the past six years trying to put me behind bars?'

'Perhaps it's his way of burying the hatchet,' suggested Maggie.

'Yes, right in the middle of my back, would be my bet. In any case, surely you wouldn't want to be seen dead with that lot.'

'Now, there's where you're wrong for once,' said Maggie.

'Why's that?'

'Because it would amuse me to see the faces of the wives of those councillors, not to mention the police officers, I've shared a bed with.'

'But it could turn out to be a trap.'

'I can't imagine how,' said Maggie, 'when we know for certain that them in the South won't give us any trouble, and anyone who could in the North is sure to be at the party.'

'That wouldn't stop them raiding our place while we're off the premises.'

'What a disappointment that will be for them,' said Maggie, 'when they discover the staff have been given the night off, and it's nothing more than the home of two decent, law-abiding citizens.'

Eamonn remained sceptical, and it wasn't until Maggie arrived back from Dublin with a new dress she wanted everyone to see her in that he finally surrendered and agreed to accompany her to the party. 'But we won't stay for more than an hour, and that's my final word on the subject,' he warned her.

When they left the house on the night of the party, Eamonn checked that every window was locked and every door was bolted before he set the alarm. He then drove slowly around the perimeter of his land, warning all the guards to be especially careful and to call him on his mobile if they spotted anything suspicious – and he meant anything.

Maggie, who was checking her hair in the car mirror, told him that if he took much longer there wouldn't be any party left to go to.

When they walked into the ballroom of the Queen's Arms half an hour later, Billy Gibson seemed genuinely pleased to see them, which only made Eamonn feel even more suspicious.

'I don't think you've met my successor,' said the Chief, before introducing Eamonn and Maggie to Jim Hogan. 'But I'm sure you know of his reputation.'

Eamonn knew of his reputation only too well, and wanted to return home immediately, but someone pressed a pint of Guinness into his hand, and a young constable asked Maggie for a dance.

While she was dancing, Eamonn looked around the room to see if there was anyone he knew. Far too many, he concluded, and couldn't wait for an hour to pass so he could go home. But then his eyes rested on Mick Burke, a local pickpocket who was serving behind the bar. Eamonn was surprised that, with Mick's record, they had let him past the front door. But at least he had found someone he could have a quiet chat to.

When the band stopped playing, Maggie joined the queue for food and filled a plate with salmon and new potatoes. She took the offering across to Eamonn, who for a few minutes looked almost as if he was enjoying himself. After a second helping he started swapping stories with one or two members of the Garda, who appeared to be hanging on his every word.

But the moment Eamonn heard eleven chime on the ballroom clock, he suddenly wanted to escape. 'Even Cinderella didn't leave the ball before twelve,' Maggie told him. 'And in any case, it would be rude to leave just as the Chief's about to deliver his farewell speech.'

The toastmaster banged his gavel and called for order. A warm round of applause greeted Billy Gibson as he stepped forward to take his place in front of the microphone. He rested his speech on the lectern and smiled down at the assembled gathering.

'My friends,' he began, '– not to mention one or two sparring partners.' He raised his glass in the direction of Eamonn, delighted to see he was still among them. 'It is with a heavy heart that I appear before you tonight, aware of how much I am indebted to all of you.' He paused. 'And I mean *all* of you.' Cheers and catcalls followed these remarks, and Maggie was delighted to see that Eamonn was joining in the laughter.

'Now, I well remember when I first joined the force. That was when things were really tough.' More cheers followed, and louder catcalls from the young. The noise died down eventually when the Chief resumed his speech, no one wishing to deny him the opportunity of reminiscing at his own farewell party.

Eamonn was still sober enough to notice the young constable entering the room, an anxious look on his face. He made his way quickly towards the stage, and although he evidently didn't feel able to interrupt Billy's speech, he carried out Mr Hogan's instructions and placed a note in the middle of the lectern.

Eamonn began to fumble for his mobile, but he couldn't find it in any of his pockets. He could have sworn he'd had it with him when he arrived.

'When I hand in my badge at midnight . . .' Billy said, glancing down at his speech to see the note in front of him. He paused and adjusted his glasses, as if trying to take in the significance of the message, then frowned and looked back up at his guests. 'I must apologise, my friends, but it seems that there's been an incident on the border that requires my personal attention. I have no choice but to leave immediately, and ask that all ranking officers join me outside. I hope our guests will continue to enjoy the party, and be assured we'll return just as soon as we've sorted the little problem out.'

Only one person reached the front door before the Chief, and he was driving out of the carpark before even Maggie realised he'd left the room. However, the Chief, siren blaring, still managed to overtake Eamonn some two miles from the border.

'Shall I have him stopped for speeding?' asked the Chief's driver.

'No, I don't think so,' said Billy Gibson. 'What's the point of this whole performance if the principal actor is unable to make an entrance?'

When Eamonn brought his car to a halt at the edge of his property a few minutes later, he found it encircled by thick blue-and-white tape proclaiming 'DANGER. DO NOT ENTER.'

He jumped out of his car and ran over to the Chief, who was receiving a briefing from a group of officers.

'What the hell is going on?' demanded Eamonn.

'Ah, Eamonn, I'm so glad you were able to make it. I was just about to call you, in case you were still at the party. It seems that about an hour ago an IRA patrol was spotted on your land.'

'Actually, that hasn't been confirmed,' said a young officer, who was listening intently to someone on a hand-phone. 'There's conflicting intelligence coming out of Ballyroney suggesting that they may have been loyalist paramilitaries.'

'Well, whoever they are, my first interest must be the protection of lives and property, and to that end I've sent in the bomb squad to make sure it will be safe for you and Maggie to return to your home.'

'That's bollocks, Billy Gibson, and you know it,' said Eamonn. 'I'm ordering you off my land before I instruct my men to forcibly remove you.'

'Well, it's not quite as easy as that,' said the Chief. 'You see, I've just had a message from the bomb squad that they've already broken into your house. You'll be relieved to know they found no one on the premises, but they were most concerned to come across an unidentifiable package in the conservatory, and a similar one in the garage.'

'But they're nothing more than . . .'

'Nothing more than what?' asked the Chief innocently.

'How did your people manage to get past my guards?' demanded Eamonn. 'They had orders to throw you off if you put so much as a toe on my land.'

'Now there's the thing, Eamonn. They must have wandered off your property for a moment without realising it, and because of the imminent danger to their lives I felt it necessary to take them all into custody. For their own protection, you understand.'

'I'll bet you don't even have a search warrant to enter my property.'

'I don't need one,' said the Chief, 'if I'm of the opinion that someone's life is in danger.'

'Well, now you know that no one's life is in danger, and never was in the first place, you can get off my property and back to your party.'

'There's my next problem, Eamonn. You see, we've just had another call, this time from an anonymous informant, to warn us that he has placed a bomb in the garage and another in the conservatory, and that they'll be detonated just before midnight. The moment I was informed of this threat, I realised that it was my duty to check the safety manual to find out what the correct procedure is in circumstances such as these.' The Chief removed a thick green booklet from an inside pocket, as if it were always with him.

'You're bluffing,' said O'Flynn. 'You don't have the authority to . . .'

'Ah, here's what I was after,' said the Chief, after he had flicked over a few pages. Eamonn looked down to see a paragraph underlined in red ink.

'Let me read you the exact words, Eamonn, so that you'll fully comprehend the terrible dilemma I'm facing. "*If an officer above the rank of Major or Chief Inspector believes that the lives of civilians may be at risk at the scene of a suspected terrorist attack, and he has a qualified member of the bomb squad present, he must first clear the area of all civilians and, having achieved this, if he deems it appropriate, carry out an isolated explosion.''* Couldn't be clearer,' said the Chief. 'Now, are you able to let me know what's in those boxes, Eamonn? If not, I must assume the worst, and proceed according to the book.'

'If you harm my property in any way, Billy Gibson, let me warn you that I'll sue you for every penny you're worth.'

'You're worrying unnecessarily, Eamonn. Let me reassure you that there's page after page in the manual concerning compensation for innocent victims. We would naturally feel it our obligation to rebuild your lovely home, brick by brick, recreating a conservatory Maggie would be proud of and a garage large enough to house all your cars. However, if we were to spend that amount of taxpayers' money, we would have to ensure that the house was built on one side of the border or the other, so that an unhappy incident such as this one could never happen again.'

'You'll never get away with it,' said Eamonn, as a heavily-built man appeared by the Chief's side, carrying a plunger.

'You'll remember Mr Hogan, of course. I introduced you at my farewell party.'

'You put a finger on that plunger, Hogan, and I'll have you facing inquiries for the rest of your working life. And you'll be able to forget any ideas of becoming Chief Constable.'

'Mr O'Flynn makes a fair point, Jim,' said the Chief, checking his watch, 'and I certainly wouldn't want to be responsible for harming your career in any way. But I see that you don't take over command for another seven minutes, so it will be my sad duty to carry out this onerous responsibility.'

As the Chief bent down to place his hand on the plunger, Eamonn leapt at his throat. It took three officers to restrain him, while he shouted obscenities at the top of his voice.

The Chief sighed, checked his watch, gripped the handle of the plunger and pressed down slowly.

The explosion could be heard for miles around as the roof of the garage – or was it the conservatory? – flew high into the air. Within moments the buildings were razed to the ground, leaving nothing in their place but smoke, dust and a pile of rubble.

When the noise had finally died away, the chimes of St Mary's could be heard striking twelve in the distance. The former Chief of Police considered it the end of a perfect day.

'You know, Eamonn,' he said, 'I do believe that was worth sacrificing my pension for.'

A Weekend to Remember

I first met Susie six years ago, and when she called to ask if I would like to join her for a drink, she can't have been surprised that my immediate response was a little frosty. After all, my memory of our last meeting wasn't altogether a happy one.

I had been invited to the Keswicks for dinner, and like all good hostesses, Kathy Keswick considered it nothing less than her duty to pair off any surviving bachelor over the age of thirty with one of her more eligible girlfriends.

With this in mind, I was disappointed to find that she had placed me next to Mrs Ruby Collier, the wife of a Conservative Member of Parliament who was seated on the left of my hostess at the other end of the table. Only moments after I had introduced myself she said, 'You've probably read about my husband in the press.' She then proceeded to tell me that none of her friends could understand why her husband wasn't in the

Cabinet. I felt unable to offer an opinion on the subject, because until that moment I had never heard of him.

The name-card on the other side of me read 'Susie', and the lady in question had the sort of looks that made you wish you were sitting opposite her at a table set for two. Even after a sideways glance at that long fair hair, blue eyes, captivating smile and slim figure, I would not have been surprised to discover that she was a model. An illusion she was happy to dispel within minutes.

I introduced myself by explaining that I had been at Cambridge with our host. 'And how do you know the Keswicks?' I enquired.

'I was in the same office as Kathy when we both worked for *Vogue* in New York.'

I remember feeling disappointed that she lived overseas. For how long, I wondered. 'Where do you work now?'

'I'm still in New York,' she replied. 'I've just been made the commissioning editor for *Art Quarterly*.'

'I renewed my subscription only last week,' I told her, rather pleased with myself. She smiled, evidently surprised that I'd even heard of the publication.

'How long are you in London for?' I asked, glancing at her left hand to check that she wore neither an engagement nor a wedding ring.

'Only a few days. I flew over for my parents' wedding anniversary last week, and I was hoping to catch the Lucian Freud exhibition at the Tate before I go back to New York. And what do you do?' she asked.

'I own a small hotel in Jermyn Street,' I told her.

I would happily have spent the rest of the evening chatting to Susie, and not just because of my passion for art, but my mother had taught me from an early age that however much you like the person on one side of you, you must be equally attentive to the one sitting on the other side.

I turned back to Mrs Collier, who pounced on me with the words, 'Have you read the speech my husband made in the Commons yesterday?'

I confessed that I hadn't, which turned out to be a mistake, because she then delivered the entire offering verbatim.

Once she had completed her monologue on the subject of the Draft Civic Amenities (Landfill) Act, I could see why her husband wasn't in the Cabinet. In fact, I made a mental note to avoid him when we retired to the drawing room for coffee.

'I much look forward to making your husband's acquaintance after dinner,' I told her, before turning my attention back to Susie, only to find that she was staring at someone on the other side of the table. I glanced across to see that the man in question was deep in conversation with Mary Ellen Yarc, an American woman who was seated next to him, and seemed unaware of the attention he was receiving.

I remembered that his name was Richard something, and that he had come with the girl seated at the other end of the table. She too, I noticed, was looking in Richard's direction. I had to confess that he had the sort of chiselled features and thick wavy hair that make it unnecessary to have a degree in quantum physics.

'So, what's big in New York at the moment?' I asked, trying to recapture Susie's attention.

She turned back to me and smiled. 'We're going to have a new Mayor at any moment now,' she informed me, 'and it could even be a Republican for a change. Frankly, I'd vote for anyone who can do something about the crime figures. One of them, I can't remember his name, keeps talking about zero tolerance. Whoever he is, he'd get my vote.'

Although Susie's conversation remained lively and informative, her attention frequently strayed back to the other side of the table. I would have assumed she and Richard were lovers, if he had given her as much as a glance.

Over pudding, Mrs Collier took a hatchet to the Cabinet, giving reasons why every one of them should be replaced – I didn't need to ask by whom. By the time she'd reached the Minister of Agriculture, I felt I'd done my duty, and glanced back to find Susie pretending to be preoccupied by her summer pudding, while actually still taking far more interest in Richard.

Suddenly he looked in her direction. Without warning, Susie grabbed my hand and began talking intently about an Eric Rohmer film she had recently seen in Nice.

Few men object to a woman grabbing their hand, particularly when that woman is graced with Susie's looks, but preferably not while she is gazing at another man.

The moment Richard resumed his conversation with our hostess, Susie immediately released my hand and dug a fork into her summer pudding.

I was grateful to be spared a third round with Mrs Collier, as Kathy rose from her place and suggested that we all go through to the drawing room. I fear this meant I had to miss out on the details of the Private Member's Bill Mrs Collier's husband was preparing to present to the House the following week.

Over coffee I was introduced to Richard, who turned out to be a banker from New York. He continued to ignore Susie – or perhaps, inexplicably, he simply wasn't aware of her presence. The girl whose name I didn't know came across to join us, and murmured in his ear, 'We shouldn't leave it too late, darling. Don't forget we're booked on the early flight to Paris.'

'I hadn't forgotten, Rachel,' he replied, 'but I'd prefer not to be the first to leave.' Someone else who had been brought up by a fastidious mother.

I felt someone touch my arm, and swung round to find Mrs Collier beaming up at me.

'This is my husband Reginald. I told him how keen you were to learn more about his Private Member's Bill.'

It must have been about ten minutes later, although it felt more like a month, that Kathy came to my rescue. 'Tony, I wonder if you'd be kind enough to give Susie a lift home. It's pouring with rain, and finding a taxi at this time of night won't be easy.'

'I'd be delighted,' I replied. 'I must thank you for including me in such charming company. It's all been quite fascinating,' I said, smiling down at Mrs Collier.

The Member's wife beamed back. My mother would have been proud of me.

In the car on the way back to her flat, Susie asked me if I had seen the Freud exhibition. 'Yes,' I said. 'I thought it was spectacular, and I'm planning to see it again before it closes.'

'I was thinking of popping in tomorrow morning,' she said, touching my hand. 'Why don't you join me?' I happily agreed, and when I dropped her off in Pimlico she gave me the sort of hug that suggests 'I would like to get to know you better.' Now, I am not an expert on many things, but I consider myself to be a world authority when it comes to hugs, as I have experienced every one – from a squeeze to a bearhug. I can interpret any message from 'I can't wait to get your clothes off' to 'Get lost.'

I arrived at the Tate early the following morning, anticipating that there would be a long queue for the exhibition, and giving myself time to pick up the tickets before Susie arrived. I had been waiting on the steps for only a few minutes when she appeared. She was wearing a short yellow dress that emphasised her slim figure, and as she climbed the steps I noticed men glance across to follow her progress. The moment she saw me, she began to run up the steps, and she greeted me with a long hug. An 'I feel I know you better already' hug.

I enjoyed the exhibition even more the second time, not least because of Susie's knowledge of Lucian Freud's work, as she took me through the different phases of his career. When we reached the last picture in the show, *Fat Women Looking Out of the Window,* I remarked a little feebly, 'Well, one thing's for certain, you'll never end up looking like that.'

'Oh, I wouldn't be so sure,' she said. 'But if I did, I'd never let you find out.' She took my hand. 'Do you have time for lunch?'

'Of course, but I haven't booked anywhere.'

'I have,' said Susie with a smile. 'The Tate has a super restaurant, and I booked a table for two, just in case . . .' She smiled again.

I don't recall much about lunch, except that when the bill came we were the last two left in the restaurant.

'If you could do anything in the world right

now,' I said – a chat-up line I've used many times in the past – 'what would it be?'

Susie remained silent for some time before replying, 'Take the shuttle to Paris, spend the weekend with you and visit the Picasso exhibition "His Early Days", which is on at the Musée d'Orsay right now. How about you?'

'Take the shuttle to Paris, spend the weekend with you, and visit the Picasso exhibition "His Early Days", which . . .'

She burst out laughing, took my hand and said, 'Let's do it!'

I arrived at Waterloo some twenty minutes before the train was due to depart. I had already booked a suite in my favourite hotel, and a table at a restaurant that prides itself on not being in the tourist guides. I bought two first-class tickets and stood under the clock, as we'd agreed. Susie was only a couple of minutes late, and gave me a hug that was a definite step towards 'I can't wait to get your clothes off.'

She held my hand as we sped through the English countryside. Once we were in France – it always makes me angry that the trains speed up on the French side – I leaned over and kissed her for the first time.

She chatted about her work in New York, the exhibitions that were a 'must', and gave me a taste of what I might expect when we visited the Picasso exhibition. 'The pencil portrait of his father sitting in a chair, which he drew when he was only sixteen, was the harbinger of all that was to come.' She continued to talk about Picasso and his work with a passion one could never gain from merely reading a book on the subject. When the train pulled into the Gare du Nord, I grabbed both our cases and jumped off to make sure we would be among the first in the taxi queue.

Susie spent most of the journey to the hotel staring out of the taxi's window, like a schoolgirl on her first visit abroad. I remember thinking how strange this was for someone who had so obviously travelled extensively.

When the taxi swung into the entrance of the Hôtel du Coeur, I told her it was the sort of place I would love to own – comfortable but unpretentious, and offering a level of service Anglo-Saxons are rarely able to match. 'And the owner, Albert, is a gem.'

'I can't wait to meet him,' she said, as the taxi came to a halt outside the front door.

Albert was standing on the steps waiting to greet

us. I knew he would be, as I would have been if he had accompanied a beautiful woman to London for the weekend.

'We have reserved your usual room, Mr Romanelli,' he said, looking as if he wanted to wink at me.

Susie stepped forward and, looking directly at Albert, said, 'And where will my room be?'

Without blinking, he smiled at her and said, 'There is an adjoining room that I'm sure you will find convenient, madame.'

'That's very thoughtful of you, Albert,' she said, 'but I would prefer to have a room on another floor.'

This time Albert was taken by surprise, although he quickly recovered, called for the reservations book and studied the entries for a few moments before saying, 'I see we have a room available overlooking the park, on the floor below Mr Romanelli's room.' He clicked his fingers and handed the two keys to a bellboy who was hovering nearby.

'Room 574 for madame, and the Napoléon suite for monsieur.'

The bellboy held the lift open for us, and once we were inside he pressed buttons 5 and 6. When the doors opened on the fifth floor, Susie said with a smile, 'Shall we meet in the foyer just before eight?'

I nodded, as my mother had never told me what to do in these circumstances.

Once I'd unpacked, I took a shower and slumped onto the redundant double bed. I flicked on the television and settled for a black-and-white French movie. I became so engrossed in the plot that I still wasn't dressed at ten to eight, when I was about to discover who had drowned the woman in the bath.

I cursed, quickly threw on some clothes, not even checking my appearance in the mirror, and rushed out of the door still wondering who the murderer could possibly be. I jumped into the lift and cursed again when the doors opened at the ground floor, because there was Susie standing in the foyer waiting for me.

I had to admit that in that long black dress, with an elegant slit down the side which allowed you a glimpse of thigh with every step she took, I was almost willing to forgive her.

In the taxi on the way to the restaurant she was at pains to tell me how pleasant her room was and how attentive the staff had been.

Over dinner – I must confess the meal was

sensational – she chatted about her work in New York, and mused over whether she would ever return to London. I tried to sound interested.

After I had settled the bill, she took my arm and suggested that as it was such a pleasant evening and she had eaten far too much, perhaps we should walk back to the hotel. She squeezed my hand, and I began to wonder if perhaps . . .

She didn't let go of my hand all the way back to the hotel. When we entered the lobby, the bell-boy ran over to the lift and held the doors open for us.

'Which floor, please?' he asked.

'Fifth,' said Susie firmly.

'Sixth,' I said reluctantly.

Susie turned and kissed me on the cheek just as the doors slid open. 'It's been a memorable day,' she said, and slipped away.

For me too, I wanted to say, but remained silent. Back in my room I lay awake, trying to fathom it out. I realised I must be a pawn in a far bigger game; but would it be a bishop or a knight that finally removed me from the board?

I don't recall how long it was before I fell asleep, but when I woke at a few minutes before six, I jumped out of bed and was pleased to see that *Le*

Figaro had already been pushed under the door. I devoured it from the first page to the last, learning all about the latest French scandals – none of them sexual, I might add – and then cast it aside to take a shower.

I strolled downstairs around eight to find Susie seated in the corner of the breakfast room, sipping an orange juice. She was dressed to kill, and although I obviously wasn't the chosen victim, I was even more determined than before to find out who was.

I slipped into the seat opposite her, and as neither of us spoke, the other guests must have assumed we had been married for years.

'I hope you slept well,' I offered finally.

'Yes, thank you, Tony,' she replied. 'And you?' she asked innocently.

I could think of a hundred responses I would have liked to make, but I knew that if I did, I would then never find out the truth.

'What time would you like to visit the exhibition?' I asked.

'Ten o'clock,' she said firmly, and then added, 'If that suits you.'

'Suits me fine,' I replied, glancing at my watch. 'I'll book a taxi for around 9.30.'

'I'll meet you in the foyer,' she said, making us sound more like a married couple by the minute.

After breakfast, I returned to my room, began to pack and phoned down to Albert to say I didn't think we'd be staying another night.

'I am sorry to hear that, monsieur,' he replied. 'I can only hope that it wasn't . . .'

'No, Albert, it was no fault of yours, that I can assure you. If ever I discover who is to blame, I'll let you know. By the way, I'll need a taxi around 9.30, to take us to the Musée d'Orsay.'

'Of course, Tony.'

I will not bore you with the mundane conversation that took place in the taxi between the hotel and the museum, because it would take a writer of far greater abilities than I possess to hold your attention. However, it would be less than gracious of me not to admit that the Picasso drawings were well worth the trip. And I should add that Susie's running commentary caused a small crowd to hang around in our wake.

'The pencil,' she said, 'is the cruellest of the artist's tools, because it leaves nothing to chance.' She stopped in front of the drawing Picasso had made of his father sitting in a chair. I was spellbound, and unable to move on for some time.

'What is so remarkable about this picture,' said Susie, 'is that Picasso drew it at the age of sixteen; so it was already clear that he would be bored by conventional subjects long before he'd left art school. When his father first saw it – and he was an artist himself – he . . .' Susie failed to finish the sentence. Instead, she suddenly grabbed my hand and, looking into my eyes, said, 'It's such fun being with you, Tony.' She leaned forward as if she were going to kiss me.

I was about to say, 'What the hell are you up to?' when I saw him out of the corner of my eye.

'Check,' I said.

'What do you mean, "Check"?' she asked.

'The knight has advanced across the board – or, to be more accurate, the Channel – and I have a feeling he's about to be brought into play.'

'What are you talking about, Tony?'

'I think you know very well what I'm talking about,' I replied.

'What a coincidence,' a voice said from behind her.

Susie swung round and put on a convincing display of surprise when she saw Richard standing there.

'What a coincidence,' I repeated.

'Isn't it a wonderful exhibition?' said Susie, ignoring my sarcasm.

'It certainly is,' said Rachel, who had obviously not been informed that she, like me, was only a pawn in this particular game, and was about to be taken by the queen.

'Well, now that we've all met up again, why don't we have lunch?' suggested Richard.

'I'm afraid we've already made other plans,' said Susie, taking my hand.

'Oh, nothing that can't be rearranged, my darling,' I said, hoping to be allowed to remain on the board for a little longer.

'But we'll never be able to find a table in a half-decent restaurant at such short notice,' Susie insisted.

'That shouldn't prove a problem,' I assured her with a smile. 'I know a little bistro where we will be welcome.'

Susie scowled as I moved out of check, and refused to talk to me as we all left the museum and walked along the left bank of the Seine together. I began chatting to Rachel. After all, I thought, we pawns must stick together.

Jacques threw his arms up in Gallic despair when he saw me standing in the doorway.

'How many, Monsieur Tony?' he asked, a sigh of resignation in his voice.

'Four,' I told him with a smile.

It turned out to be the only meal that weekend that I actually enjoyed. I spent most of the time talking to Rachel, a nice enough girl, but frankly not in Susie's league. She had no idea what was happening on the other side of the board, where the black queen was about to remove her white knight. It was a pleasure to watch the lady in full flow.

While Rachel was chatting away to me, I made every effort to listen in on the conversation that was taking place on the other side of the table, but I was only able to catch the occasional snippet.

'When are you expecting to be back in New York . . .'

'Yes, I planned this trip to Paris weeks ago . . .'

'Oh, you'll be in Geneva on your own . . .'

'Yes, I did enjoy the Keswicks' party . . .'

'I met Tony in Paris. Yes, just another coincidence, I hardly know him . . .'

True enough, I thought. In fact, I enjoyed her performance so much that I didn't even resent ending up with the bill.

After we had said our goodbyes, Susie and I

strolled back along the Seine together, but not hand in hand. I waited until I was certain Richard and Rachel were well out of sight before I stopped and confronted her. To do her justice, she looked suitably guilty as she waited to be chastised.

'I asked you yesterday, also after lunch, "If you could do anything in the world right now, what would it be?" What would your reply be this time?'

Susie looked unsure of herself for the first time that weekend.

'Be assured,' I added as I looked into those blue eyes, 'nothing you can say will surprise or offend me.'

'I would like to return to the hotel, pack my bags and leave for the airport.'

'So be it,' I said, and stepped into the road to hail a taxi.

Susie didn't speak on the journey back to the hotel, and as soon as we arrived, she disappeared upstairs while I settled the bill and asked if my bags, already packed, could be brought down.

Even then, I have to admit that when she stepped out of the lift and smiled at me, I almost wished my name was Richard.

To Susie's surprise, I accompanied her to Charles de Gaulle, explaining that I would be returning to London on the first available flight. We said goodbye below the departure board with a hug – a sort of 'Perhaps we'll meet again, but then perhaps we won't' hug.

I waved goodbye and began walking away, but couldn't resist turning to see which airline counter Susie was heading for.

She joined the queue for the Swissair check-in desk. I smiled, and headed for the British Airways counter.

Six years have passed since that weekend in Paris, and I didn't come across Susie once during that time, although her name did occasionally pop up in dinner-party conversations.

I discovered that she had become the editor of *Art Nouveau*, and had married an Englishman called Ian, who was in sports promotion. On the rebound, someone said, after an affair with an American banker.

Two years later I heard that she'd given birth to a son, followed by a daughter, but no one seemed to know their names. And finally, about a year ago, I read of her divorce in one of the gossip columns.

And then, without warning, Susie suddenly rang and suggested we might meet for a drink. When she chose the venue, I knew that she hadn't lost her nerve. I heard myself saying yes, and wondered if I'd recognise her.

As I watched her walking up the steps of the Tate, I realised that the only thing I had forgotten was just how beautiful she was. If anything, she was even more captivating than before.

We had been in the gallery for only a few minutes before I was reminded what a pleasure it was to listen to her talk about her chosen subject. I had never really come to terms with Damien Hirst, having only recently accepted that Warhol and Lichtenstein were more than just draughts-men, but I certainly left the exhibition with a new respect for his work.

I suppose I shouldn't have been surprised that Susie had booked a table for lunch in the Tate restaurant, or that she never once referred to our weekend in Paris until, over coffee, she asked, 'If you could do anything in the world right now, what would it be?'

'Spend the weekend in Paris with you,' I said, laughing.

'Then let's do it,' she said. 'There's a Hockney exhibition at the Pompidou Centre that has had glowing reviews, and I know a comfortable but unpretentious little hotel that I haven't visited in years, not to mention a restaurant that prides itself on not being in any of the tourist guides.'

I have always considered it ignoble for any man to discuss a lady as if she were simply a conquest or a trophy, but I must confess that, as I watched Susie disappear through the departure gate to catch her flight back to New York on the following Monday morning, it had been well worth the years of waiting.

She has never contacted me since.

Something for Nothing

Jake began to dial the number slowly, as he had done almost every evening at six o'clock since the day his father had passed away. For the next fifteen minutes he settled back to listen to what his mother had been up to that day.

She led such a sober, orderly life that she rarely had anything of interest to tell him. Least of all on a Saturday. She had coffee every morning with her oldest friend, Molly Schultz, and on some days that would last until lunchtime. On Mondays, Wednesdays and Fridays she played bridge with the Zaccharis who lived across the street. On Tuesdays and Thursdays she visited her sister Nancy, which at least gave her something to grumble about when he rang on those evenings.

On Saturdays, she rested from her rigorous week. Her only strenuous activity being to purchase the bulky Sunday edition of the *Times* just after lunch – a strange New York tradition, which at least gave her the chance to inform her son which stories he should check up on the following day.

For Jake, every evening the conversation would consist of a few appropriate questions, depending on the day. Monday, Wednesday, Friday: How did the bridge go? How much did you win/lose? Tuesday, Thursday: How is Aunt Nancy? Really? That bad? Saturday: Anything interesting in the *Times* that I should look out for tomorrow?

Observant readers will be aware that there are seven days in any given week, and will want to know what Jake's mother did on a Sunday. On Sunday, she always joined his family for lunch, so there was no need for him to call her that evening.

Jake dialled the last digit of his mother's number and waited for her to pick up the phone. He had already prepared himself to be told what he should look out for in tomorrow's *New York Times*. It usually took two or three rings before she answered the phone, the amount of time required for her to walk from her chair by the window to the phone on the other side of the room. When the phone rang four, five, six, seven times, Jake began to wonder if she might be out. But that wasn't possible. She was never out after six o'clock, winter or summer. She kept to a routine that was so regular it would have brought a smile to the lips of a Marine drill sergeant.

Finally, he heard a click. He was just about to say, 'Hi, Mom, it's Jake,' when he heard a voice that was certainly not his mother's, and was already in mid-conversation. Thinking he had a crossed line, he was about to put the phone down when the voice said, 'There'll be $100,000 in it for you. All you have to do is turn up and collect it. It's in an envelope for you at Billy's.'

'So where's Billy's?' asked a new voice.

'On the corner of Oak Street and Randall. They'll be expecting you around seven.'

Jake tried not to breathe in or out as he wrote down 'Oak and Randall' on the pad by the phone.

'How will they know the envelope is for me?' asked the second voice.

'You just ask for a copy of the *New York Times* and hand over a $100 bill. He'll give you a quarter change, as if you'd handed him a dollar. That way, if there's anyone else in the shop, they won't be suspicious. Don't open the envelope until you're in a safe place – there are a lot of people in New York who'd like to get their hands on $100,000. And whatever you do, don't ever contact me again.

If you do, it won't be a pay-off you'll get next time.'

The line went dead.

Jake hung up, having completely forgotten that he was meant to be ringing his mother.

He sat down and considered what to do next – if anything. His wife Ellen had taken the kids to a movie, as she did most Saturday evenings, and they weren't expected back until around nine. His dinner was in the microwave, with a note to tell him how many minutes it would take to cook. He always added one minute.

Jake found himself flicking through the telephone directory. He turned over the pages until he reached B: Bi . . . , Bil . . . , Billy's. And there it was, at 1127 Oak Street. He closed the directory and walked through to his den, where he searched the bookshelf behind his desk for a street atlas of New York. He found it wedged in between *The Memoirs of Elisabeth Schwarzkopf* and *How to Lose Twenty Pounds When You're Over Forty*.

He turned to the index in the back and quickly found the entry for Oak Street. He checked the grid reference and placed his finger on the correct square. He calculated that, were he to go, it would take him about half an hour to get over to the West Side. He checked his watch. It was 6.14.

What was he thinking of? He had no intention of going anywhere. To start with, he didn't have $100.

Jake took out his wallet from the inside pocket of his jacket, and counted slowly: $37. He walked through to the kitchen to check Ellen's petty-cash box. It was locked, and he couldn't remember where she hid the key. He took a screwdriver from the drawer beside the stove and forced the box open: another $22. He paced around the kitchen, trying to think. Next he went to the bedroom and checked the pockets of all his jackets and trousers. Another $1.75 in loose change. He left the bedroom and moved on to his daughter's room. Hesther's Snoopy moneybox was on her dressing table. He picked it up and walked over to the bed. He turned the box upside down and shook all the coins out onto the quilt: another $6.75.

He sat on the end of the bed, desperately trying to concentrate, then recalled the $50 bill he always kept folded in his driving licence for emergencies. He added up all his gatherings: they came to $117.50.

Jake checked his watch. It was 6.23. He would just go and have a look. No more, he told himself.

He took his old overcoat from the hall cupboard

and slipped out of the apartment, checking as he left that all three locks on the front door were securely bolted. He pressed the elevator button, but there was no sound. Out of order again, Jake thought, and began to jog down the stairs. Across the street was a bar he often dropped into when Ellen took the children to the movies.

The barman smiled as he walked in. 'The usual, Jake?' he asked, somewhat surprised to see him wearing a heavy overcoat when he only had to cross the road from his apartment.

'No thanks,' said Jake, trying to sound casual. 'I just wondered if you had a $100 bill.'

'Not sure if I do,' the barman replied. He rummaged around in a stack of notes, then turned to Jake and said, 'You're in luck. Just the one.'

Jake handed over the fifty, a twenty, two tens and ten ones, and received a $100 bill in exchange. Folding the note carefully in four, he slipped it into his wallet, which he returned to the inside pocket of his jacket. He then left the bar and walked out onto the street.

He ambled slowly west for two blocks until he came to a bus stop. Perhaps he would be too late, and the problem would take care of itself, he thought. A bus drew into the kerb. Jake climbed the steps, paid his fare and took a seat near the back, still uncertain what he planned to do once he reached the West Side.

He was so deep in thought that he missed his stop and had to walk almost half a mile back to Oak Street. He checked the numbers. It would be another three or four blocks before Oak Street crossed with Randall.

As he got nearer, he found his pace slowing with every step. But suddenly, there it was on the next corner, halfway up a lamppost: a white-and-green sign that read 'Randall Street'.

He quickly checked all four corners of the street, then looked at his watch again. It was 6.49.

As he stared across from the opposite side of the street, one or two people went in and out of Billy's. The light started flashing 'Walk', and he found himself being carried across with the other pedestrians.

He checked his watch yet again: 6.51. He paused at the doorway of Billy's. Behind the counter was a man stacking some newspapers. He wore a black T-shirt and jeans, and must have been around forty, a shade under six foot, with shoulders that could only have been built by spending several hours a week in the gym.

A customer brushed past Jake and asked for a packet of Marlboros. While the man behind the counter was handing him his change, Jake stepped inside and pretended to take an interest in the magazine rack.

As the customer turned to leave, Jake slipped his hand into the inside pocket of his jacket, took out his wallet and touched the edge of the $100 bill. Once the Marlboro man had left the shop, Jake put his wallet back into his pocket, leaving the bill in the palm of his hand.

The man behind the counter stood waiting impassively as Jake slowly unfolded the bill.

'The *Times*,' Jake heard himself saying, as he placed the $100 bill on the counter.

The man in the black T-shirt glanced at the money and checked his watch. He seemed to hesitate for a moment before reaching under the counter. Jake tensed at the movement, until he saw a long, thick, white envelope emerge. The man proceeded to slip it into the heavy folds of the newspaper's business section, then handed the paper over to Jake, his face remaining impassive. He took the $100 bill, rang up seventy-five cents on the cash register, and gave Jake a quarter change. Jake turned and walked quickly out of the shop, nearly knocking over a small man who looked as nervous as Jake felt.

Jake began to run down Oak Street, frequently glancing over his shoulder to see if anyone was following him. Checking again, he spotted a Yellow Cab heading towards him, and quickly hailed it.

'The East Side,' he said, jumping in.

As the driver eased back into the traffic, Jake slid the envelope out from the bulky newspaper and transferred it to an inside pocket. He could hear his heart thumping. For the next fifteen minutes he spent most of the time looking anxiously out of the cab's rear window.

When he spotted a subway entrance coming up on the right, he told the driver to pull into the kerb. He handed over $10 and, not waiting for his change, jumped out of the taxi and dashed down the subway steps, emerging a few moments later on the other side of the road. He then hailed another taxi going in the opposite direction. This time he gave the driver his home address. He congratulated himself on his little subterfuge, which he'd seen carried out by Gene Hackman in the Movie of the Week.

Nervously, Jake touched his inside pocket to be sure the envelope was still in place. Confident that no one was following him, he no longer bothered to look out of the cab's rear window. He was tempted to check inside the envelope, but there would be time enough for that once he was back in the safety of his apartment. He checked his watch: 7.21. Ellen and the children wouldn't be home for at least another half-hour.

'You can drop me about fifty yards on the left,' Jake told the driver, happy to be back on familiar territory. He cast one final glance through the back window as the taxi drew into the kerb outside his block. There was no other traffic close by. He paid the driver with the dimes and quarters he had shaken out of his daughter's Snoopy moneybox, then jumped out and walked as casually as he could into the building.

Once he was inside, he rushed across the hall and thumped the elevator button with the palm of his hand. It still wasn't working. He cursed, and started to run up the seven flights of stairs to his apartment, going slower and slower with each floor, until he finally came to a halt. Breathless, he unbolted the three locks, almost fell inside, and slammed the door quickly behind him. He rested against the wall while he got his breath back.

He was pulling the envelope out of his inside

pocket when the phone rang. His first thought was that they had traced him somehow and wanted their money back. He stared at the phone for a moment, then nervously picked up the receiver.

'Hello, Jake, is that you?'

Then he remembered. 'Yes, Mom.'

'You didn't call at six,' she said.

'I'm sorry, Mom. I did, but . . .' He decided against telling her why he didn't try a second time.

'I've been calling you for the past hour. Have you been out or something?'

'Only to the bar across the road. I sometimes go there for a drink when Ellen takes the kids to the movies.'

He placed the envelope next to the phone, desperate to be rid of her, but aware that he would have to go through the usual Saturday routine.

'Anything interesting in the *Times*, Mom?' he heard himself saying, rather too quickly.

'Not much,' she replied. 'Hillary looks certain to win the Democratic nomination for Senate, but I'm still going to vote for Giuliani.'

'Always have done, always will,' said Jake, mouthing his mother's oft-repeated comment on the Mayor. He picked up the envelope and squeezed it, to see what $100,000 felt like.

'Anything else, Mom?' he said, trying to move her on.

'There's a piece in the style section about widows at seventy rediscovering their sex drive. As soon as their husbands are safely in their graves it seems they're popping HRT and getting back into the old routine. One of them's quoted as saying, "I'm not so much trying to make up for lost time, as to catch up with him."'

As he listened, Jake began to ease open a corner of the envelope.

'I'd try it myself,' his mother was saying, 'but I can't afford the facelift that seems to be an essential part of the deal.'

'Mom, I think I can hear Ellen and the kids at the door, so I'd better say goodbye. Look forward to seeing you at lunch tomorrow.'

'But I haven't told you about a fascinating piece in the business section.'

'I'm still listening,' said Jake distractedly, slowly beginning to ease the envelope open.

'It's a story about a new scam that's being carried out in Manhattan. I don't know what they'll think of next.'

The envelope was half-open.

'It seems that a gang has found a way of tapping

into your phone while you're dialling another number . . .'

Another inch and Jake would be able to tip the contents of the envelope out onto the table.

'So when you dial, you think you've got a crossed line.'

Jake took his finger out of the envelope and began to listen more carefully.

'Then they set you up by making you believe you're overhearing a real conversation.'

Sweat began to appear on Jake's forehead, as he stared down at the almost-opened envelope.

'They make you think that if you travel to the other side of the city and hand over a $100 bill, you'll get an envelope containing $100,000 in exchange for it.'

Jake felt sick as he thought of how readily he had parted with his $100, and how easily he had fallen for it.

'They're using tobacconists and newsagents to carry out the scam,' continued his mother.

'So what's in the envelope?'

'Now that's where they're really clever,' said his mother. 'They put in a small booklet that gives advice on how you can make $100,000. And it's not even illegal, because the price on the cover is $100. You've got to hand it to them.'

I already have, Mom, Jake wanted to say, but he just slammed the phone down and stared at the envelope.

The front doorbell began to ring. Ellen and the kids must be back from the movie, and she'd probably forgotten her key again.

The bell rang a second time.

'OK, I'm coming, I'm coming!' shouted Jake. He seized the envelope, determined not to leave any trace of its embarrassing existence. As the bell rang a third time he ran into the kitchen, opened the incinerator and threw the envelope down the chute.

The bell continued to ring. This time the caller must have left a finger on the button.

Jake ran to the door. He pulled it open to find three massive men standing in the hallway. The one wearing a black T-shirt leapt in and put a knife to his throat, while the other two each grabbed an arm. The door slammed shut behind them.

'Where is it?' T-shirt shouted, holding the knife against Jake's throat.

'Where's what?' gasped Jake. 'I don't know what you're talking about.'

'Don't play games with us,' shouted the second man. 'We want our $100,000 back.'

'But there was no money in the envelope, only a book. I threw it down the incinerator chute. Listen, you can hear it for yourself.'

The man in the black T-shirt cocked his head, while the other two fell silent. There was a crunching sound coming from the kitchen.

'OK, then you'll have to go the same way,' said the man holding the knife. He nodded, and his two accomplices picked up Jake like a sack of potatoes and carried him through to the kitchen.

Just as Jake's head was about to disappear down the incinerator chute, the phone and the front doorbell began ringing at the same time . . .

Other Blighters' Efforts

It all began innocently enough, when Henry Pascoe, the First Secretary at the British High Commission on Aranga, took a call from Bill Paterson, the manager of Barclays Bank. It was late on a Friday afternoon, and Henry rather hoped that Bill was calling to suggest a round of golf on Saturday morning, or perhaps with an invitation to join him and his wife Sue for lunch on Sunday. But the moment he heard the voice on the other end of the line, he knew the call was of an official nature.

'When you come to check the High Commission's account on Monday, you'll find you've been credited with a larger sum than usual.'

'Any particular reason?' responded Henry, in his most formal tone.

'Quite simple really, old chap,' replied the bank manager. 'The exchange rate moved in your favour overnight. Always does when there's a rumour of a coup,' he added matter-of-factly. 'Feel free to call me on Monday if you have any queries.'

Henry wondered about asking Bill if he felt like a round of golf tomorrow, but thought better of it.

It was Henry's first experience of a rumoured coup, and the exchange rate wasn't the only thing to have a bad weekend. On Friday night the head of state, General Olangi, appeared on television in full-dress uniform to warn the good citizens of Aranga that, due to some unrest among a small group of dissidents in the army, it had proved necessary to impose a curfew on the island which he hoped would not last for more than a few days.

On Saturday morning Henry tuned in to the BBC World Service to find out what was really going on on Aranga. The BBC's correspondent, Roger Parnell, was always better informed than the local television and radio stations, which were simply bleating out a warning to the island's citizens every few minutes that they should not stray onto the streets during the day, because if they did, they would be arrested. And if they were foolish enough to do so at night, they would be shot.

That put a stop to any golf on Saturday, or lunch with Bill and Sue on Sunday. Henry spent a quiet weekend reading, bringing himself up to date with unanswered letters from England, clearing the fridge of any surplus food, and finally cleaning those parts of his bachelor apartment that his daily always seemed to miss.

On Monday morning, the head of state still appeared to be safely in his palace. The BBC reported that several young officers had been arrested, and that one or two of them were rumoured to have been executed. General Olangi reappeared on television to announce that the curfew had been lifted.

When Henry arrived at his office later that day, he found that Shirley, his secretary – who had experienced several coups – had already opened his mail and left it on his desk for him to consider. There was one pile marked 'Urgent, Action Required', a second, larger pile marked 'For Your Consideration', and a third, by far the largest, marked 'See and Bin'.

The itinerary for the imminent visit of the Under-Secretary of State for Foreign Affairs from the UK had been placed on top of the 'Urgent, Action Required' pile, although the Minister was only dropping in on St George's, the capital of Aranga, because it was a convenient refuelling stop on his way back to London following a trip to Jakarta. Few people bothered to visit the tiny protectorate of Aranga unless they were on their way to or from somewhere else.

This particular Minister, Mr Will Whiting, known at the Foreign Office as 'Witless Will', was, *The Times* assured its readers, to be replaced in the next reshuffle by someone who could do joined-up writing. However, thought Henry, as Whiting was staying at the High Commissioner's residence overnight, this would be his one opportunity to get a decision out of the Minister on the swimming pool project. Henry was keen to start work on the new pool that was so badly needed by the local children. He had pointed out in a lengthy memo to the Foreign Office that they had been promised the go-ahead when Princess Margaret had visited the island four years earlier and laid the foundation stone, but feared that the project would remain in the Foreign Office's 'pending' file unless he kept continually badgering them about it.

In the second pile of letters was the promised bank statement from Bill Paterson, which confirmed that the High Commission's external account was 1,123 kora better off than expected because of the coup that had never taken place that weekend. Henry took little interest in the financial affairs of the protectorate, but as First Secretary it was his duty to countersign every cheque on behalf of Her Majesty's Government.

There was only one other letter of any significance in the 'For Your Consideration' pile: an invitation to give a speech replying on behalf of the guests at the annual Rotary Club dinner in November. Every year a senior member of the High Commission staff was expected to carry out this task. It seemed that it was Henry's turn. He groaned, but placed a tick on the top right corner of the letter.

There were the usual letters in the 'See and Bin' pile – people sending out unnecessary free offers, circulars and invitations to functions no one ever attended. He didn't even bother to flick through them, but turned his attention back to the 'Urgent' pile, and began to check the Minister's programme.

August 27th

3.30 p.m.: Mr Will Whiting, Under-Secretary of State at the Foreign Office, to be met at the airport by the High Commissioner, Sir David Fleming, and the First Secretary, Mr Henry Pascoe.

4.30 p.m.: Tea at the High Commission with the High Commissioner and Lady Fleming.

6.00 p.m.: Visit to the Queen Elizabeth College, where the Minister will present the prizes to leaving sixth-formers (speech enclosed).

7.00 p.m.: Cocktail party at the High Commission. Around one hundred guests expected (names attached).

8.00 p.m.: Dinner with General Olangi at the Victoria Barracks (speech enclosed).

Henry looked up as his secretary entered the room.

'Shirley, when am I going to be able to show the Minister the site for the new swimming pool?' he asked. 'There's no sign of it on his itinerary.'

'I've managed to fit in a fifteen-minute visit tomorrow morning, when the Minister will be on his way back to the airport.'

'Fifteen minutes to discuss something which will affect the lives of ten thousand children,' said Henry, looking back down at the Minister's schedule. He turned the page.

August 28th
8.00 a.m.: Breakfast at the Residence with the

High Commissioner and leading local business rep-
resentatives (speech enclosed).

9.00 a.m.: Depart for airport.

10.30 a.m.: British Airways Flight 0177 to
London Heathrow.

'It's not even on his official schedule,' grumbled
Henry, looking back up at his secretary.

'I know,' said Shirley, 'but the High Commissioner felt that as the Minister had such a short
stopover, he should concentrate on the most
important priorities.'

'Like tea with the High Commissioner's wife,'
snorted Henry. 'Just be sure that he sits down to
breakfast on time, and that the paragraph I dic-
tated to you on Friday about the future of the
swimming pool is included in his speech.' Henry
rose from his desk. 'I've been through the letters
and marked them up. I'm just going to pop into
town and see what state the swimming pool project
is in.'

'By the way,' said Shirley, 'Roger Parnell, the
BBC's correspondent, has just called wanting to
know if the Minister will be making any official
statement while he's visiting Aranga.'

'Phone back and tell him yes, then fax him the

Minister's breakfast speech, highlighting the paragraph on the swimming pool.'

Henry left the office and jumped into his little Austin Mini. The sun was beating down on its roof. Even with both windows open, he was covered in sweat after driving only a few hundred yards from his office. Some of the locals waved at him when they recognised the Mini and the diplomat from England who seemed genuinely to care about their well-being.

He parked the car on the far side of the cathedral, which would have been described as a parish church in England, and walked the three hundred yards to the site designated for the swimming pool. He cursed, as he always did whenever he saw the patch of barren wasteland. The children of Aranga had so few sporting facilities: a brick-hard football pitch, which was transformed into a cricket square on May 1st every year; a town hall which doubled as a basketball court when the local council wasn't in session; and a tennis court and golf course at the Britannia Club, which the locals were not invited to join, and where the children were never allowed past the front gate – unless it was to sweep the drive. In the Victoria Barracks, less than half a mile away, the army had a gymnasium and half a dozen squash courts, but only officers and their guests were allowed to use them.

Henry decided there and then to make it his mission to see that the swimming pool was completed before the Foreign Office posted him to another country. He would use his speech to the Rotary Club to galvanise the members into action. He must convince them to select the swimming pool project as their Charity of the Year, and would press Bill Paterson into becoming Chairman of the Appeal. After all, as manager of the bank and secretary of the Rotary Club, he was the obvious candidate.

But first there was the Minister's visit. Henry began to consider the points he would raise with him, remembering that he had only fifteen minutes in which to convince the damn man to press the Foreign Office for more funding.

He turned to leave, and spotted a small boy standing on the edge of the site, trying to read the words chiselled on the foundation stone: '*St George's Swimming Pool. This foundation stone was laid by HRH Princess Margaret, September 12th, 1987.*'

'Is this a swimming pool?' the little boy asked innocently.

Henry repeated those words to himself as he walked back to his car, and made up his mind to include them in his speech to the Rotary Club. He checked his watch, and decided he still had time to drop into the Britannia Club, in the hope that Bill Paterson might be having lunch there. When he walked into the clubhouse, he spotted Bill, seated on his usual stool at the bar, reading an out-of-date copy of the *Financial Times*.

Bill looked up as Henry approached the bar. 'I thought you had a visiting Minister to take care of today?'

'His plane doesn't land until 3.30,' Henry said. 'I dropped by because I wanted to have a word with you.'

'Need some advice on how you should spend the surplus you made on the exchange rate last Friday?'

'No. I'll have to have a little more than that if I'm ever going to get this swimming pool project off the ground – or rather, into it.'

Henry left the club twenty minutes later, having extracted a promise from Bill that he would chair the Appeal Committee, open an account at the bank and ask head office in London if they would make the first donation.

On his way to the airport in the High Commissioner's Rolls-Royce, Henry told Sir David the
latest news about the swimming pool project. The
High Commissioner smiled and said, 'Well done,
Henry. Now we must hope that you're as successful
with the Minister as you obviously have been with
Bill Paterson.'

The two men were standing on the runway of
St George's airport, six feet of red carpet in place,
when the Boeing 727 touched down. As it was
rare for more than one plane a day to land at
St George's, and there was only one runway, 'International Airport' was, in Henry's opinion, a little
bit of a misnomer.

The Minister turned out to be a rather jolly fellow, insisting that everyone should call him Will.
He assured Sir David that he had been looking
forward with keen anticipation to his visit to
St Edward's.

'St George's, Minister,' the High Commissioner
whispered in his ear.

'Yes, of course, St George's,' replied Will, without even blushing.

Once they had arrived at the High Commission,
Henry left the Minister to have tea with Sir David
and his wife, and returned to his office. After even

such a short journey, he was convinced that Witless Will was unlikely to carry much clout back in Whitehall; but that wouldn't stop him pressing ahead with his case. At least the Minister had read the briefing notes, because he told them how much he was looking forward to seeing the new swimming pool.

'Not yet started,' Henry had reminded him.

'Funny,' said the Minister. 'I thought I read somewhere that Princess Margaret had already opened it.'

'No, she only laid the foundation stone, Minister. But perhaps all that will change once the project receives your blessing.'

'I'll do what I can,' promised Will. 'But you know we've been told to make even more cutbacks in overseas funding.' A sure sign that an election was approaching, thought Henry.

At the cocktail party that evening, Henry was able to say no more than 'Good evening, Minister,' as the High Commissioner was determined that Will would be introduced to every one of the assembled guests in under sixty minutes. When the two of them departed to have dinner with General Olangi, Henry went back to his office to check over the speech the Minister would be delivering at breakfast the following morning. He was pleased to see that the paragraph he had written on the swimming pool project remained in the final draft, so at least it would be on the record. He checked the seating plan, making sure that he had been placed next to the editor of the *St George's Echo*. That way he could be certain that the paper's next edition would lead on the British government's support for the swimming pool appeal.

Henry rose early the following morning, and was among the first to arrive at the High Commissioner's Residence. He took the opportunity to brief as many of the assembled local businessmen as possible on the importance of the swimming pool project in the eyes of the British government, pointing out that Barclays Bank had agreed to open the fund with a substantial donation.

The Minister arrived for breakfast a few minutes late. 'A call from London,' he explained, so they didn't sit down to eat until 8.15. Henry took his place next to the editor of the local paper and waited impatiently for the Minister to make his speech.

Will rose at 8.47. He spent the first five minutes talking about bananas, and finally went on to say:

'Let me assure you that Her Majesty's Government have not forgotten the swimming pool project that was inaugurated by Princess Margaret, and we hope to be able to make an announcement on its progress in the near future. I was delighted to learn from Sir David,' he looked across at Bill Paterson, who was seated opposite him, 'that the Rotary Club have taken on the project as their Charity of the Year, and several prominent local businessmen have already generously agreed to support the cause.' This was followed by a round of applause, instigated by Henry.

Once the Minister had resumed his seat, Henry handed the editor of the local paper an envelope which contained a thousand-word article, along with several pictures of the site. Henry felt confident that it would form the centre-page spread in next week's *St George's Echo.*

Henry checked his watch as the Minister sat down: 8.56. It was going to be close. When Will disappeared up to his room, Henry began pacing up and down the hallway, checking his watch as each minute passed.

The Minister stepped into the waiting Rolls at 9.24 and, turning to Henry, said, 'I fear I'm going to have to forgo the pleasure of seeing the swimming pool site. However,' he promised, 'I'll be sure to read your report on the plane, and will brief the Foreign Secretary the moment I get back to London.'

As the car sped past a barren plot of land on the way to the airport, Henry pointed out the site to the Minister. Will glanced out of the window and said, 'Admirable, worthwhile, important,' but never once did he commit himself to spending one penny of government money.

'I'll do my damnedest to convince the mandarins at the Treasury,' were his final words as he boarded the plane.

Henry didn't need to be told that Will's 'damnedest' was unlikely to convince even the most junior civil servant at the Treasury.

A week later, Henry received a fax from the Foreign Office giving details of the changes the Prime Minister had made in his latest reshuffle. Will Whiting had been sacked, to be replaced by someone Henry had never heard of.

Henry was going over his speech to the Rotary Club when the phone rang. It was Bill Paterson.

'Henry, there are rumours of another coup brewing, so I was thinking of waiting until Friday before changing the High Commission's pounds into kora.'

'Happy to take your advice, Bill – the money market is beyond me. By the way, I'm looking forward to this evening, when we finally get a chance to launch the Appeal.'

Henry's speech was well received by the Rotarians, but when he discovered the size of the donations some of the members had in mind, he feared it could still be years before the project was completed. He couldn't help remembering that there were only another eighteen months before his next posting was due.

It was in the car on the way home that he recalled Bill's words at the Britannia Club. An idea began to form in his mind.

Henry had never taken the slightest interest in the quarterly payments that the British government made to the tiny island of Aranga. The Foreign Office allocated £5 million a year from its contingency fund, made up of four payments of £1.25 million, which was automatically converted into the local currency of kora at the current exchange rate. Once Henry had been informed of the rate by Bill Paterson, the Chief Administrator at the High Commission dealt with all the

Commission's payments over the next three months. That was about to change.

Henry lay awake that night, all too aware that he lacked the training and expertise to carry out such a daring project, and that he must pick up the knowledge he required without anyone else becoming aware of what he was up to.

By the time he rose the following morning, a plan was beginning to form in his mind. He started by spending the weekend at the local library, studying old copies of the *Financial Times*, noting in particular what caused fluctuating exchange rates and whether they followed any pattern.

Over the next three months, at the golf club, cocktail parties in the Britannia Club, and whenever he was with Bill, he gathered more and more information, until finally he was confident that he was ready to make his first move.

When Bill rang on the Monday morning to say that there would be a small surplus of 22,107 kora on the current account because of the rumours of another coup, Henry gave orders to place the money in the Swimming Pool Account.

'But I usually switch it into the Contingency Fund,' said Bill.

'There's been a new directive from the Foreign

Office – K14792,' said Henry. 'It says that surpluses can now be used on local projects, if they've been approved by the Minister.'

'But that Minister was sacked,' the bank manager reminded the First Secretary.

'That may well be the case, but I've been instructed by my masters that the order still applies.' Directive K14792 did in fact exist, Henry had discovered, although he doubted that when the Foreign Office issued it they had had swimming pools in mind.

'Fine by me,' said Bill. 'Who am I to argue with a Foreign Office directive, especially when all I have to do is move money from one High Commission account to another within the bank?'

The Chief Administrator didn't comment on any missing money during the following week, as he had received the same number of kora he had originally expected. Henry assumed he'd got away with it.

As there wasn't another payment due for three months, Henry had ample time to refine his plan. During the next quarter, a few of the local businessmen came up with their donations, but Henry quickly realised that even with this influx of cash, they could only just about afford to start digging. He would have to deliver something a great deal more substantial if he hoped to end up with more than a hole in the ground.

Then an idea came to him in the middle of the night. But for Henry's personal coup to be effective, he would need to get his timing spot on.

When Roger Parnell, the BBC's correspondent, made his weekly call to enquire if there was anything he should be covering other than the swimming pool appeal, Henry asked if he could have a word with him off the record.

'Of course,' said the correspondent. 'What do you want to discuss?'

'HMG is a little worried that no one has seen General Olangi for several days, and there are rumours that his recent medical check-up has found him to be HIV positive.'

'Good God,' said the BBC man. 'Have you got any proof?'

'Can't say I have,' admitted Henry, 'although I did overhear his personal doctor being a little indiscreet with the High Commissioner. Other than that, nothing.'

'Good God,' the BBC man repeated.

'This is, of course, strictly off the record. If it

were traced back to me, we would never be able to speak again.'

'I never disclose my sources,' the correspondent assured him indignantly.

The report that came out on the World Service that evening was vague, and hedged with 'ifs' and 'buts'. However, the next day, when Henry visited the golf course, the Britannia Club and the bank, he found the word 'AIDS' on everyone's lips. Even the High Commissioner asked him if he had heard the rumour.

'Yes, but I don't believe it,' said Henry, without blushing.

The kora dropped 4 per cent the following day, and General Olangi had to appear on television to assure his people that the rumours were false, and were being spread by his enemies. All his appearance on television did was to inform anyone who hadn't already heard them about the rumours, and as the General seemed to have lost some weight, the kora dropped another 2 per cent.

'You did rather well this month,' Bill told Henry on Monday. 'After that false alarm about Olangi's HIV problem, I was able to switch 118,000 kora into the Swimming Pool Account, which means my committee can go ahead and instruct the architects to draw up some more detailed plans.'

'Well done,' said Henry, passing the praise on to Bill for his personal coup. He put the phone down aware that he couldn't risk repeating the same stunt again.

Despite the architects' plans being drawn up and a model of the pool placed in the High Commissioner's office for all to see, another three months went by with only a trickle of small donations coming in from local businessmen.

Henry wouldn't normally have seen the fax, but he was in the High Commissioner's office, going over a speech Sir David was due to make to the Banana Growers' Annual Convention, when it was placed on the desk by the High Commissioner's secretary.

The High Commissioner frowned and pushed the speech to one side. 'It hasn't been a good year for bananas,' he grunted. The frown remained in place as he read the fax. He passed it across to his First Secretary.

'*To all Embassies and High Commissions: The government will be suspending Britain's membership of the*

Exchange Rate Mechanism. Expect an official announcement later today.'

'If that's the way of things, I can't see the Chancellor lasting the day,' commented Sir David. 'However, the Foreign Secretary will remain in place, so it's not our problem.' He looked up at Henry. 'Still, perhaps it would be wise if we were not to mention the subject for at least a couple of hours.'

Henry nodded his agreement and left the High Commissioner to continue working on his speech.

The moment he had closed the door of the High Commissioner's office, he ran along the corridor for the first time in two years. As soon as he was back at his desk, he dialled a number he didn't need to look up.

'Bill Paterson speaking.'

'Bill, how much have we got in the Contingency Fund?' he asked, trying to sound casual.

'Give me a second and I'll let you know. Would you like me to call you back?'

'No, I'll hold on,' said Henry. He watched the second hand of the clock on his desk sweep nearly a full circle before the bank manager spoke again.

'A little over £1 million,' said Bill. 'Why did you want to know?'

'I've just been instructed by the Foreign Office to switch all available monies into German marks, Swiss francs and American dollars immediately.'

'You'd be charged a hefty fee for that,' said the bank manager, suddenly sounding rather formal. 'And if the exchange rate were to go against you . . .'

'I'm aware of the implications,' said Henry, 'but the telegram from London doesn't leave me with any choice.'

'Fair enough,' said Bill. 'Has this been approved by the High Commissioner?'

'I've just left his office,' said Henry.

'Then I'd better get on with it, hadn't I?'

Henry sat sweating in his air-conditioned office for twenty minutes until Bill called back.

'We've converted the full amount into Swiss francs, German marks and American dollars, as instructed. I'll send you the details in the morning.'

'And no copies, please,' said Henry. 'The High Commissioner isn't keen that this should be seen by any of his staff.'

'I quite understand, old boy,' said Bill.

The Chancellor of the Exchequer announced the suspension of Britain's membership of the

Exchange Rate Mechanism from the steps of the Treasury in Whitehall at 7.30 p.m., by which time all the banks in St George's had closed for the day.

Henry contacted Bill the moment the markets opened the following morning, and instructed him to convert the francs, marks and dollars back into sterling as quickly as possible, and let him know the outcome.

It was to be another twenty minutes of sweating before Bill called back.

'You made a profit of £64,312. If every Embassy around the world has carried out the same exercise, the government will be able to cut taxes long before the next election.'

'Quite right,' said Henry. 'By the way, could you convert the surplus into kora, and place it in the Swimming Pool Account? And Bill, I assured the High Commissioner the matter would never be referred to again.'

'You have my word on it,' replied the bank manager.

Henry informed the editor of the *St George's Echo* that contributions to the swimming pool fund were still pouring in, thanks to the generosity of local businessmen and many private individuals. In truth the outside donations made up only about half of what had been raised to date.

Within a month of Henry's second coup, a contractor had been selected from a shortlist of three, and lorries, bulldozers and diggers rolled onto the site. Henry paid a visit every day so that he could keep an eye on progress. But it wasn't long before Bill was reminding him that unless more funds were forthcoming, they wouldn't be able to consider his plan for a high diving board and changing rooms for up to a hundred children.

The *St George's Echo* continually reminded their readers of the appeal, but after a year, just about everyone who could afford to give anything had already done so. The trickle of donations had dried up almost entirely, and the income raised from bring-and-buy sales, raffles and coffee mornings was becoming negligible.

Henry began to fear that he would be sent to his next posting long before the project was completed, and that once he left the island Bill and his committee would lose interest and the job might never be finished.

Henry and Bill visited the site the following day, and stared down into a fifty-by-twenty-metre hole in the ground, surrounded by heavy equipment that had been idle for days and would soon have to be transferred to another site.

'It will take a miracle to raise enough funds to finish the project, unless the government finally keeps its promise,' the First Secretary remarked.

'And we haven't been helped by the kora remaining so stable for the past six months,' added Bill.

Henry began to despair.

At the morning briefing with the High Commissioner the following Monday, Sir David told Henry that he had some good news.

'Don't tell me. HMG has finally kept its promise, and . . .'

'No, nothing as startling as that,' said Sir David, laughing. 'But you are on the list for promotion next year, and will probably be given a High Commission of your own.' He paused. 'One or two good appointments are coming up, I'm told, so keep your fingers crossed. And by the way, when Carol and I go back to England for our annual leave tomorrow, try to keep Aranga off the front pages – that is, if you want to get Bermuda rather than the Ascension Islands.'

Henry returned to his office and began to go through the morning post with his secretary. In the 'Urgent, Action Required' pile was an invitation to accompany General Olangi back to his place of birth. This was an annual ritual the President carried out to demonstrate to his people that he hadn't forgotten his roots. The High Commissioner would usually have accompanied him, but as he would be back in England at the time, the First Secretary was expected to represent him. Henry wondered if Sir David had organised it that way.

From the 'For Your Consideration' pile, Henry had to decide between accompanying a group of businessmen on a banana fact-finding tour around the island, or addressing St George's Political Society on the future of the euro. He placed a tick on the businessmen's letter and wrote a note suggesting to the Political Society that the Controller was better placed than he to talk about the euro.

He then moved on to the 'See and Bin' pile. A letter from Mrs Davidson, donating twenty-five kora to the swimming pool fund; an invitation to the church bazaar on Friday; and a reminder that it was Bill's fiftieth birthday on Saturday.

'Anything else?' asked Henry.

'Just a note from the High Commissioner's office with a suggestion for your trek up into the hills with the President: take a case of fresh water, some anti-malaria pills and a mobile phone. Otherwise you could become dehydrated, break out in a fever and be out of contact all at the same time.'

Henry laughed. 'Yes, yes and yes,' he said, as the phone on his desk rang.

It was Bill, who warned him that the bank could no longer honour cheques drawn on the Swimming Pool Account, as there hadn't been any substantial deposits for over a month.

'I don't need reminding,' said Henry, staring down at Mrs Davidson's cheque for twenty-five kora.

'I'm afraid the contractors have left the site, as we're unable to cover their next stage payment. What's more, your quarterly payment of £1.25 million won't be yielding any surplus while the President looks so healthy.'

'Happy fiftieth on Saturday, Bill,' said Henry.

'Don't remind me,' the bank manager replied. 'But now you mention it, I hope you'll be able to join Sue and me for a little celebration that evening.'

'I'll be there,' said Henry. 'Nothing will stop me.'

That evening, Henry began taking his malaria tablets each night before going to bed. On Thursday, he picked up a crate of fresh water from the local supermarket. On Friday morning his secretary handed him a mobile phone just before he was due to leave. She even checked that he knew how to operate it.

At nine o'clock, Henry left his office and drove his Mini to the Victoria Barracks, having promised that he'd check in with his secretary the moment they arrived at General Olangi's village. He parked his car in the compound, and was escorted to a waiting Mercedes near the back of the motorcade that was flying the Union Jack. At 9.30, the President emerged from the palace and walked over to the open-topped Rolls-Royce at the front of the motorcade. Henry couldn't help thinking that he had never seen the General looking healthier.

An honour guard sprang to attention and presented arms as the motorcade swept out of the compound. As they drove slowly through St George's, the streets were lined with children waving flags, who had been given the day off school so they could cheer their leader as he set off on the long journey to his birthplace.

Henry settled back for the five-hour drive up into the hills, dozing off from time to time, but was rudely woken whenever they passed through a village, where the ritual cheering children would be paraded to greet their President.

At midday, the motorcade came to a halt in a small village high in the hills where the locals had prepared lunch for their honoured guest. An hour later they moved on. Henry feared that the tribesmen had probably sacrificed the best part of their winter stores to fill the stomachs of the scores of soldiers and officials who were accompanying the President on his pilgrimage.

When the motorcade set off again, Henry fell into a deep sleep and began dreaming about Bermuda, where, he was confident, there would be no need to build a swimming pool.

He woke with a start. He thought he'd heard a shot. Had it taken place in his dream? He looked up to see his driver jumping out of the car and fleeing into the dense jungle. Henry calmly opened the back door, stepped out of the limousine, and, seeing a commotion taking place in front of him, decided to go and investigate. He had walked only a few paces when he came across the massive figure of the President, lying motionless at the side of the road in a pool of blood, surrounded by soldiers. They suddenly turned and, seeing the High Commissioner's representative, raised their rifles.

'Shoulder arms!' said a sharp voice. 'Try to remember that we are not savages.' A smartly dressed army captain stepped forward and saluted. 'I am sorry for any inconvenience you have suffered, First Secretary,' he said, in a clipped Sandhurst voice, 'but be assured that we wish you no harm.'

Henry didn't comment, but continued to stare down at the dead President.

'As you can see, Mr Pascoe, the late President has met with a tragic accident,' continued the captain. 'We will remain with him until he has been buried with full honours in the village where he was born. I'm sure that is what he would have wished.'

Henry looked down at the prostrate body, and doubted it.

'May I suggest, Mr Pascoe, that you return to the capital immediately and inform your masters of what has happened.'

Henry remained silent.

'You may also wish to tell them that the new President is Colonel Narango.'

Henry still didn't voice an opinion. He realised that his first duty was to get a message through to the Foreign Office as quickly as possible. He nodded in the direction of the captain and began walking slowly back to his driverless car.

He slipped in behind the wheel, relieved to see that the keys had been left in the ignition. He switched on the engine, turned the car around and began the long journey back down the winding track to the capital. It would be nightfall before he reached St George's.

After he had covered a couple of miles and was certain that no one was following him, he brought the car to a halt by the side of the road, took out his mobile phone and dialled his office number.

His secretary picked up the phone.

'It's Henry.'

'Oh, I'm so glad you phoned,' Shirley said. 'So much has happened this afternoon. But first, Mrs Davidson has just called to say that it looks as if the church bazaar might raise as much as two hundred kora, and would it be possible for you to drop in on your way back so they can present you with the cheque? And by the way,' Shirley added before Henry could speak, 'we've all heard the news.'

'Yes, that's what I was calling about,' said Henry. 'We must contact the Foreign Office immediately.'

'I already have,' said Shirley.

'What did you tell them?'

'That you were with the President, carrying out official duties, and would be in touch with them just as soon as you returned, High Commissioner.'

'High Commissioner?' said Henry.

'Yes, it's official. I assumed that's what you were calling about. Your new appointment. Congratulations.'

'Thank you,' said Henry casually, not even asking where he'd been appointed to. 'Any other news?'

'No, not much else happening this end. It's a typically quiet Friday afternoon. In fact, I was wondering if I could go home a little early this evening. You see, I promised to drop in and help Sue Paterson prepare for her husband's fiftieth.'

'Yes, why not,' said Henry, trying to remain calm. 'And do let Mrs Davidson know that I'll make every effort to call in at the bazaar. Two hundred kora should make all the difference.'

'By the way,' Shirley asked, 'how's the President getting on?'

'He's just about to take part in an earth-moving ceremony,' said Henry, 'so I'd better leave you.'

Henry touched the red button, then immediately dialled another number.

'Bill Paterson speaking.'

'Bill, it's Henry. Have you exchanged our quarterly cheque yet?'

'Yes, I did it about an hour ago. I got the best rate I could, but I'm afraid the kora always strengthens whenever the President makes his official trip back to his place of birth.'

Henry avoided adding 'And death', simply saying, 'I want the entire amount converted back into sterling.'

'I must advise you against that,' said Bill. 'The kora has strengthened further in the last hour. And in any case, such an action would have to be sanctioned by the High Commissioner.'

'The High Commissioner is in Dorset on his annual leave. In his absence, I am the senior diplomat in charge of the mission.'

'That may well be the case,' said Bill, 'but I would still have to make a full report for the High Commissioner's consideration on his return.'

'I would expect nothing less of you, Bill,' said Henry.

'Are you sure you know what you're doing, Henry?'

'I know exactly what I'm doing,' came back the immediate reply. 'And while you're at it, I also require that the kora we are holding in the Contingency Fund be converted into sterling.'

'I'm not sure . . .' began Bill.

'Mr Paterson, I don't have to remind you that there are several other banks in St George's, who for years have made it clear how much they would like to have the British government's account.'

'I shall carry out your orders to the letter, First Secretary,' replied the bank manager, 'but I wish it to be placed on the record that it is against my better judgement.'

'Be that as it may, I wish this transaction to be carried out before the close of business today,' said Henry. 'Do I make myself clear?'

'You most certainly do,' said Bill.

It took Henry another four hours to reach the capital. As all the streets in St George's were empty, he assumed that the news of the President's death must have been announced, and that a curfew was in force. He was stopped at several checkpoints –

grateful to have the Union Jack flying from his bonnet – and ordered to proceed to his home immediately. Still, it meant he wouldn't have to drop into Mrs Davidson's bazaar and pick up the cheque for two hundred kora.

The moment Henry arrived back home he switched on the television, to see President Narango, in full-dress uniform, addressing his people.

'Be assured, my friends,' he was saying, 'you have nothing to fear. It is my intention to lift the curfew as soon as possible. But until then, please do not stray out onto the streets, as the army has been given orders to shoot on sight.'

Henry opened a tin of baked beans and remained indoors for the entire weekend. He was sorry to miss Bill's fiftieth, but he felt on balance it was probably for the best.

HRH Princess Anne opened St George's new swimming pool on her way back from the Commonwealth Games in Kuala Lumpur. In her speech from the poolside, she said how impressed she was by the high diving board and the modern changing facilities.

She went on to single out the work of the Rotary

Club and to congratulate them on the leadership they had shown throughout the campaign, in particular the chairman, Mr Bill Paterson, who had received an OBE for his services in the Queen's Birthday Honours.

Sadly, Henry Pascoe was not present at the ceremony, as he had recently taken up his post as High Commissioner to the Ascensions – a group of islands which isn't on the way to anywhere.

The Reclining Woman

'You may wonder why this sculpture is numbered "13",' said the curator, a smile of satisfaction appearing on his face. I was standing at the back of the group, and assumed we were about to be given a lecture on artists' proofs.

'Henry Moore,' the curator continued, in a voice that made it clear he believed he was addressing an ignorant bunch of tourists who might muddle up Cubism with sugar lumps, and who obviously had nothing better to do on a bank holiday Monday than visit a National Trust house, 'would normally produce his works in editions of twelve. To be fair to the great man, he died before approval was given for the only casting of a thirteenth example of one of his masterpieces.'

I stared across at the vast bronze of a nude woman that dominated the entrance of Huxley Hall. The magnificent, curvaceous figure, with the trademark hole in the middle of her stomach, head resting in a cupped hand, stared out imperiously at a million visitors a year. She was, to quote the handbook, classic Henry Moore, 1952.

I continued to admire the inscrutable lady, wanting to lean across and touch her – always a sign that the artist has achieved what he set out to do.

'Huxley Hall,' the curator droned on, 'has been administered by the National Trust for the past twenty years. This sculpture, *The Reclining Woman*, is considered by scholars to be among the finest examples of Moore's work, executed when he was at the height of his powers. The sixth edition of the sculpture was purchased by the fifth Duke – a Yorkshireman, like Moore – for the princely sum of £1,000. When the Hall was passed on to the sixth Duke, he discovered that he was unable to insure the masterpiece, because he simply couldn't afford the premium.

'The seventh Duke went one better – he couldn't even afford the upkeep of the Hall, or the land that surrounded it. Shortly before his demise, he avoided leaving the eighth Duke with the burden of death duties by handing over the Hall, its contents and its thousand-acre grounds to the National Trust. The French have never understood that if you wish to kill off the aristocracy, death duties are far more effective than revolutions.' The curator laughed at his little *bon mot*, and one or two at the front of the crowd politely joined in.

'Now, to return to the mystery of the edition of thirteen,' continued the curator, resting a hand on *The Reclining Woman*'s ample bottom. 'To do this, I must first explain one of the problems the National Trust faces whenever it takes over someone else's home. The Trust is a registered charity. It currently owns and administers over 250 historic buildings and gardens in the British Isles, as well as more than 600,000 acres of countryside and 575 miles of coastline. Each piece of property must meet the Trust's criterion of being "of historic interest or natural beauty". In taking over the responsibility for maintaining the properties, we also have to insure and protect their fabric and contents without bankrupting the Trust. In the case of Huxley Hall, we have installed the most advanced security system available, backed up by guards who work around the clock. Even so, it is impossible to protect all our many treasures for twenty-four hours a day, every day of the year.

'When something is reported missing, we naturally inform the police immediately. Nine times out of ten the missing item is returned to us within days.' The curator paused, confident that someone would ask why.

'Why?' asked an American woman, dressed in tartan Bermuda shorts and standing at the front of our group.

'A good question, madam,' said the curator condescendingly. 'It's simply because most petty criminals find it almost impossible to dispose of such valuable booty, unless it has been stolen to order.'

'Stolen to order?' queried the same American woman, bang on cue.

'Yes, madam,' said the curator, only too happy to explain. 'You see, there are gangs of criminals operating around the globe who steal masterpieces for clients who are happy that no one else should ever see them, as long as they can enjoy them in private.'

'That must come expensive,' suggested the American woman.

'I understand that the current rate is around a fifth of the work's market value,' confirmed the curator. This seemed to finally silence her.

'But that doesn't explain why so many treasures are returned so quickly,' said a voice from the middle of the crowd.

'I was about to come to that,' said the curator, a little sharply. 'If an artwork has not been stolen to order, even the most inexperienced fence will avoid it.'

He quickly added, 'Because . . .' before the American woman could demand 'Why?'

'. . . all the leading auctioneers, dealers and galleries will have a full description of the missing piece on their desks within hours of its being stolen. This leaves the thief in possession of something no one is willing to handle, because if it were to come onto the market the police would swoop within hours. Many of our stolen masterpieces are actually returned within a few days, or dumped in a place where they are certain to be found. The Dulwich Art Gallery alone has experienced this on no fewer than three separate occasions in the past ten years, and, surprisingly, very few of the treasures are returned damaged.'

This time, several 'Whys?' emanated from the little gathering.

'It appears,' said the curator, responding to the cries, 'that the public may be inclined to forgive a daring theft, but what they will not forgive is damage being caused to a national treasure. I might add that the likelihood of a criminal being charged if the stolen goods are returned undamaged is also much reduced.

'But, to continue my little tale of the edition of thirteen,' he went on. 'On September 6th 1997, the day of Diana, Princess of Wales's funeral, just at the moment the coffin was entering Westminster Abbey, a van drove up and parked outside the main entrance of Huxley Hall. Six men dressed in National Trust overalls emerged and told the guard on duty that they had orders to remove *The Reclining Woman* and transport her to London for a Henry Moore exhibition that would shortly be taking place in Hyde Park.

'The guard had been informed that because of the funeral, the pick-up had been postponed until the following week. But as the paperwork all seemed to be in order, and as he wanted to hurry back to his television, he allowed the six men to remove the sculpture.

'Huxley Hall was closed for the two days after the funeral, so no one gave the incident a thought until a second van appeared the following Tuesday with the same instructions to remove *The Reclining Woman* and transport her to the Moore exhibition in Hyde Park. Once again, the paperwork was in order, and for some time the guards assumed it was simply a clerical error. One phone call to the organisers of the Hyde Park exhibition disabused them of this idea. It became clear that the masterpiece had been stolen by a gang of professional criminals. Scotland Yard was immediately informed.

'The Yard,' continued the curator, 'has an entire department devoted to the theft of works of art, with the details of many thousands of pieces listed on computer. Within moments of being notified of a crime, they are able to alert all the leading auctioneers and art dealers in the country.'

The curator paused, and placed his hand back on the lady's bronze bottom. 'Quite a large piece to transport and deliver, you might think, even though the roads were unusually empty on the day of the theft, and the public's attention was engaged elsewhere.

'For weeks, nothing was reported of *The Reclining Woman*, and Scotland Yard began to fear that they were dealing with a successful "stolen to order" theft. But some months later, when a petty thief called Sam Jackson was picked up trying to remove a small oil of the second Duchess from the Royal Robing Room, the police obtained their first lead. When the suspect was taken back to the local station to be questioned, he offered the arresting officer a deal.

'"And what could *you* possibly have to offer, Jackson?" the Sergeant asked incredulously.

'"I'll take you to *The Reclining Woman*," said Jackson, "if in return you only charge me with breaking and entering" – for which he knew he had a chance of getting off with a suspended sentence.

'"If we recover *The Reclining Woman*," the Sergeant told him, "you've got yourself a deal." As the portrait of the second Duchess was a poor copy that would only have fetched a few hundred pounds at a boot sale, the deal was struck. Jackson was bundled into the back of a car, and guided three police officers across the Yorkshire border and on into Lancashire, where they drove deeper and deeper into the countryside until they came to a deserted farmhouse. From there, Jackson led the police on foot across several fields and into a valley, where they found an outbuilding hidden behind a copse of trees. The police forced the lock and pulled open the door, to discover they were in an abandoned foundry. Several scraps of lead piping were lying on the floor, probably stolen from the roofs of churches and old houses in the vicinity.

'The police searched the building, but couldn't find any trace of *The Reclining Woman*. They were just about to charge Jackson with wasting police time when they saw him standing in front of a large lump of bronze.

'"I didn't say you'd get it back in its original condition," said Jackson. "I only promised to take you to it."'

The curator waited for the slower ones to join in the 'ums' and 'ahs', or simply to nod their understanding.

'Disposing of the masterpiece had obviously proved difficult, and as the criminals had no wish to be apprehended in possession of stolen goods to the value of over a million pounds, they had simply melted down *The Reclining Woman*. Jackson denied knowing who was responsible, but he did admit that someone had tried to sell him the lump of bronze for £1,000 – ironically, the exact sum the fifth Duke had paid for the original masterpiece.

'A few weeks later, a large lump of bronze was returned to the National Trust. To our dismay, the insurance company refused to pay a penny in compensation, claiming that the stolen bronze had been returned. The Trust's lawyers studied the policy carefully, and discovered that we were entitled to claim for the cost of restoring damaged items to their original state. The insurance company gave in, and agreed to pay for any restoration charges.

'Our next approach was to the Henry Moore Foundation, asking if they could help in any way. They studied the large lump of bronze for several days, and after weighing and chemically testing it, they agreed with the police laboratory that it could well be the metal which was cast into the original sculpture bought by the fifth Duke.

'After much deliberation, the Foundation agreed to make an unprecedented exception to Henry Moore's usual practice, and to cast a thirteenth edition of *The Reclining Woman*, provided the Trust was willing to cover the foundry's costs. We naturally agreed to this request, and ended up with a bill for a few thousand pounds, which was covered by our insurance policy.

'However, the Foundation did make two provisos before agreeing to create this unique thirteenth edition. Firstly, they insisted that we never allow the statue to be put up for sale, publicly or privately. And secondly, if the stolen sixth edition were ever to reappear anywhere in the world, we would immediately return the thirteenth edition to the Foundation so that it could be melted down.

'The Trust agreed to abide by these terms, which is why you are able to enjoy the masterpiece you see before you today.'

A ripple of applause broke out, and the curator gave a slight bow.

I was reminded of this story a few years later, when I attended a sale of modern art at Sotheby Parke-Bernet in New York, where the third edition of *The Reclining Woman* came under the hammer and was sold for $1,600,000.

I am assured that Scotland Yard has closed the file on the missing sixth edition of *The Reclining Woman* by Henry Moore, as they consider the crime solved. However, the Chief Inspector who had been in charge of the case did admit to me that if an enterprising criminal were able to convince a foundry to cast another edition of *The Reclining Woman*, and to mark it '6/12', he could then dispose of it to a 'stolen to order' customer for around a quarter of a million pounds. In fact, no one can be absolutely sure how many sixth editions of *The Reclining Woman* are now in private hands.

The Grass is Always
Greener . . .

Bill woke with a start. It was always the same following a long sleep-in over the weekend. Once the sun had risen on Monday morning they would expect him to move on. He had slept under the archway of Critchley's Bank for more years than most of the staff had worked in the building.

Bill would turn up every evening at around seven o'clock to claim his spot. Not that anyone else would have dared to occupy his pitch after all these years. Over the past decade he had seen them come and go, some with hearts of gold, some silver and some bronze. Most of the bronze ones were only interested in the other kind of gold. He had sussed out which was which, and not just by the way they treated him.

He glanced up at the clock above the door: ten to six. Young Kevin would appear through that door at any moment and ask if he would be kind enough to move on. Good lad, Kevin – often slipped him a bob or two, which must have been a sacrifice, what with another baby on the way. He certainly wouldn't have been treated with the same consideration by most of the posher ones who came in later.

Bill allowed himself a moment to dream. He would have liked to have Kevin's job, dressed in that heavy, warm coat and peaked hat. He would still have been on the street, but with a real job and regular pay. Some people had all the luck. All Kevin had to do was say, 'Good morning, sir. Hope you had a pleasant weekend.' Didn't even have to hold the door open since they'd made it automatic.

But Bill wasn't complaining. It hadn't been too bad a weekend. It didn't rain, and nowadays the police never tried to move him on – not since he'd spotted that IRA man parking his van outside the bank all those years ago. That was his army training.

He'd managed to get hold of a copy of Friday's *Financial Times* and Saturday's *Daily Mail*. The *Financial Times* reminded him that he should have invested in Internet companies and kept out of clothes manufacturers, because their stocks were dropping rapidly following the slowdown in High

Street sales. He was probably the only person attached to the bank who read the *Financial Times* from cover to cover, and certainly the only one who then used it as a blanket.

He'd picked up the *Mail* from the bin at the back of the building – amazing what some of those yuppies dropped in that bin. He'd had everything from a Rolex watch to a packet of condoms. Not that he had any use for either. There were quite enough clocks in the City without needing another one, and as for the condoms – not much point in those since he'd left the army. He had sold the watch and given the condoms to Vince, who worked the Bank of America pitch. Vince was always bragging about his latest conquests, which seemed a little unlikely given his circumstances. Bill had decided to call his bluff and give him the condoms as a Christmas present.

The lights were being switched on all over the building, and when Bill glanced through the plate-glass window he spotted Kevin putting on his coat. Time to gather up his belongings and move on: he didn't want to get Kevin into any trouble, on account of the fact he hoped the lad would soon be getting the promotion he deserved.

Bill rolled up his sleeping bag – a present from

the Chairman, who hadn't waited until Christmas
to give it to him. No, that wasn't Sir William's style.
A born gentleman, with an eye for the ladies –
and who could blame him? Bill had seen one or
two of them go up in the lift late at night, and he
doubted if they were seeking advice on their PEPs.
Perhaps he should have given *him* the packet of
condoms.

He folded up his two blankets – one he'd bought
with some of the money from the watch sale, the
other he'd inherited when Irish died. He missed
Irish. Half a loaf of bread from the back of the
City Club, after he'd advised the manager to get
out of clothes manufacturers and into the Internet, but he'd just laughed. He shoved his few possessions into his QC's bag – another dustbin job,
this time from the back of the Old Bailey.

Finally, like all good City men, he must check
his cash position – always important to be liquid
when there are more sellers than buyers. He
fumbled around in his pocket, the one without a
hole, and pulled out a pound, two 10p pieces and
a penny. Thanks to government taxes, he wouldn't
be able to afford any fags today, let alone his usual
pint. Unless of course Maisie was behind the bar
at The Reaper. He would have liked to reap her,

he thought, even though he was old enough to be her father.

Clocks all over the city were beginning to chime six. He tied up the laces of his Reebok trainers – another yuppie reject: the yuppies all wore Nikes now. One last glance as Kevin stepped out onto the pavement. By the time Bill returned at seven that evening – more reliable than any security guard – Kevin would be back home in Peckham with his pregnant wife Lucy. Lucky man.

Kevin watched as Bill shuffled away, disappearing among the early-morning workers. He was good like that, Bill. He would never embarrass Kevin, or want to be the cause of him losing his job. Then he spotted the penny underneath the arch. He picked it up and smiled. He would replace it with a pound coin that evening. After all, wasn't that what banks were meant to do with your money?

Kevin returned to the front door just as the cleaners were leaving. They arrived at three in the morning, and had to be off the premises by six. After four years he knew all of their names, and they always gave him a smile.

Kevin had to be out on the pavement by six o'clock on the dot, shoes polished, clean white shirt, the bank's crested tie and the regulation brass-buttoned long blue coat – heavy in winter, light in summer. Banks are sticklers for rules and regulations. He was expected to salute all board members as they entered the building, but he had added one or two others he'd heard might soon be joining the board.

Between six and seven the yuppies would arrive with, 'Hi, Kev. Bet I make a million today.' From seven to eight, at a slightly slower pace, came the middle management, already having lost their edge after dealing with the problems of young children, school fees, new car or new wife: 'Good morning,' not bothering to make eye contact. From eight to nine, the dignified pace of senior management, having parked their cars in reserved spaces in the carpark. Although they went to football matches on a Saturday like the rest of us, thought Kevin, they had seats in the directors' box. Most of them realised by now that they weren't going to make the board, and had settled for an easier life. Among the last to arrive would be the bank's Chief Executive, Phillip Alexander, sitting in the back of a chauffeur-driven Jaguar, reading the *Financial Times*. Kevin was expected to run out onto the pavement and open the car door for Mr

Alexander, who would then march straight past him without so much as a glance, let alone a thank-you.

Finally, Sir William Selwyn, the bank's Chairman, would be dropped off in his Rolls-Royce, having been driven up from somewhere in Surrey. Sir William always found time to have a word with him. 'Good morning, Kevin. How's the wife?'

'Well, thank you, sir.'

'Let me know when the baby's due.'

Kevin grinned as the yuppies began to appear, the automatic door sliding open as they dashed through. No more having to pull open heavy doors since they'd installed that contraption. He was surprised they bothered to keep him on the payroll – at least, that was the opinion of Mike Haskins, his immediate superior.

Kevin glanced around at Haskins, who was standing behind the reception desk. Lucky Mike. Inside in the warmth, regular cups of tea, the odd perk, not to mention a rise in salary. That was the job Kevin was after, the next step up the bank's ladder. He'd earned it. And he already had ideas for making reception run more efficiently. He turned back the moment Haskins looked up, reminding himself that his boss only had five months, two weeks and four days to go before he was due to retire. Then Kevin would take over his job – as long as they didn't bypass him and offer the position to Haskins's son.

Ronnie Haskins had been appearing at the bank pretty regularly since he'd lost his job at the brewery. He made himself useful, carrying parcels, delivering letters, hailing taxis and even getting sandwiches from the local Pret A Manger for those who wouldn't or couldn't risk leaving their desks.

Kevin wasn't stupid – he knew exactly what Haskins's game was. He intended to make sure Ronnie got the job that was Kevin's by right, while Kevin remained out on the pavement. It wasn't fair. He had served the bank conscientiously, never once missing a day's work, standing out there in all weathers.

'Good morning, Kevin,' said Chris Parnell, almost running past him. He had an anxious look on his face. He should have my problems, thought Kevin, glancing round to see Haskins stirring his first cup of tea of the morning.

'That's Chris Parnell,' Haskins told Ronnie, before sipping his tea. 'Late again – he'll blame it on British Rail, always does. I should have been given his job years ago, and I would have been, if like him I'd been a Sergeant in the Pay Corps, and not a Corporal in the Greenjackets. But management didn't seem to appreciate what I had to offer.'

Ronnie made no comment, but then, he had heard his father express this opinion every workday morning for the past six weeks.

'I once invited him to my regimental reunion, but he said he was too busy. Bloody snob. Watch him, though, because he'll have a say in who gets my job.'

'Good morning, Mr Parker,' said Haskins, handing the next arrival a copy of the *Guardian*.

'Tells you a lot about a man, what paper he reads,' Haskins said to Ronnie as Roger Parker disappeared into the lift. 'Now, you take young Kevin out there. He reads the *Sun*, and that's all you need to know about him. Which is another reason I wouldn't be surprised if he doesn't get the promotion he's after.' He winked at his son. 'I, on the other hand, read the *Express* – always have done, always will do.

'Good morning, Mr Tudor-Jones,' said Haskins, as he passed a copy of the *Telegraph* to the bank's Chief Administrator. He didn't speak again until the lift doors had closed.

'Important time for Mr Tudor-Jones,' Haskins informed his son. 'If he doesn't get promoted to the board this year, my bet is he'll be marking time until he retires. I sometimes look at these jokers and think I could do their jobs. After all, it wasn't my fault my old man was a brickie, and I didn't get the chance to go to the local grammar school. Otherwise I might have ended up on the sixth or seventh floor, with a desk of my own and a secretary.

'Good morning, Mr Alexander,' said Haskins as the bank's Chief Executive walked past him without acknowledging his salutation.

'Don't have to hand him a paper. Miss Franklyn, his secretary, picks the lot up for him long before he arrives. Now he wants to be Chairman. If he gets the job, there'll be a lot of changes round here, that's for sure.' He looked across at his son. 'You been booking in all those names, the way I taught you?'

'Sure have, Dad. Mr Parnell, 7.47; Mr Parker, 8.09; Mr Tudor-Jones, 8.11; Mr Alexander, 8.23.'

'Well done, son. You're learning fast.' He poured himself another cup of tea, and took a sip. Too hot, so he went on talking. 'Our next job is to deal with the mail – which, like Mr Parnell, is

late. So, I suggest . . .' Haskins quickly hid his cup
of tea below the counter and ran across the foyer.
He jabbed the 'up' button, and prayed that one
of the lifts would return to the ground floor before
the Chairman entered the building. The doors slid
open with seconds to spare.

'Good morning, Sir William. I hope you had a
pleasant weekend.'

'Yes, thank you, Haskins,' said the Chairman, as
the doors closed. Haskins blocked the way so that
no one could join Sir William in the lift, and he
would have an uninterrupted journey to the four-
teenth floor.

Haskins ambled back to the reception desk to
find his son sorting out the morning mail. 'The
Chairman once told me that the lift takes thirty-
eight seconds to reach the top floor, and he'd
worked out that he'd spend a week of his life in
there, so he always read the *Times* leader on the
way up and the notes for his next meeting on the
way down. If he spends a week trapped in there,
I reckon I must spend half my life,' he added, as
he picked up his tea and took a sip. It was cold.
'Once you've sorted out the post, you can take it
up to Mr Parnell. It's his job to distribute it, not
mine. He's got a cushy enough number as it is, so

there's no reason why I should do his work for him.'

Ronnie picked up the basket full of mail and headed for the lift. He stepped out on the second floor, walked over to Mr Parnell's desk and placed the basket in front of him.

Chris Parnell looked up, and watched as the lad disappeared back out of the door. He stared at the pile of letters. As always, no attempt had been made to sort them out. He must have a word with Haskins. It wasn't as if the man was run off his feet, and now he wanted his boy to take his place. Not if *he* had anything to do with it.

Didn't Haskins understand that his job carried real responsibility? He had to make sure the office ticked like a Swiss clock. Letters on the correct desks before nine, check for any absentees by ten, deal with any machinery breakdowns within moments of being notified of them, arrange and organise all staff meetings, by which time the second post would have arrived. Frankly, the whole place would come to a halt if he ever took a day off. You only had to look at the mess he always came back to whenever he returned from his summer holiday.

He stared at the letter on the top of the pile. It

was addressed to 'Mr Roger Parker'. 'Rog', to him. He should have been given Rog's job as Head of Personnel years ago – he could have done it in his sleep, as his wife Janice never stopped reminding him: 'He's no more than a jumped-up office clerk. Just because he was at the same school as the Chief Cashier.' It wasn't fair.

Janice had wanted to invite Roger and his wife round to dinner, but Chris had been against the idea from the start.

'Why not?' she had demanded. 'After all, you both support Chelsea. Is it because you're afraid he'll turn you down, the stuck-up snob?'

To be fair to Janice, it had crossed Chris's mind to invite Roger out for a drink, but not to dinner at their home in Romford. He couldn't explain to her that when Roger went to Stamford Bridge he didn't sit at the Shed end with the lads, but in the members' seats.

Once the letters had been sorted out, Chris placed them in different trays according to their departments. His two assistants could cover the first ten floors, but he would never allow them anywhere near the top four. Only *he* got into the Chairman and Chief Executive's offices.

Janice never stopped reminding him to keep his

eyes open whenever he was on the executive floors. 'You can never tell what opportunities might arise, what openings could present themselves.' He laughed to himself, thinking about Gloria in Filing, and the openings she offered. The things that girl could do behind a filing cabinet. That was one thing he didn't need his wife to find out about.

He picked up the trays for the top four floors, and headed towards the lift. When he reached the eleventh floor, he gave a gentle knock on the door before entering Roger's office. The Head of Personnel glanced up from a letter he'd been reading, a preoccupied look on his face.

'Good result for Chelsea on Saturday, Rog, even if it was only against West Ham,' Chris said as he placed a pile of letters in his superior's in-tray. He didn't get any response, so he left hurriedly.

Roger looked up as Chris scurried away. He felt guilty that he hadn't chatted to him about the Chelsea match, but he didn't want to explain why he had missed a home game for the first time that season. He should be so lucky as only to have Chelsea on his mind.

He turned his attention back to the letter he had been reading. It was a bill for £1,600, the first month's fee for his mother's nursing home.

Roger had reluctantly accepted that she was no longer well enough to remain with them in Croydon, but he hadn't been expecting a bill that would work out at almost £20,000 a year. Of course he hoped she'd be around for another twenty years, but with Adam and Sarah still at school, and Hazel not wanting to go back to work, he needed a further rise in salary, at a time when all the talk was of cutbacks and redundancies.

It had been a disastrous weekend. On Saturday he had begun to read the McKinsey report, outlining what the bank would have to do if it was to continue as a leading financial institution into the twenty-first century.

The report had suggested that at least seventy employees would have to participate in a downsizing programme – a euphemism for 'You're sacked.' And who would be given the unenviable task of explaining to those seventy individuals the precise meaning of the word 'downsizing'? The last time Roger had had to sack someone, he hadn't slept for days. He had felt so depressed by the time he put the report down that he just couldn't face the Chelsea match.

He realised he would have to make an appointment to see Godfrey Tudor-Jones, the bank's Chief

Administrator, although he knew that Tudor-Jones would brush him off with, 'Not my department, old boy, people problems. And you're the Head of Personnel, Roger, so I guess it's up to you.' It wasn't as if he'd been able to strike up a personal relationship with the man, which he could now fall back on. He had tried hard enough over the years, but the Chief Administrator had made it all too clear that he didn't mix business with pleasure – unless, of course, you were a board member.

'Why don't you invite him to a home game at Chelsea?' suggested Hazel. 'After all, you paid enough for those two season tickets.'

'I don't think he's into football,' Roger had told her. 'More a rugby man, would be my guess.'

'Then invite him to your club for dinner.'

He didn't bother to explain to Hazel that Godfrey was a member of the Carlton Club, and he didn't imagine he would feel at ease at a meeting of the Fabian Society.

The final blow had come on Saturday evening, when the headmaster of Adam's school had phoned to say he needed to see him urgently, about a matter that couldn't be discussed over the phone. He had driven there on the Sunday morning, apprehensive about what it could possibly be that couldn't be discussed over the phone. He knew that Adam needed to buckle down and work a lot harder if he was to have a chance of being offered a place at any university, but the headmaster told him that his son had been caught smoking marijuana, and that the school rules on that particular subject couldn't be clearer – immediate expulsion and a full report to the local police the following day. When he heard the news, Roger felt as if he were back in his own headmaster's study.

Father and son had hardly exchanged a word on the journey home. When Hazel had been told why Adam had come back in the middle of term she had broken down in tears, and proved inconsolable. She feared it would all come out in the *Croydon Advertiser*, and they would have to move. Roger certainly couldn't afford a move at the moment, but he didn't think this was the right time to explain to Hazel the meaning of negative equity.

On the train up to London that morning, Roger couldn't help thinking that none of this would have arisen if he had landed the Chief Administrator's job. For months there had been talk of Godfrey joining the board, and when he eventually did, Roger would be the obvious candidate to take his place. But he needed the extra cash right now, what with his mother in a nursing home and having to find a sixth-form college that would take Adam. He and Hazel would have to forget celebrating their twentieth wedding anniversary in Venice.

As he sat at his desk, he thought about the consequences of his colleagues finding out about Adam. He wouldn't lose his job, of course, but he needn't bother concerning himself with any further promotion. He could hear the snide whispers in the washroom that were meant to be overheard.

'Well, he's always been a bit of a lefty, you know. So, frankly, are you surprised?' He would have liked to explain to them that just because you read the *Guardian*, it doesn't automatically follow that you go on Ban the Bomb marches, experiment with free love and smoke marijuana at weekends.

He returned to the first page of the McKinsey report, and realised he would have to make an early appointment to see the Chief Administrator. He knew it would be no more than going through the motions, but at least he would have done his duty by his colleagues.

He dialled an internal number, and Godfrey Tudor-Jones's secretary picked up the phone.

'The Chief Administrator's office,' said Pamela, sounding as if she had a cold.

'It's Roger. I need to see Godfrey fairly urgently. It's about the McKinsey report.'

'He has appointments most of the day,' said Pamela, 'but I could fit you in at 4.15 for fifteen minutes.'

'Then I'll be with you at 4.15.'

Pamela replaced the phone and made a note in her boss's diary.

'Who was that?' asked Godfrey.

'Roger Parker. He says he has a problem and needs to see you urgently. I fitted him in at 4.15.'

He doesn't know what a problem is, thought Godfrey, continuing to sift through his letters to see if any had 'Confidential' written on them. None had, so he crossed the room and handed them all back to Pamela.

She took them without a word passing between them. Nothing had been the same since that week-end in Manchester. He should never have broken the golden rule about sleeping with your secretary. If it hadn't rained for three days, or if he'd been able to get a ticket for the United match, or if her skirt hadn't been quite so short, it might never have happened. If, if, if. And it wasn't as if the earth had moved, or he'd had it more than once. What a wonderful start to the week to be told she was pregnant.

As if he didn't have enough problems at the moment, the bank was having a poor year, so his bonus was likely to be about half what he'd budgeted for. Worse, he had already spent the money long before it had been credited to his account.

He looked up at Pamela. All she'd said after her initial outburst was that she hadn't made up her mind whether or not to have the baby. That was all he needed right now, what with two sons at Tonbridge and a daughter who couldn't make up her mind if she wanted a piano or a pony, and didn't understand why she couldn't have both, not to mention a wife who had become a shopaholic. He couldn't remember when his bank balance had last been in credit. He looked up at Pamela again, as she left his office. A private abortion wouldn't come cheap either, but it would be a damn sight cheaper than the alternative.

It would all have been so different if he had taken over as Chief Executive. He'd been on the shortlist, and at least three members of the board had made it clear that they supported his application. But the board in its wisdom had offered the position to an outsider. He had reached the last three, and for the first time he understood what it must feel like to win an Olympic silver medal when you're the clear favourite. Damn it, he was just as well qualified for the job as Phillip Alexander, and he had the added advantage of having worked for the bank for the past twelve years. There had been hints of a place on the board as compensation, but that would bite the dust the moment they found out about Pamela.

And what was the first recommendation Alexander had put before the board? That the bank should invest heavily in Russia, with the cataclysmic result that seventy people would now be losing their jobs and everyone's bonus was having to be readjusted. What made it worse was that Alexander was now trying to shift the blame for his decision onto the Chairman.

Once again, Godfrey's thoughts returned to Pamela. Perhaps he should take her out to lunch and try to convince her that an abortion would be the wisest course of action. He was about to pick up the phone and suggest the idea to her when it rang.

It was Pamela. 'Miss Franklyn just called. Could you pop up and see Mr Alexander in his office?'

This was a ploy Alexander used regularly, to ensure you never forgot his position. Half the time, whatever needed to be discussed could easily have been dealt with over the phone. The man had a bloody power-complex.

On the way up to Alexander's office, Godfrey remembered that his wife had wanted to invite him to dinner, so she could meet the man who had robbed her of a new car.

'He won't want to come,' Godfrey had tried to explain. 'You see, he's a very private person.'

'No harm in asking,' she had insisted. But Godfrey had turned out to be right: '*Phillip Alexander thanks Mrs Tudor-Jones for her kind invitation to dinner, but regrets that due to . . .* '

Godfrey tried to concentrate on why Alexander wanted to see him. He couldn't possibly know about Pamela – not that it was any of his business in the first place. Especially if the rumours about his own sexual preferences were to be believed. Had he been made aware that Godfrey was well in excess of the bank's overdraft limit? Or was he going to try to drag him onside over the Russian fiasco? Godfrey could feel the palms of his hands sweating as he knocked on the door.

'Come in,' said a deep voice.

Godfrey entered to be greeted by the Chief Executive's secretary, Miss Franklyn, who had joined him from Morgans. She didn't speak, just nodded in the direction of her boss's office.

He knocked for a second time, and when he heard 'Come,' he entered the Chief Executive's office. Alexander looked up from his desk.

'Have you read the McKinsey report?' he asked. No 'Good morning, Godfrey.' No 'Did you have a pleasant weekend?' Just 'Have you read the McKinsey report?'

'Yes, I have,' replied Godfrey, who hadn't done much more than speed-read through it, checking the paragraph headings and then studying in more detail the sections that would directly affect him. On top of everything else, he didn't need to be one of those who were about to be made redundant.

'The bottom line is that we can make savings of three million a year. It will mean having to sack up to seventy of the staff, and halving most of the bonuses. I need you to give me a written assessment on how we go about it, which departments can afford to shed staff, and which personnel we would risk losing if we halved their bonuses. Can you have that ready for me in time for tomorrow's board meeting?'

The bastard's about to pass the buck again, thought Godfrey. And he doesn't seem to care if he passes it up or down, as long as he survives. Wants to present the board with a *fait accompli,* on the back of my recommendations. No way.

'Have you got anything on at the moment that might be described as priority?'

'No, nothing that can't wait,' Godfrey replied. He didn't think he'd mention his problem with Pamela, or the fact that his wife would be livid if he failed to turn up for the school play that evening, in which their younger son was playing an angel. Frankly, it wouldn't have mattered if he were playing Jesus. Godfrey would still have to be up all night preparing his report for the board.

'Good. I suggest we meet up again at ten o'clock tomorrow morning, so you can brief me on how we should go about implementing the report.' Alexander lowered his head and returned his attention to the papers on his desk – a sign that the meeting was over.

Phillip Alexander looked up once he heard the door close. Lucky man, he thought, not to have any real problems. He was up to his eyes in them. The most important thing now was to make sure he continued to distance himself from the Chairman's disastrous decision to invest so heavily in Russia. He had backed the move at a board meeting the previous year, and the Chairman had made sure that his support had been minuted. But the moment he found out what was happening over at the Bank of America and Barclays, he had put an immediate stop on the bank's second instalment – as he continually reminded the board.

Since that day Phillip had flooded the building with memos, warning every department to be sure it covered its own positions, and urging them all to retrieve whatever money they could. He kept the memos flowing on a daily basis, with the result that by now almost everyone, including several members of the board, was convinced that he had been sceptical about the decision from the outset.

The spin he'd put on events to one or two board members who were not that close to Sir William was that he hadn't felt he could go against the Chairman's wishes when he'd only been in the Chief Executive's job for a few weeks, and that had been his reason for not opposing Sir William's recommendation for a £500 million loan to the Nordsky Bank in St Petersburg. The situation could still be turned to his advantage, because if the Chairman was forced to resign, the board might feel an internal appointment would be the best course of action, given the circumstances. After all, when they had appointed Phillip as Chief Executive, the Deputy Chairman, Maurice Kington, had made it clear that he doubted if Sir William would serve his full term – and that was before the Russian débâcle. About a month later, Kington had resigned; it was well known in the City that he only resigned when he could see trouble on the horizon, as he had no intention of giving up any of his thirty or so other directorships.

When the *Financial Times* published an unfavourable article about Sir William, it covered itself by opening with the words: '*No one will deny that Sir William Selwyn's record as Chairman of Critchley's Bank has been steady, even at times impressive. But recently there have been some unfortunate errors, which appear to have emanated from the Chairman's office.*' Alexander had briefed the journalist with chapter and verse of those 'unfortunate errors'.

Some members of the board were now whispering 'Sooner rather than later.' But Alexander still had one or two problems of his own to sort out.

Another call last week, and demands for a further payment. The damn man seemed to know just how much he could ask for each time. Heaven knows, public opinion was no longer so hostile towards homosexuals. But with a rent boy it was still different – somehow the press could make it sound far worse than a heterosexual man paying a prostitute. And how the hell was he to know the boy was under age at the time? In any case, the law had changed since then – not that the tabloids would allow that to influence them.

And then there was the problem of who should become Deputy Chairman now that Maurice Kington had resigned. Securing the right replacement would be crucial for him, because that person would be presiding when the board came to appoint the next Chairman. Phillip had already made a pact with Michael Butterfield, who he knew would support his cause, and had begun dropping hints in the ears of other board members about Butterfield's qualifications for the job: 'We need someone who voted against the Russian loan . . . Someone who wasn't appointed by Sir William . . . Someone with an independent mind . . . Someone who . . .'

He knew the message was getting through, because one or two directors had already dropped into his office and suggested that Butterfield was the obvious candidate for the job. Phillip was happy to fall in with their sage opinion.

And now it had all come to a head, because a decision would have to be made at tomorrow's board meeting. If Butterfield was appointed Deputy Chairman, everything else would fall neatly into place.

The phone on his desk rang. He picked it up and shouted, 'I said no calls, Alison.'

'It's Julian Burr again, Mr Alexander.'

'Put him through,' said Alexander quietly.

'Good morning, Phil. Just thought I'd call in and wish you all the best for tomorrow's board meeting.'

'How the hell did you know about that?'

'Oh, Phil, surely you must realise that not everyone at the bank is heterosexual.' The voice paused. 'And one of them in particular doesn't love you any more.'

'What do you want, Julian?'

'For you to be Chairman, of course.'

'What do you want?' repeated Alexander, his voice rising with every word.

'I thought a little break in the sun while you're moving up a floor. Nice, Monte Carlo, perhaps a week or two in St Tropez.'

'And how much do you imagine that would cost?' Alexander asked.

'Oh, I would have thought ten thousand would comfortably cover my expenses.'

'Far too comfortably,' said Alexander.

'I don't think so,' said Julian. 'Try not to forget that I know exactly how much you're worth, and that's without the rise in salary you can expect once you become Chairman. Let's face it, Phil, it's far less than the *News of the World* would be willing to offer me for an exclusive. I can see the headline now: "Rent Boy's Night with Chairman of Family Bank".'

'That's criminal,' said Alexander.

'No. As I was under age at the time, I think you'll find it's you who's the criminal.'

'You can go too far, you know,' said Alexander.

'Not while you have ambitions to go even further,' said Julian, with a laugh.

'I'll need a few days.'

'I can't wait that long – I want to catch the early flight to Nice tomorrow. Be sure that the money has been transferred to my account before you go into the board meeting at eleven, there's a good chap. Don't forget it was you who taught me about electronic transfers.'

The phone went dead, then rang again immediately.

'Who is it this time?' snapped Alexander.

'The Chairman's on line two.'

'Put him through.'

'Phillip, I need the latest figures on the Russian loans, along with your assessment of the McKinsey report.'

'I'll have an update on the Russian position on your desk within the hour. As for the McKinsey report, I'm broadly in agreement with its recommendations, but I've asked Godfrey Tudor-Jones to let me have a written opinion on how we should go about implementing it. I intend to present his report at tomorrow's board meeting. I hope that's satisfactory, Chairman?'

'I doubt it. I have a feeling that by tomorrow it will be too late,' the Chairman said without explanation, before replacing the phone.

Sir William knew it didn't help that the latest Russian losses had exceeded £500 million. And now the McKinsey report had arrived on every director's desk, recommending that seventy jobs, perhaps even more, should be shed in order to make a saving of around £3 million a year. When would management consultants begin to understand that human beings were involved, not just numbers on a balance sheet – among them seventy loyal members of staff, some of whom had served the bank for more than twenty years?

There wasn't a mention of the Russian loan in the McKinsey report, because it wasn't part of their brief; but the timing couldn't have been worse. And in banking, timing is everything.

Phillip Alexander's words to the board were indelibly fixed in Sir William's memory: 'We mustn't allow our rivals to take advantage of such a one-off windfall. If Critchley's is to remain a player on the international stage, we have to move quickly while there's still a profit to be made.' The short-term gains could be enormous, Alexander had assured the board – whereas in truth the opposite had turned out to be the case. And within moments of things falling apart, the little shit had begun digging himself out of the Russian hole, while dropping his Chairman right into it. He'd been on holiday at the time, and Alexander had phoned him at his hotel in Marrakech to tell him that he had everything under control, and there was no need for him to rush home. When he did eventually return, he found that Alexander had already filled in the hole, leaving him at the bottom of it.

After reading the article in the *Financial Times*, Sir William knew his days as Chairman were numbered. The resignation of Maurice Kington had been the final blow, from which he knew he couldn't hope to recover. He had tried to talk him out of it, but there was only one person's future Kington was ever interested in.

The Chairman stared down at his handwritten letter of resignation, a copy of which would be sent to every member of the board that evening.

His loyal secretary Claire had reminded him that he was fifty-seven, and had often talked of retiring at sixty to make way for a younger man. It was ironic when he considered who that younger man might be.

True, he was fifty-seven. But the last Chairman hadn't retired until he was seventy, and that was what the board and the shareholders would remember. It would be forgotten that he had taken over an ailing bank from an ailing Chairman, and increased its profits year on year for the past decade. Even if you included the Russian disaster, they were still well ahead of the game.

Those hints from the Prime Minister that he was being considered for a peerage would quickly be forgotten. The dozen or so directorships that are nothing more than routine for the retiring Chairman of a major bank would suddenly evaporate, along with the invitations to Buck House, the Guildhall and the centre court at Wimbledon – the one official outing his wife always enjoyed.

He had told Katherine over dinner the night before that he was going to resign. She had put down her knife and fork, folded her napkin and said, 'Thank God for that. Now it won't be necessary to go on with this sham of a marriage any longer. I shall wait for a decent interval, of course, before I file for divorce.' She had risen from her place and left the room without uttering another word.

Until then, he'd had no idea that Katherine felt so strongly. He'd assumed she was aware that there had been other women, although none of his affairs had been all that serious. He thought they had reached an understanding, an accommodation. After all, so many married couples of their age did. After dinner he had travelled up to London and spent the night at his club.

He unscrewed the top of his fountain pen and signed the twelve letters. He had left them on his desk all day, in the hope that before the close of business some miracle would occur which would make it possible for him to shred them. But in truth he knew that was never likely.

When he finally took the letters through to his secretary, she had already typed the recipients' names on the twelve envelopes. He smiled at Claire, the best secretary he'd ever had.

'Goodbye, Claire,' he said, giving her a kiss on the cheek.

'Goodbye, Sir William,' she replied, biting her lip.

He returned to his office, picked up his empty briefcase and a copy of *The Times*. Tomorrow he would be the lead story in the Business Section – he wasn't quite well enough known to make the front page. He looked around the Chairman's office once again before leaving it for the last time. He closed the door quietly behind him and walked slowly down the corridor to the lift. He pressed the button and waited. The doors opened and he stepped inside, grateful that the lift was empty, and that it didn't stop on its journey to the ground floor.

He walked out into the foyer and glanced towards the reception desk. Haskins would have gone home long ago. As the plate-glass door slid open he thought about Kevin sitting at home in

Peckham with his pregnant wife. He would have liked to have wished him luck for the job on the reception desk. At least that wouldn't be affected by the McKinsey report.

As he stepped out onto the pavement, something caught his eye. He turned to see an old tramp settling down for the night in the far corner underneath the arch.

Bill touched his forehead in a mock salute. 'Good evening, Chairman,' he said with a grin.

'Good evening, Bill,' Sir William replied, smiling back at him.

If only they could change places, Sir William thought, as he turned and walked towards his waiting car.